A FATAL FALL

The cable car suddenly jolted to a stop and they swung in midair high over the city. Indy glanced at Oron, who shrugged at his wordless question. He didn't know what had happened, either.

Indy looked over the side.

"Don't even think about jumping out of here," Oron said. "It's at least a hundred feet and it's steep. You wouldn't make it and even if you did live, you wouldn't be any better off."

Indy believed him. But there was another option. "I'm going up." Before Oron could respond, Indy climbed out the window and onto the top of the car. He reached up, grabbed the cable, and pulled himself hand over hand.

But he'd only gone a dozen yards or so when it dawned on him that he'd taken a bigger challenge than he'd thought. The angle was steep, and the cable was greasy. More important, there was no end in sight.

Better go back.

Just then he heard a noise and felt the cable vibrate. The car was moving forward again, coming right at him. Panicking, he climbed hand over hand, his legs kicking below him as if he were running a race—a race he was losing.

Shudders of fear rippled through him. He was losing his grip. It didn't matter. The race was over. He dangled from one hand, spun around, let go. . . .

Bantam Books by Rob MacGregor
Ask your bookseller for those you have missed.

INDIANA JONES™

and the

SEVEN VEILS

by
Rob MacGregor

BANTAM BOOKS
NEW YORK · TORONTO · LONDON · SYDNEY · AUCKLAND

INDIANA JONES AND THE SEVEN VEILS

A Bantam Falcon Book / December 1991

ISBN 0-553-29334-6

Published simultaneously in the United States and Canada

*Bantam Books are published by Bantam Books, a division of
Bantam Doubleday Dell Publishing Group, Inc. Its trademark,
consisting of the words "Bantam Books" and the portrayal of a
rooster, is Registered in U.S. Patent and Trademark Office and in
other countries. Marca Registrada. Bantam Books, 666 Fifth
Avenue, New York, New York 10103.*

PRINTED IN THE UNITED STATES OF AMERICA

RAD   0 9 8 7 6 5 4

For Daemian & Dean

As a topic for controversy and conjecture the Colonel's fate enjoys in Brazil a popularity accorded elsewhere only to the sea-serpent. Nothing so stimulates the Brazilian's power of invention, nothing so enlarges his credulity, as a conversation about Colonel Fawcett. Enough legend has grown up around the subject to form a new and separate branch of folklore. Everyone has his own theory; and since the best sort of theory is clearly one based on personal experience or private information, personal experience and private information are coined for the occasion. It became harder than ever to believe that Fawcett had really existed; under this battery of apocryphal sidelights our *ignis fatuus* threatened to vanish altogether.

—Peter Fleming,
Brazilian Adventure

Vision is the art of seeing things invisible.

—Jonathan Swift

PROLOGUE

14 August, 1925

I'm anxious to get moving. My bruises and sores are healed and I have new hope. The canoe is stocked with supplies: rifles, ammunition, clothing, and food. The amounts of the latter are meagre, but the fish are plentiful in the river and when we take to the land, we will hunt game.

I'm waiting now in the canoe for my two companions. They're not the pair I'd have chosen as my travel mates, but there is little choice at this point. Harry Walters is the name of one of them. He seems to survive on rum, but he claims to know this treacherous jungle like the back of his hand. We'll see.

The other is a woman, Maria.

Most of my colleagues would scoff at the very idea of taking a woman into the jungle. I can hear them now: She'll get in the way. She won't have the courage, the will, or the determination of a man. *Women are trouble, a distraction, prone to faintness of heart and physical weakness. Maybe true.* But they don't know Maria.

From my observations of this woman these past few weeks, she knows nothing of the expected weakness of her sex, not the physical, nor the mental, nor the emotional. She's a levelheaded lady if there ever was one. She's extremely patient, honourable, and trustworthy. I'm not sure yet that I can say the same qualities are true for Walters.

Maria and I have taken walks together, and by God she's more of a man than half the men I've met in my day. I am particularly impressed by her familiarity with and knowledge of the jungle, as well as her fleetness of foot. But I am most enthralled by something which she has only hinted at: the place where she came from. She is my guide, after all, and her former home is where we are headed.

But I am getting ahead of myself. Let me backtrack, for I did not arrive at this juncture without great effort and considerable discomfort. It's all in my other journals, but I'll summarize it here. The jungle, I should begin, is no place to venture alone, and after months of trekking through this harsh land, which conspires daily to kill anyone who would dare challenge it, I was indeed desperate and alone. My son, lame from a bad ankle and feverish from malaria, turned back some weeks ago, and I sent our last guide with him. God save them.

I followed a river upstream for several days, but saw it was veering from the direction I was headed. I left it and marched directly north toward uncharted territory. On the third day I ran out of water, and for the next two or three days my only source of liquid was the dew I licked from *leaves. How I questioned myself over and over about my decision to go on alone! I called myself a fool, an idiot, a madman, and more names than I care to mention. I wandered aimlessly and soon found myself talking to old friends and even animals that appeared and vanished. Finally, I could walk no further, and crawled. Insects chewed on me. I desperately needed water, and knew I had but hours to live. I fought against death, and refused to give up. But I must have lost conscious ness.*

When I awoke I found myself in a mission outpost on the Rio Tocantins. Maria had found me and dragged me through the jungle. She nursed me back to health, so I can say nothing against her.

Indeed, she is clearly a most unique individual. She claims that she knew that I was coming and needed help, and that she had gone out to search for me. Under normal conditions, I would say her comments were just so much poppycock. However, I am beginning to understand that survival in the jungle requires a certain sharpness of the senses that we citizens of the civilised world have disposed of in favor of logic and analysis. So maybe she did actually sense my imminent arrival.

Now about Walters. He's an Englishman like myself, but he has lived in and out of the jungle for years. From what I gather, he is charged with locating Indians for the missionaries. He gives the heathens pots and pans, trinkets, and clothing, and prepares them for their eventual submission and conversion.

I was surprised to learn from Walters that he is something of a religious mercenary. Within a few miles of one another are Protestant and Catholic missions, and Walters works for both of them. Be-

sides laying the groundwork for the missionaries, he also spies on each of them, gathering information about the competition's activities and progress. This I find rather humorous, but Walters considers it to be normal jungle communication between rival clergies. Oddly enough, this foul-mouthed drunkard is the missionaries' most important link to the outside world. Since money isn't much good in the jungle, the missionaries pay him mostly in rum, which they obtain from traders.

One day a few months ago, Walters showed up at the Catholic mission with a young woman who was not from any tribe anyone had ever seen. He isn't the sort who scares easily, but he has confessed to me that he was extremely frightened the day he encountered her. He had almost finished a bottle of rum when the woman suddenly appeared in his camp. He was sure he was seeing things. Her skin was white, and her long chestnut hair reflected a reddish tinge in the firelight. She talked in a strange language that was like nothing he'd ever heard. When he reached for his gun, she swiftly vanished as strangely as she had appeared.

Walters thought he must have encountered the jungle spirit, Yaro, guardian of jungle beasts. According to the Indian legend, she lures men into the jungle at night where she kills them and feeds their body parts to her animal children. Walters vowed to stay awake all night, but eventually he dozed off. When he awoke at the first light, she was standing over him. He saw that she was no spirit, but he didn't know what she was. Without a word, he packed his gear and returned to the mission. She followed him.

The woman, of course, is the one I mentioned, Maria. That is the name the missionaries gave her *when they baptised her. I had been recovering at the mission for a couple of weeks when I heard Walters's tale. I was fascinated and uplifted, because I knew immediately where she had come from, the place which has been my destination all along. My destiny.*

I speak, of course, of the lost city known as Z.
    —From the journal of Colonel Percy Fawcett

1

CAMOZOTZ'S REVENGE

Tikal, Guatemala—March 7, 1926

The torchlight flickered in the close quarters. The tunnel was tight, the air choked with dust and the dank smell of earth. After two days of slowly removing one stone after another from the clogged passage, Indy had reached the end. A hole the size of his arm now opened into a dark chamber inside the pyramid.

"Can you see anything yet?" a woman's voice asked from behind him. The hole grew brighter as she thrust the torch closer to the opening.

"Hey, get that torch out of my face," Indy said in a hoarse voice. "You're burning my hat."

"Sorry."

He shook his head, annoyed by her impatience. While Deirdre Campbell was every bit as knowledgeable as the graduate students who had accompanied him and Professor Bernard to Guatemala, she lacked the patience of her mother, who had been one of Britain's most distinguished archaeologists. She could also be as stubborn as he was, something he liked to attribute to her Scottish upbringing.

Carefully, Indy brushed away several stones with a gloved hand. He was anxious to get inside the pyramid, but he didn't want to bulldoze his way inside, either. There could be traps at the entrance awaiting an unwary intruder.

"What's that?" Deirdre asked.

"What?"

"I see something. It's above the hole, not in it."

Indy scowled, but now he saw the glint of green. "Give me more light."

"Maybe you should take your hat off," she said.

He leaned closer and carefully picked away the pebbles from around the object. Then he pulled a stiff-bristled brush from his knapsack and scraped at the dirt and rubble.

After a few minutes, he took off one of his gloves and felt a polished jade surface. He exchanged the brush for one with softer bristles and whisked away crumbled bits of dried mud. He knew it was something unusual, something significant and precious.

"What is it, Indy?"

"Take a look." He moved aside and they both stared at a jade mask that was half animal, half man. It had white almond-shaped eyes that curved upward on the outside, an extra pair of ears, and a sharp nose. "It's Camozotz, the bat god."

"Oh, my God." Deirdre's voice was a whisper.

"Friendly looking fellow, isn't he?" The bat god was one of the lords of Xibalba, the underworld, and ruler of the House of Bats. In legend, as recorded in the *Popol Vuh*, the Mayan book of mythology, he beheaded the father of the twin heroes.

"Maybe we've found the entrance to Xibalba," he said. "Can you see him, Esteban?" he asked the Mayan, who was squatting behind Deirdre.

Esteban nodded and Indy wondered what he was thinking.

"It must have been placed above the doorway to guard the inner chambers," Deirdre said. "Don't you think?"

Deirdre's pale blue eyes were glazed with wonder. Her face, smudged with dirt, was framed by cascading auburn hair. *Even after digging a hole she looks great,* he thought.

"Good guess."

Now he had a choice to make. Bernard no doubt would want to see the mask in place, but Indy wanted to get into the pyramid as soon as possible, and he couldn't clear the opening any further without removing the mask. He was about to tell Deirdre to go and get Bernard when the mask slipped a couple of inches. He caught it and carefully removed it from the wall.

"Well, that takes care of that."

"Takes care of what?" she asked.

"Never mind." He took off his shirt and wrapped the jade mask with it. "Take this down to Bernard for me, and tell him I've broken through." He carefully handed her the mask as he took the torch from her. "The entrance will be open by the time he gets here."

"Where is he?"

"Down by the river cleaning up."

"I hope he's dressed."

"Knock first."

She uttered a short, curt laugh. "Right."

"You know what I mean. Just make a lot of noise so he hears you coming."

It seemed almost as if Bernard didn't like getting dirty. He hadn't spent more than a couple of minutes in the tunnel since they'd discovered the entrance to the rock-filled passage. Instead, he'd placed Indy in charge of the excavation and requested reports every couple of hours.

A smile brightened Deirdre's face and she leaned toward Indy. "Why don't we both go? You can give the mask to Dr. Bernard, then we can take a swim in that pool I found about half mile down from the bend. It's nice and private."

He couldn't miss the implications, but her timing was terrible. "Just get Bernard, will you," he said, impatiently. "And be careful with the artifact."

"Sorry I mentioned it," she snapped, turning away. "I bet John will go with me for a swim." She stomped out of the tunnel without another word.

Swell. Go swim with John, he thought. For the past two days, she'd shadowed him everywhere. She hadn't given him a minute alone, and he knew why. She was playing defensive.

She'd caught him with his arms around Katherine, one of the graduate students. Actually, Katherine had started it. They'd literally bumped into each other on the trail between the camp and the river where the dinner dishes were being washed. Katherine was an attractive blonde and he knew that if Deirdre weren't here with him, he'd be tempted by her. They'd started a casual conversation and then her arms slipped around him. He didn't exactly fight her off, but he hadn't been pursuing her either. The next thing he knew he was kissing her, and when he opened his eyes

Deirdre was standing in the trail, her hands on her hips.

Katherine immediately moved off in one direction and Deirdre stormed away in the other. He followed Deirdre and apologized to her, but she said he was only apologizing for getting caught, that he wasn't sincere. But the next morning, the day he began the excavation of the tunnel, she'd taken a new tack. She stayed by his side like a watchdog, and hadn't given Katherine a chance to even wink at him.

He knew the pattern; he understood it. He and Deirdre had spent almost a year together in a relationship that had gone from hot to cold and back again several times. There'd been talk of marriage, but after Deirdre's initial enthusiasm she'd said she needed more time to think about it. Then, as the fall classes began, Indy had begun seeing another woman from time to time. When Deirdre found out about it, she was angry. Then, suddenly, she wanted to get married. Indy felt she was pushing him into a corner, and told her he wanted to wait. Since then, there'd been no more talk about marriage.

Although neither of them had said it, this trip was the turning point. They'd either decide to commit to each other, or go their own ways. And right now it wasn't looking good for a future together.

Indy noticed the silent Mayan watching him. He was a stocky man with a barrel chest, dark eyes, and black hair that fell over his forehead, accenting his high cheekbones. "Women," Indy muttered.

"Can't live with them, can't live without them," Esteban answered in slow English.

Indy laughed and couldn't stop. "Old Mayan saying, right?"

He turned back to the wall and continued removing rocks. He tried to concentrate, but still felt giddy, a relief from the tension that had built up between him and Deirdre, and he laughed as he handed one rock after another to Esteban, who took them outside. *Where the hell would a Mayan pick up that phrase?* he wondered, and laughed again.

By the time the opening was large enough to crawl through, he'd regained his serious demeanor. He took the torch, pushed it into the hole, and craned his neck. He saw a narrow chamber, its walls painted with ornately costumed Mayan figures as well as birds, monkeys, and jaguars. Vertical rows of glyphs separated the paintings, and hanging on the wall opposite the door was a green shield the size of a man's torso.

Indy considered climbing into the chamber for a closer look, but decided against it. Bernard wouldn't appreciate finding him already inside. Instead, he busied himself with expanding the size of the opening so that it finally was large enough to walk through with only a slight bend at the waist.

"Where's Bernard?" he muttered after a few minutes of digging.

Although the Englishman had assured Indy that they would be "jolly good" partners on the dig, it was just talk. There was nothing equal in their association. After Deirdre's mother's death the previous year, Bernard, whose specialty was Mayan civilization, had replaced her as chairman of the archaeology department at the University of London, thus becoming Indy's boss. Here at the ruins of Tikal, Bernard was in charge of the dig, and Indy was his excavator.

"Maybe I'll just take a quick look around while we're waiting."

"It's dangerous," Esteban said.

Indy turned to the Mayan. "Oh? How dangerous?"

"You will see."

The Mayans who were working with them were uneducated in the intricacies of field work, but they knew the jungle, and Indy was sure they knew more about Mayan ways than any archaeologist. He also suspected that some of them had done their share of pillaging.

"Will you come inside with me?"

Esteban considered the question. "Camozotz was guarding the entrance."

"Yeah, but he's gone now."

Esteban didn't answer. In the torchlight, his face with its high cheekbones and black eyes looked chiseled from stone. Indy had chosen Esteban to work with him not because he had any experience in field archaeology, but because he was the grandson of an old shaman and knowledgeable in Mayan lore. But now he realized that that very knowledge might be a hindrance.

Indy stuck his head through the hole and started to climb into the darkened chamber, hoping that Esteban would follow him. He sniffed the ancient air and his imagination ran wild with possibilities of what lay ahead.

"Jones! You in there, Jones?" Bernard's deep, authoritative voice boomed into the tunnel.

Nice timing, Indy thought as he quickly withdrew from the room. "Right here, Dr. Bernard."

Bernard was a burly man with thinning, gray-streaked hair and thick glasses. The confines of the tunnel forced him to hunch over so far that he looked like a bear that had just risen partially up on its haunches. He was followed by his assistant, a young Mayan named Carlos, whom Bernard treated like a servant. When Bernard saw the opening, he looked as if he were about to take a swipe at Indy with his big paw. "Jones, did you already go inside?"

"No, sir. I've been waiting right here. Didn't Deirdre tell you?"

"Tell me what? I didn't see her."

"That's odd."

Indy cursed under his breath. Deirdre had probably run off to her swimming hole with John just to spite him. Christ, if something happened to the mask, he was responsible, and he knew that with Bernard as his boss it could cost him his job. He considered not telling him about it, but quickly realized that could make matters worse. Better to be up front.

"So you didn't see the jade mask?"

"What mask?"

He described the discovery and explained why he'd removed the mask.

"My God," Bernard said, softly. "Camozotz."

"Yeah. That's what Deirdre said. I didn't know he was so popular."

Bernard looked blankly at him as if he didn't comprehend Indy's sense of humor.

"I guess I should go look for her." Exactly what he didn't feel like doing.

Bernard surprised him. "Don't worry about it. I came up from the river by way of one of the side trails. She probably missed me." He peered into the opening. "Let's get on with it. I'll have plenty of time to examine the mask."

"Fine with me." Indy stretched a leg into the hole, but Bernard grasped him by the arm.

"I'll go first, if you don't mind."

"Be careful. The place could be booby-trapped."

"Nonsense. We shouldn't have any trouble with that sort of thing. The Mayans were a peace-loving people, not like the Aztecs. They didn't go around ripping the hearts out of their slaves or turning their pyramids into booby traps."

"What about that mask? Camozotz isn't exactly the friendliest Mayan god. It could've been put there as a warning."

"Of course it was a warning. The priests knew that no one would dare intrude on Camozotz's territory without their approval. That's the charm of the Mayans. They didn't need anything more than a warning."

Indy didn't like the way Bernard talked down to him, as if he were one of his students. Expert or not, Bernard's views of the Mayans were limited. To Bernard the Mayans were a dead culture; the fact that two Mayans were by their sides right now was irrelevant. No doubt he'd never even considered asking someone like Esteban to talk about his people. In Bernard's eyes, that was sociology, not archaeology.

Bernard crouched low and backed into the hole. He wriggled and pushed and huffed as if he'd just run a mile. Finally, he disappeared from sight. As Indy followed him, he heard Esteban and Carlos speaking Tzotzil, a Mayan dialect. Then Carlos stuck his head through the hole and looked around. He said something else to Esteban and while Indy didn't understand it all, whatever it was must have been convincing, because both men crept into the chamber.

"Let's stay together and not disturb anything," Bernard said when they were all inside the room. "Not on our first look around."

The flickering torches cast waves of light through the room. The painted walls, which rose about twenty-five feet, curved inward. "Impressive," Bernard commented. "You see the figures painted blue? Those are the Nine Lords of Darkness. The red ones are figures of Mayan royalty."

Indy was tempted to say that the professor wasn't telling him anything he didn't know, but he kept quiet. After Bernard had approved his request to join the excavation team, Indy had spent his spare hours enhancing his knowledge of the Mayans. What intrigued him most was the argument over whether ancient cultures, like the Mayans', arose independently or were influenced by other cultures. More than one nineteenth-century archaeologist had speculated that the Mayans were influenced by survivors of Atlantis. The same was said about Egypt, which would explain why both cultures had built pyramids. The problem with that theory was that Egypt's pyramids were several thousand years older than those of the Mayans.

Still, Indy didn't discount the possibility of outside influences having affected the development of the Mayan culture. The Mayans' own myths, after all, spoke of a bearded man with red hair and white skin who arrived on a raft from the east and brought knowledge of crafts and arts. He was incorporated into the Mayan hierarchy as Quetzalcoatl, the god of culture.

Indy looked around the barren room. "I wonder if someone beat us here."

Bernard moved over to the intricately carved shield attached to the wall. "I don't think so. Why would they leave this?" His voice echoed in the chamber. "It's jade with gold inlay." He ran his hands lightly over the shield. "I'm going to take it down."

"I thought you didn't want to remove anything yet."

"I don't want it to fall. Our presence alone could be enough to disturb it."

"Be careful," Indy said.

"It won't budge." Bernard stepped to one side and pulled the pointed bottom of the shield toward him. As he did, a small arrow shot from the wall. It whizzed past Indy's ear. Carlos gasped and staggered several steps, and Indy saw the arrow protruding from his neck.

"Good God. What happened?" Bernard gaped at his wounded assistant.

Indy caught the man as he stumbled and lowered him to the floor. "Booby-trapped," Indy snarled.

With a quick jerk, Esteban pulled the arrow from the man's neck. Blood spurted from the wound. It was already too late. Carlos's eyes were wide and his body shuddered. He coughed frothy blood. Within seconds, the shaking stopped. He was dead.

Jesus, Indy thought. *Just what we didn't need.* And so much for peace-loving Mayans.

"You bastards," Esteban shouted. "I warned you, and now look!"

Bernard acted as if he didn't hear him. He was staring at the wall where the shield was. It appeared to be a revolving door, which had turned inward. Before Indy could say anything, a vibration resonated across the room, seeming to emanate from the tunnel.

"What's that?" Bernard yelled.

"I don't know, but we better get out of here." Indy dragged the body by the shoulders toward the tunnel; Esteban picked up the feet. Just as he ducked through the opening, Indy glanced up and saw that Bernard had gone through the doorway.

"Dr. Bernard! This way."

"No! This way, Jones," Bernard responded.

"Cuidado!" Esteban yelled, as he jerked back on the body, pulling Indy out of the tunnel.

At that moment, a massive stone block dropped, sealing the tunnel shut. For a moment, all Indy could think was that his leg had nearly been crushed. He set down the body and shoved against the rock. It was useless; the rock was unmovable. They were trapped inside the pyramid.

Bernard peered through the doorway. "What's going on?"

Indy pointed at the wall where the tunnel had been. "Look for yourself."

Suddenly, the stone floor beneath Indy's feet shook violently and dropped from under him.

2

BAT TIME

A fraction of a second before the floor dropped away, Indy dove headlong toward the doorway where Bernard was standing. His leap, however, fell short, and he grasped for the nearest object, Bernard's calf. The professor lost his balance, and toppled over backwards. Indy slid further into the hole as his weight dragged Bernard with him.

Bernard shook his leg, smashing Indy's hands against the corner of the floor. Indy's grasp slid down Bernard's leg until he was hanging from the professor's boot. His grip was weakening; he couldn't hold on much longer.

Out of the corner of his eye, Indy saw Esteban hanging from the edge of the hole. Using his powerful upper body, the Mayan raised himself up until his chest fell forward on the floor. He swung his legs over the side, and rolled out of the hole.

"Jones, let go of me, let go of me," Bernard yelled as he skidded further toward the hole.

Indy looked down and saw Carlos's body ten feet below him, skewered on a bed of razor-sharp stakes. "Stop kicking," he yelled back to Bernard, but to no avail. But just as he lost his grip, Esteban reached out and grabbed him by the wrist.

"Hang on, Dr. Jones."

"You too."

Esteban slowly pulled him up until Indy flopped onto the remaining section of floor. He rolled onto his back, exhaled, and opened his eyes. *"Gracias, amigo."*

"You survived your first confrontation with Camozotz, Dr. Jones. *Tiene mucho suerte.*"

"I guess he doesn't like unexpected guests." Then Indy remembered Bernard and sat up. "Are you all right, Dr. Bernard?"

The professor was lying on his back; his chest was rising and falling as he tried to catch his breath. "You almost killed me, Jones," he blustered. "Mark my words, you'll pay for this."

Without another word, Bernard rolled over and crawled into the next room. *Swell, just swell,* Indy thought. Bernard was vowing vengeance, and probably walking into another booby-trapped room. And how the hell were they going to get out of here?

Indy moved carefully along the edge of the hole to the revolving door. At first, all he saw was the outer wall of an earlier pyramid that had been covered over by the newer one. Then he spotted a low opening leading into the older pyramid. He crawled into it and spotted Bernard standing at the center, staring intently at a massive stone sarcophagus which was covered with relief carvings. Diffused light seeped into the chamber from somewhere above. Scattered about the chamber were several skeletons, probably servants who'd been buried alive as part of their master's funeral.

"Jones, it's the funerary crypt of a king from the

Late Classical period, and it's still sealed." Bernard's voice shook with excitement as he pointed at the carvings. "I'm sure it contains a trove of priceless artifacts. Can you just imagine."

Indy was as much surprised by Bernard's shift in temperament from venomous anger to twittering delight as by the discovery itself. Bernard's reputation was that of a cautious man, who had risen to his position by aggressively courting the right people and never offending any of them. But in the last few minutes, he had expressed more of his true nature than Indy had seen in the months he'd known him.

After a moment, Bernard took control of himself and assumed his usual quiet, studied demeanor. He cleared his throat, and straightened his shoulders. "Sorry about what happened out there. I guess I overreacted."

"That's okay. This is quite a discovery, but—"

"Yes. There's so much we can learn here. For a change we beat the *huaqueros*. We are truly fortunate."

"Not that fortunate," Indy interjected. "We're trapped in here."

"What?"

"That's what I was trying to show you before the floor fell in. The tunnel's blocked."

"Good God," Bernard muttered.

"Camozotz has caught us," Esteban said from behind them.

"I don't believe in superstitions, mister," Bernard snapped as he looked over his shoulder. "We'll get out of here."

"Any ideas?" Indy asked.

Bernard pointed toward the top of the pyramid. Indy could tell he was struggling to maintain his calm, authoritative demeanor. "There's light seeping in somewhere up there. We'll call for help. They can dig us out."

Indy saw a narrow stairway leading to the ceiling of the pyramid fifty or sixty feet above them. "Let's see if we can get up there."

Bernard frowned at the stairs. "You lead the way. You seem to know more about this sort of thing than I do. I've never gotten trapped inside anything before."

Indy ignored the jibe and motioned Esteban to follow him with the torch. The stone steps were steep, as if the Mayans were a long-legged race. Actually, the opposite was true, a fact which puzzled early researchers. A popular theory had been that giants of another race had built the pyramids in ancient times, but that wasn't giving the Mayans their due. Indy favored a simpler explanation, that the stairways of the temples were built in such a manner to emphasize that the elevated realms of the spiritual world were a steep climb, not easily attained.

As they ascended, the stairs became progressively more slippery. The steps were narrow and dropped straight down on either side of them. "Watch your step. There's a black crud on the stones."

"I smell it," Bernard said.

They were almost halfway to the top when Indy heard a fluttering noise. He glanced up to see a dark shape swoop past him. Then another.

"Murciélagos!" Esteban called. "Bats, no?"

Indy ducked as another dove past his head. "Flying rats, Esteban."

"Jones, let's keep moving," Bernard said. "I don't like it here much."

Indy ducked his head to avoid the bats that were careening down in growing numbers. He was glad he was wearing a hat. He took another step and slipped and his forearm slid through the thick black slime. The stench was overpowering.

Pushing himself off the steps, he scraped the crud from his arm as best he could. But as he did so, a bat struck the crown of his hat, knocking it from his head. Esteban reached out and caught it, but he slipped and nearly knocked Indy off the steps.

"Careful. The hat can be replaced," Indy said, tugging at the brim to secure the fedora to his head.

Just then, Bernard screamed in panic as a bat tangled in his hair. Indy swatted it away, then grabbed Bernard by the arm before he tumbled over the side. The air swarmed with bats; their high squeals shrieked in his ears as they zipped past him.

"Pull your shirt over your head, and keep low," Indy yelled.

Bernard did as Indy said, then rubbed his arms with his hands, fast and hard. "I've really got to get out of here."

"I don't like bats much either," Indy said as he crouched down next to Bernard.

"It's not just the bats. I've never told anyone this, but I don't like closed spaces. That's why you did all the excavating of the tunnel."

Indy was baffled. "What about all the other pyramids you've excavated?"

"I've always been fortunate to have others doing the actual digging. I can go inside for a few minutes, then I have to get out."

"Well, don't hold your breath. We may be a little bit longer today."

"I should've listened to the gossip. I was warned that you had a way of attracting trouble."

"Up here," Esteban called.

Indy looked up and glimpsed the Mayan's face peering down through a rectangular hole above them. "I also have a way of getting out of trouble." He climbed the remaining steps, then pulled himself up through the hole. Bernard was right behind him, and it took all Indy's strength to pull him through.

They found themselves atop a stone platform that had probably been an altar. The bats were no longer bothering them, but they weren't much closer to getting out. Above them was the capstone of the outside pyramid.

"Very interesting," Bernard said, studying the thick wood beams and stone blocks over their heads. "You can see the workmanship is not as good on the outside pyramid. They used mud as mortar, instead of limestone. It goes to show you that some of the largest of the pyramids were built at the time when the Mayan decline was already underway."

Indy saw the glazed look in Bernard's eyes. It was as if he were assuming his intellectual mantle as a way of escaping any thought of their predicament. "How are you feeling?"

"Feeling? Fine. Fine. By the way, thanks for helping me out of the fix back there."

Indy didn't answer. He was staring intently at the ceiling, following Esteban's gaze. "Thank God for the bats," he said, softly.

"What are you talking about?" Bernard asked.

Just above one of the beams was a crack in the stone ceiling through which sunlight filtered. "There's the bat entrance," Indy said, "and our way out."

"We certainly can't get through that hole, even if we could get up there," Bernard said.

"Don't think we have much choice," Indy said as he unhitched his whip. Before Bernard could respond, Indy snared the beam with the whip and swung out from the platform.

"Jones, are you crazy?"

Indy curled a leg over the beam, and pulled himself upright. "That was the easy stuff. The tricky part's going to be making the hole wide enough to get through. Once I'm out, I'll get help and a rope and we'll lift you out."

"I hope you know what you're doing."

Indy stood up and walked along the beam. It was plenty wide, and the ceiling was just over his head in case he needed to catch his balance. He'd taken only a couple of steps when he realized he had company. Something was nipping at his lower back. He stopped and wobbled, then grimaced as he reached under his shirt and felt a bat burrowing its teeth into his skin. Rocking unsteadily, he ripped it free, and flung it away.

"Disgusting."

As he reached the far side of the beam, he peered through the hole. From the reddish tinge of the light he knew that the sun was low in the sky. He reached up and felt along the narrow slit, a crack between two stone slabs. How the hell was he going to get through there? The stones were at least a foot thick and there was soil and vegetation around them. He'd need a sledgehammer, and even that might not help.

"How does it look, Jones?" Bernard yelled.

"Not good."

"Call for help, for Christ's sake. They'll hear you down below."

Indy wasn't so sure about that. The base of the pyramid was a couple of hundred feet away and chances were his voice would be absorbed by the

thick jungle growth on the outside of the unexca-
vated pyramid.

He cupped one hand over his mouth and yelled
through the hole. He shouted until he was dizzy
and his lungs were ready to give out. Catching his
breath, he was about to try again when Esteban
called out to him. "Dr. Jones! Behind you!"

"Behind me?" he muttered. "Nothing is—"

His yelling had attracted the bats, which were
darting about just below the ceiling. One swooped
past his ear. Another struck the back of his hat,
knocking it forward over his eyes. "Creepy little
bastards are driving me batty," he growled. He
tottered a moment, caught his balance, then
crouched down on the beam and wrapped his legs
around it just as several more bats screeched past
his ear.

"Dr. Jones," Esteban called again. "Catch."

Indy turned to see the Mayan standing on the
edge of the stone platform, holding out the torch
as more bats darted through the holes in the floor
of the platform behind him.

"Catch?"

The torch flew through the air, flipping end over
end toward him, but Esteban had underestimated
the power of his throw, and all Indy could do was
block it from striking him. The torch dropped onto
the beam with the burning end landing on his foot.

"AHH!" He snatched it up. "Thanks, Esteban.
Thanks a lot."

He brushed cinders off his boot, but he didn't
have long to fuss about it. The bats were sweeping
in a black mass toward him, and he jabbed the
torch at them. One, then another and another
were singed by the flames before the message rippled through the flying horde, and they swerved

away, darting back down through the hole in the altar.

"You okay, Jones?" Bernard called.

"Yeah. I think I scared them off." Just then he heard a chorus of squeals and the bats were on him again. He swung the torch, but it slipped out of his hand. Cursing, he pressed down against the beam. He squeezed his eyes shut, and gripped his hat on either side of his head.

When he didn't feel anything, he opened an eye. The bats, one after another, were soaring through the hole above his head and out of the pyramid. Indy looked up through the hole and realized it was dusk.

Bat time.

Before he had time to think what to do next he heard voices. "Dr. Jones, Dr. Bernard, where are you?"

Indy raised himself up on the beam. The voice was faint and distant. He balanced on the beam, gripping the crack in the ceiling, and yelled as loud as he could. He didn't know if anyone could hear him; he just kept yelling.

Finally, he stopped to catch his breath. He could hear responses. Louder, clearer now. He recognized John's voice, and wondered for a moment what had happened to Deirdre. Then he saw the flickering of a torchlight.

"Where are you?" John called.

He was close, so close Indy could see his legs through the crack. "Right under your feet."

The light blazed above him. "Dr. Jones, are you all right?"

"Just great. Be even better when you get us out of here."

"We didn't know what happened to you and Dr. Bernard. The entrance is blocked."

"Yeah. We know," Indy said patiently.

"Then we heard you calling. Sorry we couldn't make it any faster. It's so steep and overgrown. It's like scaling a mountain in the dark."

"How many are with you?"

"All of us are here. We've got picks and shovels and rope."

"Good. Let me talk to Deirdre."

"We thought she was with you. No one's seen her since after lunch."

Just what they needed. Trouble on top of trouble. "Get us out of here and we'll go look for her," he said evenly. "If you can loosen a couple of the blocks and pull them out, we should be able to squeeze out of here."

"Gotcha."

"Jones, what's going on?" Bernard called out from the platform. "Who's missing?"

"Deirdre."

"I'm holding you responsible if she isn't found. You sent her to the river unaccompanied."

"We'll find her," Indy replied, but his voice was drowned out by the pounding which had begun on the stones above his head. He edged along the beam as dirt rained down on him.

What a day, he thought. After nearly two weeks of monotonously hacking away at the jungle around the base of the pyramid and two days of digging out the tunnel, everything had happened at once. And all the bad stuff was going to be his fault. He could already tell. Suddenly, he was jarred from his reverie as a stone block crashed onto the beam, then struck the altar, barely missing Bernard and Esteban.

Indy winced as another block ripped loose and tumbled to the altar. Indy was reminded of a similar experience a year ago in Scotland, when he and

Deirdre had been trapped in Merlin's Cave and had escaped through an ancient blocked-up chimney. That time Deirdre had barely made it out alive. This time, he wished she were here with him now that they were escaping.

Light from the torches streamed into the pyramid. It had taken the students less than fifteen minutes to open the new entrance. Indy heard more voices; they seemed to be arguing. But they were too far from the hole for him to tell what was being said. Then everyone was silent.

"What the devil are they doing, Jones?" Bernard yelled.

"I don't know."

Just then an arm stretched down and a rope with a wide loop at the end was tossed to him. "Here, take it," John shouted.

His voice sounded strained. He'd probably had an argument with one of other students about how to tie the knot, Indy thought. But he could put up with a petty annoyance. They were getting out. That was what mattered. He tossed the rope down to Esteban.

"Give it me," Bernard said, taking the rope from the Mayan and looping the rope under his arms. "I'll get to the top and take charge."

Indy shouted up through the hole when Bernard was ready. The professor swung past Indy, nearly striking the far wall, but the hands at the top pulled fast and Bernard quickly disappeared through the gap.

If Carlos hadn't been killed and Deirdre weren't missing, they'd have cause to celebrate their rescue and the discovery of the treasures. But Indy sensed that it wasn't going to be that sort of a night.

"Dr. Jones, I don't like it," Esteban called to him. "Something is wrong up there."

What else could be wrong? "I'll go up next." He walked along the beam until he was just below the hole. He looked up, but the light from the torches prevented him from seeing anything.

"Here you go, Dr. Jones," John said as he dropped the rope down to him. Indy slipped it under his arms, but didn't bother waiting for the lift. He reached up through the hole, grabbed the edge of the stone, and chinned himself up. Hands grasped his shoulders and pulled him the rest of the way.

"I've got some good news and bad news," John said.

"What is it?"

"Deirdre is okay, but . . ."

Bernard stepped forward into the light and finished the sentence. "Look who brought her here, Jones. We've got serious trouble."

Indy squinted as his eyes adjusted to the torchlight. The first thing he saw was the barrel of a rifle aimed at his head.

3

Huaqueros

A one-eyed man grinned at Indy as he aimed his weapon at him. Two cartridge belts were strapped in an X from his shoulders to his belt. His companions were armed with guns and machetes, and didn't look any friendlier than One Eye.

"So you have found the way in for us, *amigos*," One Eye said.

"Indy, I'm sorry," Deirdre blurted.

"Are you all right?"

"They didn't hurt me. They were watching us from across the river."

"*Sí*, the *señorita* is right," One Eye said. "We were here first. It is our treasure."

"So you steal from the dead for a living," Indy sneered.

"Just like you," One Eye snapped back. "No different."

"There's a big difference." Deirdre's voice was vehement. "Archaeologists record and preserve and analyze. That's how we learn about the past."

"Nicely put," Indy said. "Don't think he'll buy it, though."

One Eye laughed. "But this treasure is ours."

Indy grinned at the *huaquero* and tipped his hat. "Help yourself. There's nothing down there. We already looked."

"I do not believe you." One Eye reached into a canvas satchel and held up the jade mask. It was no longer wrapped in Indy's shirt; One Eye was wearing the shirt. "You see the reason I doubt your word, *amigo*?"

"They took it from me, Indy," Deirdre said, haplessly.

"Don't worry about it." Indy turned to the *huaquero*. "That's all there was. Trust me."

"That I will not do. Take that whip off. You are going with us, and if you are lying you will die."

Indy slowly unhitched his whip, stalling for time. If they opened the crypt and Bernard was right about the treasure, Indy knew he was dead. He cursed himself for leaving his revolver back in the camp. Then he remembered that Esteban was still inside the pyramid, and that glimmer of hope set his mind churning. He dropped the whip to the ground.

"Look, all I saw was a jade shield and a carved stone. It's not worth going in there. The place is cursed. One of our men died, and we were lucky to survive."

"You lie, and I don't believe in curses, except my own, *chigador*." He cackled and his partners guffawed. Then One Eye picked two of his men to accompany him and Indy into the pyramid. The other three *huaqueros* set off to the camp with Deirdre, Bernard, and the others in tow.

After two of the men were lowered through the hole and reached the stone altar, it was Indy's turn, then One Eye followed. They lowered themselves through the opening in the platform, then One Eye motioned for the man nearest him to remain on the steps. The other *huaquero* was carrying a torch, and led the way as they descended the stairs. All the while One Eye kept his rifle aimed at Indy's back.

When they reached the floor, One Eye and his partner crunched over the skeletons as if they weren't there and headed directly to the sarcophagus. The *huaquero* chief examined it a moment and smiled. "It looks like no one has opened it yet. You think I would not know that there is a fortune underneath this stone? Maybe after we clean it out, we will leave you inside it."

He looked at his companion, laughed, and slapped him on the back. The man, who had a mouthful of jagged teeth, grinned maniacally.

"Some greedy gringos will find you some day. They will be so disappointed that one of their own kind was sleeping here and all the gold is gone."

They laughed again. They seemed to be having a great time. Then One Eye turned to the crypt. "Let's have a look."

He jabbed his rifle at Indy and told him to take one end of the stone cover. It was about twelve feet long and four feet wide and heavy as lead. Indy and Jagged Teeth lifted it with a refrain of grunts and slid it slowly to one side.

"Be careful," Indy cautioned, but to no avail. The *huaquero* let his end of the carved sarcophagus crash onto the stone floor. The sarcophagus slipped from Indy's hands and broke into three pieces.

"Nice going," Indy growled, but the two men were gaping at the contents of the crypt. What Indy glimpsed was worthy of detailed study and documentation. But he knew that wasn't going to happen. Surrounding the skeleton were jade necklaces, a gold incense burner with the heads of gods on the outside surface, a carved soapstone jar, formations of obsidian stones and quartz crystals, bone objects and teeth, a jade mosaic mask, and several gold figurines.

One Eye rummaged through the crypt, carelessly examining the objects, stuffing the gold and jade pieces in his sack. Covering the top of the skull was a jeweled headdress. One Eye snatched it, and beneath it was a pile of gold discs. He greedily scooped them up. Then he pulled several jade rings off the skeleton and the finger bones snapped like pretzels.

Indy couldn't take any more. "Filthy grave robbers," he yelled, and he barreled into the two men. He caught them off guard and knocked them to the ground. He kicked One Eye's rifle out of his grasp and punched Jagged Teeth in the jaw, then struggled for his weapon. But One Eye pulled a revolver from inside his shirt and jammed it at Indy's head. "It is all over, *chigador.*" He cocked the trigger.

Indy glimpsed movement beyond One Eye, and suddenly the third *huaquero* tumbled down the steps. His hands were bound behind his back and his mouth was gagged. Then a gun fired and One Eye screamed in pain as he buckled over grabbing his stomach. Jagged Teeth looked around, and when he couldn't find the source of the gunfire, he dashed for the hole in the wall.

He disappeared into the next room, the one with the missing floor. An instant later, his cry echoed through the pyramid as he plummeted into the pit.

Indy grabbed the bag of artifacts, and raced for

the stairway. He was halfway up when One Eye yelled. Indy turned and saw the *huaquero* sitting up and aiming his rifle. He fired and the bullet struck a stair, missing Indy's head by an inch or two. Indy took two quick steps up, but slipped, and slid down several stairs as artifacts spilled from the canvas satchel.

He looked back and saw One Eye taking aim at him. He heard a shot. The *huaquero*'s body jerked, then keeled over. Indy looked up to see Esteban lowering his rifle. Quickly, but carefully, Indy scaled the steps. "Thanks. I was getting worried there. Let's get out of here."

Esteban pointed to the spilled artifacts. "You want me to get them?"

"We'll come back later. We've got to help the others."

They climbed up to the altar, then crawled out of the pyramid along the rope, which had been tied to the trunk of a tree. They were about to head down the side of the mound when Esteban froze.

"What's wrong?"

"I think I'm standing on a snake, Dr. Jones. I can't see."

Indy cautiously stepped forward, then smiled as he reached down and snatched up his whip.

"Thanks. I may need it."

Even though the night was warm and they were all sitting around a campfire, no one was roasting marshmallows, telling stories, or singing songs. The mood was apprehensive, and the faces flickering in the fire light were solemn and worried. Deirdre knew that her expression was drained of emotion. She, after all, had already experienced hours of terror.

Indy had told her there might be *huaqueros* around, but the grave robbers were rarely violent and they stayed away when archaeologists were at a site. So he'd said.

They'd caught her by the river and taken her to their encampment, where they'd tied her to a tree. The one with the bad teeth wanted to rape her, but the leader slapped him and said that they were going to stick to their business. When they had the treasures in the pyramid they could have all the women they wanted.

Their plan was to hold her until morning, then take control of the dig. They already knew that the entrance had been found, and how many were in the camp. A short time later, Deirdre found out why they knew so much. Manuel, the Mayan cook from the camp, showed up and told them that the archaeologists were trapped in the pyramid, but that they'd found another way out and everyone was climbing to the top to dig them out.

But now what was going on in the pyramid? The thought that the *huaqueros* might be about to murder Indy made her want to bolt for the pyramid and somehow snatch him from death. She, after all, was at least partially responsible for their troubles, and if Indy died she'd always feel at fault. She hadn't gone directly to the river as she'd said she would. Instead, she'd stopped in the camp and shown John the mask, and she'd flirted with him. She didn't have any feelings one way or another about John, but she'd wanted to make Indy jealous.

Across from her, Dr. Bernard stared into the flames and looked as if he were in shock. Next to him was John, holding hands with Katherine. She was looking back at Deirdre now, and Deirdre knew by her expression that Katherine blamed her for everything.

Deirdre had spoken to her only once since she'd come upon Katherine kissing Indy. She'd told her to keep her hands off him, but Katherine had laughed at her, and said it wasn't the first time she'd been alone with him. Deirdre knew Katherine was lying, and suspected that she had instigated the whole thing. Still, things hadn't been right with her and Indy since that moment. They were supposed to work everything out on this trip, but nothing was getting worked out. Everything was only getting worse. Much worse.

Her thoughts were interrupted by Manuel, who told the *huaqueros* that two men were approaching from the pyramid. Only two, she thought.

The horses neighed and two of the guards hurried off. A moment later, a startled yell cut through the air. Then silence. A minute passed, then two. The remaining guard looked uneasy. He called out to his companions. There was no answer.

As the seconds passed, Deirdre's hopes surged and her heart pounded. Blood rushed through her head. She was dizzy with joy. Indy was out there. He was alive!

The guard and Manuel conferred. The betrayer hurried toward the horses, and the guard trailed after him into the shadows, his rifle ready. No one was guarding the prisoners, and Deirdre edged away from the fire, watching as Manuel circled the horses. The guard positioned himself on one knee several yards away.

Then Deirdre fit everything together, and panicked. Indy and whoever was with him probably thought there were just three guards. They didn't know that Manuel was with the *huaqueros*, and now Indy was approaching them.

Deirdre crept forward, shadowing the two men. Suddenly, Indy stepped into view. Before Manuel could react, Indy's whip unfurled and lashed around his upper body. Just then Esteban crawled out from between the legs of a horse. "It's Manuel, Dr. Jones."

"Sí, sí," the Mayan whispered. "I want to help."

The guard aimed his rifle.

Deirdre rushed forward. "Indy!" she yelled, as she crashed into the *huaquero*.

Everything seemed to happen in slow motion. Deirdre hurtled over the man, and as she did the *huaquero*'s gun fired and she heard a cry of pain from Indy. Then someone else was struggling with the *huaquero*. She heard a groan, and the two men fell apart.

Slowly, she rose to her feet and saw Esteban standing over the other man. A knife protruded from the *huaquero's* chest. They looked a moment at each other, then they both raced over to Indy. Miraculously, he was sitting up and holding his shoulder with one hand and his whip, still wrapped about the Mayan, with the other.

"Just grazed me," he said, staring up at Deirdre. "I owe you one."

Relief flooded over her. Relief and exhaustion. "I think we're even."

But she knew at that moment that this had better be her last adventure with Indy. She didn't think she would survive another.

4

ANCIENT MARINERS

The room was crowded with penguins, a typical opening night for a museum exhibition. No, maybe not so typical. There was more than the usual number of newspapermen; they stood out because they never played the penguin game and several wore hats with press cards.

Indy tugged at his starched collar, swiveled his neck uncomfortably, then adjusted his black bow tie. He didn't much care for wearing a tux, especially with his arm in a sling. But when he'd arrived in New York a week ago, he'd promised Marcus Brody he'd show up, at least for a while. So here he was, a winged penguin attending "New Evidence of Ancient Forays to the Americas," an exhibition that was probably going to turn out to be a major embarrassment.

He wandered about, lost in thought, and only pretending to look at the exhibits. Things had not gone well since he'd taken his leave from teaching. His field work at Tikal had been cut short after the near-disastrous encounter with the band of *hua-*

queros. Although the grave robbers had been caught, the Guatemalan army had moved in and confiscated all the artifacts.

If that wasn't bad enough, Bernard had blamed Indy for everything. Indy had been responsible for hiring the Mayan workers, and had taken on a man who was associated with the *huaqueros.* There were a dozen responses Indy could make to that accusation, but he knew it wouldn't do any good. It would only get him into even hotter water.

To top it off, he hadn't seen Deirdre since they'd arrived in New York. She was staying with a friend who was attending Columbia University, and every time he called or stopped by the Greenwich Village apartment, she was out. He knew she was avoiding him, but he couldn't say why. He'd thought everything had been cleared up between them. Then, on the train trip to New York, she had gotten cooler and cooler toward him by the hour, until at Grand Central Station she'd told him that she didn't want to see him for a while.

Just as his thoughts touched on Deirdre, he saw a slender woman with red hair wearing a royal blue dress. She was studying an inscription on a triangular-shaped stone. He moved toward her, and with each step his anticipation grew. Deirdre had come to the opening knowing he'd be here. Things were going to work out. The woman sensed his presence as he stopped behind her. She turned, and he realized he was mistaken. Even though her trim figure matched Deirdre's, the woman was at least ten years older and didn't look anything like her.

Indy looked down at the stone, embarrassed by his mistake. "Excuse me."

"Do you think the Phoenicians were in Iowa twenty-five hundred years ago?" the woman asked. "That's when they say this stone plaque was made."

"Maybe the Indians gave them the plaque as an award," Indy said, starting to move away.

The woman gave him a puzzled look. "But seriously, do you think it's possible? I mean, it is a Punic text and it was found in Iowa."

"Anything's possible, but don't count on it," Indy said, then excused himself. He meandered through the crowd, then saw a hand raised in greeting.

"There you are, Indy. Glad you could make it."

"Evening, Marcus."

They shook hands and Brody clasped his shoulder. He was a kindly man who had always treated Indy like a son. "How are you feeling?"

"Fine. The sling comes off in a couple of days. Just a minor flesh wound."

"You were lucky. I had a long chat with your father yesterday. I told him what happened."

"You did?" Indy wished he hadn't. "What did he say?"

A pained look crossed Brody's face. He shrugged. "You know how he is."

Yeah. Indy knew. It wasn't worth talking about.

"By the way, he knows Victor Bernard and he doesn't think much of him." Brody brightened as if the comment was some consolation for Indy's nonexistent relationship with his father. "I understand that Victor is being very insensible about the unfortunate affair in Tikal."

"So I've heard." Indy didn't feel like talking about his father or Bernard.

He turned and looked at a collection of Roman coins from the fourth century that had been found on the coast of Massachusetts. "I bet they couldn't buy much with those coins back then."

"But don't you think it's all very interesting, Indy? Look over here." Brody pointed to a stone inscribed with glyphs. "This is a reproduction of one of the Libyan inscriptions from California. It dates back to around 232 B.C., to the time of the pharaoh Ptolemy III, and was found on the outskirts of the Mojave Desert. It says: 'All men, Take care, Take Care. Great desert.' We've also got photographs and replicas of inscriptions in Nordic runes, Phoenician, and Iberian-Celtic. Some date back as far as 500 B.C., and they're from all over the Americas, from Vermont to Brazil. It's truly amazing."

Brody sounded awed, and with good reason. The exhibition was a visual display of virtually every anomalous artifact that had been discovered in the Americas in the past hundred years. Placed together, they were a bold attempt to virtually rewrite American history. But not many scientists were buying it. For the past week, detractors had been condemning the exhibition before it even opened, and Brody was probably going to end up looking like a fool by the time the press was through with him.

"Marcus, you know, these Libyan inscriptions could be Zuni," Indy said in a gentle voice. "Their writing was a lot alike."

"Oh, I know. It's interesting that you point it out, because the Zuni Indians may well have learned their written language from Libyan explorers and colonists."

Indy nodded. He hoped Brody's reputation wouldn't be too greatly damaged. "Well, you've got quite a turnout tonight. That must please you."

"Yes, indeed. It's going to be quite controversial, you know. Some of our colleagues are not so pleased with me."

"Really?"

"You wouldn't believe it. But I don't pay them any heed. I'm convinced that these inscriptions deserve attention. I went to quite a bit of work pulling all of this together. It took me two years."

"You've done a good job, Marcus. Who knows, maybe you'll be remembered as the man who redefined American history. World history, for that matter."

Brody reddened. "Well, I just see it as an educational service," he said modestly. He gazed past Indy a moment, fixing his attention across the room. "I've got to start the press conference now, but there's something I need to talk to you about. Can you come see me tomorrow? It's a confidential matter."

Indy nodded, wondering what Brody was up to now. "Of course."

He moved over to a replica of a six-foot-tall statue from San Agustin, Colombia. On the headdress was carved a series of glyphs resembling Viking runes. Maybe it was someone's idea of a joke. Next to it was a table with two figurines that had been discovered in a Mound Builder burial site in Iowa. They wore the high-crowned hats, called *hennins*, that were donned by Phoenicians during rituals and celebrations. Also on the table was a comparison between the alphabets used by Phoenician colonists in Spain and the script found in Davenport, Iowa in 1874, the one the redhead had been so curious about. Indy had to admit the resemblance was remarkable, but then so were the redhead and Deirdre until he'd taken a closer look.

He examined a series of photographs of underground stone-slab chambers from Mystery Hill, New Hampshire. They reminded him of Celtic *dunans,* "little fortresses" that were found in Scotland. Next to the photos was a report dated September 18, 1917 by Harold W. Krueger. It explained that while archaeologists had labeled the cellars as less than a century old, the stones had been penetrated by the roots of a tree estimated to date from A.D. 1690, plus or minus ninety years. An addendum to the report said that other evidence suggested that the megalithic chambers were Celtic in origin and dated back to the second millennium B.C.

Nearby was a pedestal on which rested a stone lintel found at one of the cellars. On it were carved a series of short lines tilting back and forth and poorly spaced, with a single horizontal line running through the marks. It was purportedly a Celtic ogham inscription.

Suddenly, Indy's interest was piqued. He ran his finger over the inscription. To the casual viewer, ogham didn't look much like an alphabet. But Indy readily identified the script and slowly translated the letters. He took out a pad and pen and wrote them down. During the past year, while teaching a class in Celtic archaeology, he had become fascinated with ogham. What he saw was an Iberian form of Celtic in which no vowels were included, and had to be added to make sense.

When Indy was finished, the letters read: PY HD T BL, HS Y S TH SN. He played with the sentence, adding and removing vowels until words were formed. Now it read: "Pay heed to Bel, his eye is the sun." He looked over at the translation written on a card next to the lintel. It said the same thing, adding that Bel was the Celtic sun god, sometimes equated with Apollo.

While Indy had once thought that his linguistics background had served only to delay his entrance into archaeology, he had come to realize that the years he'd spent studying ancient written languages were now invaluable. In fact, his specialization was epigraphy, the study of ancient inscriptions. He refused to call himself an epigraphist, though. The word sounded too much like the study of a certain farm animal.

But what was ogham script doing on a stone found in Vermont? Maybe Brody actually was onto something significant.

"Hello, Indy."

He spun on his heels at the sound of the familiar voice. "Deirdre!"

"How are you, Indy?"

"Better. I've been trying to see you."

She was wearing a powder blue gown that fell off her shoulders; he thought she looked great. She ran a hand through her auburn mane. "I know. I've needed time to think."

"About what?"

"About us, and I've made a decision."

"Yeah?"

She nodded. "I just wanted to say good-bye."

"What are you talking about?"

"It's over, Indy. Our lives are going in different directions."

"What do you mean? What are you going to do?"

She shrugged. "I don't know. Maybe I'll drop out of the university and stay here in New York and get a job."

"Deirdre, I know you're mad about what happened with Katherine, but it really wasn't my fault."

"Don't even mention her name around me," she snapped.

Indy kept his voice low and spoke rapidly. "It

just happened. I'm sorry about it. How many times do I have to apologize?"

"I'm sorry too, Indy. But it's not just that. It's a lot of things. It's too late."

With that, she walked away. Indy was about to go after her when he felt a hand on his shoulder. "Jones, I didn't expect to see you here."

"Dr. Bernard, uh . . ." Indy looked after Deirdre, but she'd disappeared in the crowd. "I didn't expect to see you, either."

Bernard laughed. "I just wanted to see how far Marcus Brody has gone in his fantasy."

"I guess you don't agree with what he's doing here," Indy said, wondering how he was going to straighten things out with Deirdre.

"This ogham stuff is pure nonsense. The lines were probably made by a plow or a tree root."

"No, I don't think so. That's ogham."

Bernard smiled benignly. "I suppose if one tries hard enough, it's possible to read anything into those lines. But you'd have to be a palm reader."

Bernard laughed again and made an expansive gesture with his hand to take in the entire exhibition. "No, Jones, I'd say what we have here is a mixture of blatant fraud, shoddy hoax, and inexcusable misinterpretation."

Indy didn't like the way Bernard so easily dismissed the entire exhibit, and he felt compelled to defend Brody. "I think Marcus Brody has done us all a service. We should look carefully at what he's presented. Some of it might be valid."

Bernard clasped a hand on Indy's shoulder. "I know all this may look intriguing to a young mind, but don't get misled by it. That's the problem with an exhibition like this. It's wild speculation, and it just confuses people. The Americas have been my specialty for thirty years, and I'll stake my reputation that neither Egyptians, Libyans, Phoenicians, nor Celts took tours here two thousand years ago."

Brody mounted a podium across the room as camera bulbs flashed. Above his head a banner read: ANCIENT FORAYS. "I think I'll go hear what he has to say," Indy said.

"Wait a minute," Bernard said. "Do you want to go back to Guatemala? I'm restarting the excavation of the pyramid. I'm sure there's much more to be uncovered."

"I don't doubt it, but don't you think it's a bit dangerous just now?"

"This time we'll have armed guards."

"I'm surprised you're asking me to join you. I had the impression that—"

Bernard waved a hand. "Don't worry about it." He reached into a pocket on the inside of his jacket and pulled out a sheet of paper. "I just want you to sign a petition I have here."

"What is it?"

"It's for the board of directors of this museum. It condemns this exhibition, requests it be closed immediately, and demands the removal of Marcus Brody from his position."

"Brody is an old friend of mine. I can't sign anything like that. Besides, I already told you, I think it's a worthwhile exhibition."

"Then I don't think you're going back to Tikal with me, Jones."

"I don't see what Tikal has to do with your petition."

"It has everything to do with it. A committee has been formed, of which I am the chairman, and any archaeologist who refuses to sign it will no longer be doing fieldwork for any of the major American, British, or European universities."

"You can't do that."

"Jones, you don't understand power and influence. If you did, you would put your name on this list right now."

"I'm not impressed," Indy said, and he walked away.

Indy approached the crowd surrounding the podium where Brody was speaking, and listened as he tried to calm his anger. Brody began by saying that the exhibition was dedicated to a woman he'd met many years ago while teaching a class in Nordic mythology at a Midwestern university. The woman later became his wife and source of inspiration for his study of Nordic heritage in the Americas. Indy knew Brody's wife had died of pneumonia a few years after they were married.

"But as I studied the subject, I discovered that the Norse sailors were only one of a number of early explorers who ventured to the Americas, and some of them apparently arrived here long before the Vikings."

Brody spoke enthusiastically about the evidence he'd gathered and with the utmost confidence that what he presented was true, in spite of the critics.

"Not only do we have evidence in stone of Egyptian, Libyan, Celtic, and Norse adventures in both North and South America, but there are also legends from the time of the conquest about a tribe of white Indians living in the Amazon. Could these have been descendants of any early colony? An intriguing thought, and even as I speak a great British explorer, Colonel P. H. Fawcett, is seeking such a lost city in an unexplored region of the Amazon. Just imagine what we could learn from such a tribe if we found it still in existence today."

A reporter called out to Brody. "If we forget about legends and the Jack Fawcetts of the world and just look at the hard evidence, are you saying that there is enough here to prove that our history books are wrong, that we've been misled? And my second question is: Isn't this exhibition a slap in the face to Christopher Columbus?"

Brody patted his forehead with a handkerchief, and took a sip of water. "Well, sir, we have not been consciously misled. At least, I hope not. What we are talking about goes beyond known American history into the realms of archaeology, the study of prehistoric culture. As has always been the case, when new evidence comes to light, the old theories fall away. And no, this exhibition is not an intent to insult Columbus. The fact is, Columbus never claimed to be the first to sail across the Atlantic, and if he were with us today, I'm sure he'd find this exhibition an interesting one."

"This is utter nonsense," Bernard piped. Heads turned as the bearlike man moved through the crowd toward the podium. "What you see here is not scientific proof of anything. It's simply speculation, supported by highly questionable evidence. Granted, some of these markings may actually be man-made. But believe me, they are simply meaningless scratches made by primitive Indians to amuse themselves."

The pop of a flashgun accented his comment as a photographer snapped his picture. Bernard seemed ill at ease in his penguin suit. "There's good reason our history books begin with Columbus. Libyans didn't go to California. Phoenicians didn't colonize Iowa. Celts went from Spain to the British Isles, but not to New England or South America. And Vikings didn't go to Minnesota or Oklahoma, much less Argentina and Colombia. A tribe of white Indians in the Amazon?" He smiled indulgently. "It's rubbish. Legendary lies."

"Now wait a minute, Dr. Bernard," Brody sputtered. "This is not a debate; this is an opening of an exhibition. You were not invited here to—"

"I understand that, Marcus. But we have a large contingent of the press here this evening, and I want them to understand that there is no record of cross-Atlantic trips by ancient mariners. The Vikings made it as far as Greenland. That is all. The Egyptians, Celts, and Libyans left no record of journeys across South America."

"Thank you, Dr. Bernard," Brody said, taking a new tack. "I'm sure your opinion will be duly reported. Now, I hope that all of you let your curiosity wander and seriously consider what you see here. Please enjoy yourselves, and thank you for coming." With that he stepped down from the podium.

Indy headed toward Brody, but several reporters and photographers immediately clustered around the museum director, while others peppered Bernard with questions. Indy decided he'd seen enough for tonight. Besides, he'd already promised Marcus that he'd meet him tomorrow, and he had a feeling that the confidential matter was somehow going to be related to the exhibition.

As Indy stepped through the door and moved out into the Manhattan night, he had an urge to stop by the apartment where Deirdre was staying. He wasn't giving up on her so easily. But then he decided he'd give her a night to think it over. He'd see her first thing tomorrow, and they'd work out their problems as they'd done before. He'd take her to Brody's office with him and then they'd have lunch and everything would be okay.

It would be just fine.

It had to be.

5

MESSAGES

On the subway heading uptown to Brody's office, Indy tried to take his mind off Deirdre by paging through the *Times* for an article on the exhibition. But thoughts of their deteriorating relationship kept gnawing at his mind like a jungle parasite drilling through his inner ear. He'd stopped by the apartment, and was told by Deirdre's friend that she'd gone out. If it hadn't been for his appointment with Brody, he would've asked to wait inside for her. That was what he'd do later on if she wasn't home, and he'd stay until she showed up.

Finally, on page twenty-six of the third section of the *Times,* he found a four-paragraph article, entitled "Exhibition Speculates on Early Voyages." It began: *"Ancient Forays* is an exhibition of farfetched ideas about who discovered America. It is suggested that an assortment of ancient cultures, from the Phoenicians and Egyptians to the Libyans and Celts, discovered America two thousand years before the voyage of Columbus. These claims are supported by fuzzy photographs and inscrutable stones."

The article went on to say that the exhibition took itself too seriously. "If the displays had been presented as mere curiosities rather than earth-shaking evidence, we would be less prone to pan this exhibition as an example of bad science which unfortunately it is."

Poor Marcus, Indy thought.

He picked up a copy of the *Herald-Tribune*, which someone had left behind on the seat next to him. He winced as he moved his arm. He'd discarded the sling this morning, but his arm was still tender from where the *huaquero*'s bullet had torn through skin and muscle. He thumbed through the paper until he found another less-than-flattering review. "The exhibition should be called *Modern Forays up Mount Molehill* for making much ado about nothing," the writer said. In the last paragraph, the reporter noted that if ever there was a written language that looked like chicken scratches, it was the Celtic ogham. Which was just the point, Indy thought. It did look like chicken scratches, but it was every bit as much of a written language as were Nordic runes. And as in the case of the runes, not only were the letters of the ogham alphabet used for written communication, but each one held mystical significance.

The train slowed as it approached Indy's stop. As he stood up, he saw someone across the aisle reading the *Post*. The front-page headlines read: LIBYANS COLONIZED OLD WEST 500 B.C.—WON RACE WITH PHOENICIANS, EGYPTIANS, CELTS.

"Oh God. What a nightmare," Indy muttered as he hurried out of the subway and headed for the stairway to the street. He could just imagine Bernard clucking his tongue at the *Post* article and condemning Brody.

Five minutes later, Indy arrived at the archaeology museum, a massive Gothic building that had been constructed in the 1880's and overlooked Central Park. Its wide-spanning steps at the front entrance led up to a series of stone pillars and beyond them, a pair of twenty-foot-high black doors. The structure looked as if it were built for the gods. However, to accommodate those less than godly in stature, smaller doors had been inset into the larger ones.

Indy passed through the foyer, and headed to the second floor. He approached the secretary at the desk outside of Brody's office and was about to tell her who he was when he recognized the pretty blonde.

"Brenda!"

"Professor Jones, what a surprise. I didn't know you were in New York until a few minutes ago when Mr. Brody said he was expecting you."

"I didn't know you were working here."

"For three months now."

Brenda had been a secretary in the archaeology department at the University of London when Indy joined the staff a year ago. He remembered her quizzing him once about life in America and particularly in New York. She'd gotten a faraway look on her face, and then walked away. A couple of months later she'd quit, and he remembered hearing she'd moved to New York.

"How do you like the city?"

"Oh, I love it. Everything is so . . . so American."

"You could say that. Glad you like it. You're working for a nice man, too. Is he in?"

"He certainly is. I'll tell him you're here," she said, pushing her chair away from her desk.

Brody greeted Indy at the door of his office. "Come in. Come in. Welcome. Excuse the mess."

Brody's desk was cluttered with books and magazines and stacks of papers. Stone and ceramic artifacts littered the floor, and Indy had to watch where he stepped. There were pots and vases, urns, and statues, ranging in size from several inches tall to nearly Indy's height. The office always looked as if it were part warehouse and part office, and Indy would've been amazed to see it in any other condition.

"Quite a surprise seeing Brenda at your front desk," he said as Brody showed him to a chair.

"She came with excellent recommendations, and you know I'm partial to Londoners."

Indy noticed the *Times* was turned to the review of the exhibition, and stacked under it were several other newspapers.

Brody noticed his gaze. "Well, I think the opening was a big success. An excellent turnout, and all the papers covered it."

"I know," Indy said. "I read a couple of them. They were . . ." Indy tried to think of some way to put it delicately. ". . . interesting."

Brody leaned against the corner of his desk. "Oh, I know it wasn't all favorable, but the articles will generate curiosity and discussion. Moreover, the exhibition will bring people into the museum. Too often we serve only a small audience. I want to open our doors to people who have never visited the museum."

"You're probably right, but Marcus, you should know that Victor Bernard is involved in some committee that—"

Brody waved a hand. "I know all about the committee. It's a group of scientists who organized last year after John Scopes was convicted of teaching evolution. I supported them, of course, but now they're becoming fanatics in their own right."

"But what do they have against you? What's wrong with presenting new ideas on prehistory in the Americas?"

"Nothing, of course, but they say my exhibition is taking fraudulent evidence and presenting it as fact."

Indy shrugged. "Some of those stone inscriptions are controversial, but it's very easy to call something a fraud that you don't understand or want to understand."

"Exactly my point." Brody stabbed a finger at Indy. "The committee, unfortunately, seems bent on opposing anyone who suggests ideas that are outside of what they consider the gospel truth of science. They're sounding as self-righteous as the antievolutionists. It's science as religion and it's a scandal."

"Knowing that Bernard is involved leads me to suspect that his opposition to diffusion theory has something to do with it."

"Oh, of course it does. It has everything to do with it. Bernard's reputation is based on the concept that civilization in the Americas arose independently of any outside influences. He's argued against diffusion theory for years, and he's very convincing. But he refuses to look at any evidence to the contrary."

Indy nodded. He knew all about Bernard's reputation. "How is your board of directors handling the criticism?"

"Very well so far. They're backing me one hundred percent. But they're under a lot of pressure right now."

"I can imagine."

Brody moved behind his desk and sat down. "Well, enough talk about the museum. I've asked you here for another reason." He opened a desk drawer and took out several ragged sheets of paper that were clipped together. "What I have here is very exciting and at the same time very disturbing. It's a section of Jack's journal."

"Who?" Indy asked.

"Fawcett, of course."

"Oh, I didn't know the colonel was back from the Amazon."

"That's just it. He's not. Take a look at this." Brody handed Indy the sheaf of papers.

Indy knew that Colonel Fawcett was an old chum from Brody's college days in London, and that they'd kept track of each other over the years. In England, Fawcett was something of a celebrity. In the past year there'd been much hoopla in the press about his search for a lost city which he called Z. The explorer had heard stories of a red-haired, blue-eyed tribe descended from colonists who had come from a land east of South America and brought with them a written language resembling ogham. They'd built magnificent stone cities surrounded by walls. But since Fawcett had set out into unexplored jungle almost a year ago, nothing had been heard from him. Recently Indy had seen speculation in the press that either Fawcett had found his lost city and stayed, or he was dead.

When Brody passed the papers over to him, Indy noticed that the date at the top of the first sheet was August 14, 1925, seven months ago. He read the journal entry, which detailed Fawcett's recovery from injuries and dehydration at a mission and his renewed plans to set out for his destination. Indy was intrigued by Fawcett's description of his new partners, especially the woman who seemed almost too good to be true. A creature of the jungle, a guide, and a beautiful woman altogether in one neat package. It occurred to him that if Fawcett was still unaccounted for, it was more than a bit peculiar that Brody possessed a few pages of his journal.

"How did you get this, Marcus?"

"It was sent to me."

"By whom?"

"I'm not sure. But tell me, what do you think of it? When I read it, I thought it was the sort of story that would intrigue you."

Indy shrugged. He hoped someone wasn't trying to con Brody. "Truthfully, it sounds a bit like fiction. Are you certain that Fawcett wrote this?"

Brody nodded. "That much I'm sure of. I know his handwriting well. The pages must have been torn from his journal. They were sent to me from Bahia, Brazil."

Indy frowned. "But why would they be sent to you?"

"Well, you see, before Jack set sail, we had a long talk. I promised him that if I could be of any help at any time, he should feel free to contact me."

"That was nice of you."

"Yes, but I didn't really expect him to take me seriously."

"What are you going to do?"

Brody threaded and unthreaded his fingers. "Well, I was wondering if you could help me get to the bottom of it."

"I had a feeling you were thinking something of the sort."

"It seems you do have the time, now that the dig ended early," Brody said hopefully.

Indy rubbed the back of his neck. "Marcus, I'm an archaeologist, not a private detective. I don't know anything about looking for a missing person."

"But Indy, this is no ordinary missing person. And we know where he went."

"Yeah. To a mythical city in the Amazon. I think you should look for someone else. I'm not really the right person for the job."

Brody opened his desk again, and the creases in his frown seemed to deepen. "There's something else I haven't shown you yet, and I think you may change your mind when you see it."

Now what? Indy wondered, as Brody unfolded a piece of paper and handed it to Indy.

" 'If you want your friend alive, come here,' " he read. " 'Come fast. Or friend die.' "

"What do you make of the signature?" Brody asked.

Indy's gaze fixed on what was below the crudely written English. It vaguely looked like a bird's head, and below it was a vertical line with two horizontal bars touching the left side.

"I'm not sure it's a signature, Marcus," Indy said cautiously. He had an idea what it might be, but he wasn't going to say anything quite yet.

"Come on, Indy. You know what it is. That's the Eye of Bel."

Exactly. The Eye of Bel was a common symbol used by ancient Celts to invoke protection from their sun god. "I suppose you could say that."

"And what about the symbol right below it? Do you know what that is?"

"All right. It looks like ogham. The symbol for the letter—"

"Z, right? I knew it," Brody crowed. "Jack must be on to something really important. I bet he's found the city."

Indy raised a hand. "Wait a minute. Fawcett was looking for a lost city, a ruin, not an inhabited one."

Brody rubbed his hands together. "Not exactly. You see, Jack believed there were several ancient stone cities in the Serra do Roncador, or Snoring Mountains, and that at least one of them was still inhabited. In fact, in the conversation I had with him, he said he believed that the inhabited city was founded around 500 B.C. by Celtic druids. As you know, the Celts journeyed from Iberia, or what is now part of Portugal and Spain, to Britain and Scandinavia."

Indy nodded impatiently. He didn't need a lesson in Celtic history. He was teaching it.

"Anyhow, a contingent of druids apparently sailed from the Danish island of Zealand along the European coast to North Africa, then crossed the Atlantic and followed the South American coast. After more than two years at sea, they set out on a journey inland, where they founded the city of Z. Named, of course, after Zealand."

This wasn't any Celtic history that Indy had ever heard of. "Marcus, where did Fawcett get this idea?"

Brody suddenly looked uncomfortable. "Well, I came up with that part about Zealand myself. It seems to fit the rest of the tale."

Indy looked at the note again and tapped his

finger against the ogham letter. "Marcus, I hate to disappoint you, but this isn't a Z. It's D, the letter D."

Brody was crestfallen. "It is? Oh. Well, whatever." Then he brightened. "The point is, Jack's on the right track. Can't you see the significance, Indy? A lost city in the Amazon where ogham is still in use. A city settled by ancient Celts. If you could find that city, not only could you rescue Colonel Fawcett, but you could prove once and for all that Europeans arrived in the Americas almost twenty-five hundred years ago."

"That would be something. But to tell you the truth, I find all this a little hard to believe."

"Why?"

"Well, what would motivate these druids to spend months or years at sea, and who knows how long journeying through the jungle, just to find a new home?" Indy leaned forward. "Frankly, Marcus, it doesn't make sense, and no offense meant, but if you ask me the colonel was a little off his bean."

"Now wait a minute, Indy. Before you go castigating poor Jack give him a chance. As a matter of fact, he did have an answer for that very question of yours."

Indy sat back. "So what is it?"

"Jack thought that the druids made the journey because they were hoping to reunite with descendants of their ancestors."

"In the Amazon?" Indy asked skeptically.

"According to Jack, the druids were descendants of priests—initiates of secret knowledge—who had survived the destruction of Atlantis. But they weren't the only survivors. Other initiates had also survived and gone westward where they built cities in the Amazon. Eleven thousand years ago."

"So are you saying these druids, who went to the Amazon twenty-five hundred years ago, were looking for their distant relatives?"

"In a manner of speaking, yes." Brody crossed his arms. "And their descendants are still alive today. This note with the ogham is proof of it. So what do you think? Are you interested?"

Indy fiddled with the note that had accompanied the journal excerpt. Maybe the whole thing was a forgery just to get Brody into more trouble. "I wouldn't know where to start, Marcus. This letter doesn't even have a return address."

"I know, but the envelope does." Brody smiled and held it up. Written on the back of it was Hotel Paraíso, Bahia, Brazil.

"That's where you start. That is, if you're interested."

Indy tried to think of a way of turning him down that wouldn't offend his old friend. "I'd like to, Marcus, I really would. But there's a time problem. This could take months, and I'm sure Bernard would fire me if I didn't return for the fall semester."

"Don't worry. I've already made arrangements for you to fly into the jungle. You'll save weeks. There's an English pilot, named Larry Fletcher, who lives on a farm outside of Bahia. He raises . . . what did he say now?" Brody frowned and crossed his arms. "Guavas. He raises guavas on a farm outside of Bahia, and is willing to fly you into the jungle. I understand his airplane is amphibious so he can land on rivers and lakes."

"How do you know about this guy, Marcus?"

"Through the English Flying Club. It's very reputable. They contacted him for me."

"That would save some time, I suppose. But still, it seems like a long shot."

"Why don't you take Deirdre with you?"

"Deirdre? I don't think she can afford it."

"Don't worry. I'll support the expenses. You see, I feel bad because a couple of years ago, when Jack needed money for the expedition, I turned him down. But since then I've been the recipient of a modest inheritance, and well, I'd go myself, but this is a very bad time for me with all the museum politics I have to deal with now because of the exhibition."

The problem with taking Deirdre was that she'd just ended their relationship. But maybe, if he asked her about taking a trip to Brazil, she'd reconsider and give him another chance. "Tell you what, Marcus. I'll ask her. If she's for it, we'll leave right away. But we won't go scouring the Amazon unless I find the person who sent this journal, or someone else who knows where to look for Fawcett."

"Wonderful. I'll wire Fletcher that you're on your way." Brody stood up and shook Indy's hand and patted him on the back. "I'm sure Deirdre will be happy to accompany you. She's quite an adventurer from what you've told me about her."

She was that. But Indy wondered if she was more interested in adventures of her own undertaking. He'd soon find out.

It was the middle of the lunch hour and Washington Square was filled with people eating bag lunches when Indy rapped on the front door of the apartment in a brownstone facing the square. If no one answered, he was going to sit on the stoop and wait until Deirdre showed up. It was their last chance to work things out. If she still wanted nothing to do with him, then that was it. But he had to see her face to face one more time.

After several seconds the door opened a crack. "Deirdre?"

"She's not here, Indy. She's gone."

"Angie, if she's in there, let me talk to her. I'm not going to leave until I've seen her."

"Just a minute." She closed the door.

Finally, he thought.

When the door reopened, it was Angie again, and she started to hand Indy something.

"Where is she?"

"I told you, she's gone. She left you this letter."

He took the folded sheet of paper, and opened it up.

"Listen, I've got to get ready for work," Angie said. "Good luck to you." She closed the door; the bolt slid shut. But he wasn't concerned about Angie; he was already reading the letter.

> *Dear Indy,*
> *In case you come by again, I thought it was best if I left you a note. I meant what I said last night. It's over between us. I've decided to go back to London. I'm going to drop out of the university and move home to Scotland. I hope you'll understand. It's not your fault—in spite of Katherine. It's just me.*
> *I wanted to tell you in person this morning when you came to the door, but I couldn't bring myself to do it. It was hard enough saying good-bye at the museum. I'll miss you, but I think it's for the better. I hope I've made the right decision.*
> *Well, my ship is leaving at one. I've got to go. I wish you only the best.*
> *Deirdre*

Indy pulled his pocket watch from his hip pocket. If he hurried, he might still get to the boat in time. He didn't know what he would say to her, but he had to see her before she was gone from his life for good. He caught a taxi and urged the driver to go as fast as he could to the docks.

It seemed to take forever.

Finally, they arrived. He threw some money on the front seat and dashed away. He heard the deep, resonating blast of a ship's horn, signaling that it was leaving port.

No. She couldn't get away like this.

A crowd was gathered. Hands waved, and the ship was slowly pulling away from the pier. His heart pounded, but at the same time it was sinking, along with his hopes of ever seeing her again.

He pushed his way through the crowd and looked up at the passengers lining the railing. He could make out their smiles as they pointed and waved. He searched the faces, but he didn't see Deirdre's. Maybe she'd missed the ship. But, if she'd gone alone, there was no one for her to wave to on the dock. She was probably already in her cabin.

The ship edged further away. He felt lost, alone. He never knew he'd feel this way about a woman. Not even Deirdre.

Snap out of it, he told himself. *She's gone. Forget about her. The world's full of women.*

It didn't work. He felt like diving over the pier and swimming after the ship.

"Indy?"

He was hearing things. He turned. "Deirdre!" He looked at her, looked out to the ship, and back again.

"I couldn't do it," she said.

He saw the tears in her eyes. "I'm glad. Real glad."

They embraced and kissed as if they were lovers who'd been separated for months.

"Let's get out of here," she whispered.

"I don't want to let you go."

"I'm not going anywhere without you."

He drew back from her, tilted his head to the side. "In that case, how would you like to go to Brazil with me? Tomorrow."

She laughed. "Brazil? Are you serious?"

"Of course I am. I'll tell you all about it."

She laughed again. "That's the Indiana Jones I know."

6

Surprises at Sea

The majestic S.S. *Mauretania* dwarfed the sail-boats that moved alongside it in New York harbor. It was not only a massive vessel, but the fastest in the world. Two years earlier, it had set a new cross-Atlantic record of just over five days, averaging 26.25 knots. On this journey the British cruise ship would sail the 4,743 nautical miles from New York to Rio de Janeiro in eight days, arriving on Shrove Tuesday, the high point of Rio's Carnival.

"Indy, this is going to be so much fun," Deirdre said as they gazed at the city skyline in the waning late afternoon light. "A week of relaxing and enjoying ourselves. Then Rio and Carnival."

Indy stretched his left arm, testing its strength. It was still tender to the touch, but improving rapidly. "I'm sure we'll have a gay old time." He was glad Deirdre was so pleased about the trip, but he also wanted her fully aware of the potential dangers. "You've got to remember, though, this isn't a vacation. It's not going to be easy when we get to the jungle. If we get that far, that is."

She slipped a hand around his waist and gazed out at the Statue of Liberty, receding in the distance. "As long as I'm with you, I don't care. But let's not think about that now. We're on a cruise and it's wonderful."

"Mr. Jones. Mr. Indiana Jones," a deep voice boomed along the deck.

Indy waved a hand. "Over here."

"Morning, folks." A tall, lanky Negro dressed in white and wearing a black bow tie approached them. "My name's Oron. I'm your steward. Can I show you to your cabin now?"

"Glad to meet you, Oron," Indy said. "Lead the way."

When they reached the upper deck, they moved down a passageway past several doors. "Here we are," Oron said, handing Indy the key. "Your luggage is already inside. Do you want me to hang your clothes up in the closet?"

"No, thanks. We can handle it." Indy passed him some change. He knew tipping wasn't required until the end of the voyage, but a little extra incentive for good service never hurt.

"Thank you, Mr. Jones, Miss Deirdre." The steward touched the bill of his cap. "I hope you both have a nice trip."

Indy noticed Oron's accent and asked him where he was from. "As a matter of fact, I'm from the place where you're going. Born in Rio fifty years ago this month. They've been calling me the Brazil nut lately, because I'm so happy to be going home. Been away now three years."

"That's a long time," Deirdre said.

"I know, but I ain't complaining. I love the sea, and the *Mauretania* is a wonderful ship."

"Maybe I'll ask you a few questions about your country later on," she said.

"Be more than happy to help in any way I can."

Indy closed the door and gave Deirdre a hug. "It's going to be a good trip."

They moved about the suite peering into the closet and bathroom, and examining the paintings on the wall. Deirdre lifted a complimentary bottle of Bordeaux that was cooling in a bucket of ice. "Should we open it?"

"Let's wait a while." Indy flopped down on the queen-size bed and sank into the soft mattress. "Great room. We could stay right here for a week and send out for meals."

Deirdre reached for his hand and pulled him up. "You're crazy. It's no time for a nap. This is a cruise ship. We've got to enjoy all the amenities. First, I want to see all the shops before dinner. Then after we eat, we'll go to the ballroom."

"Who said anything about a nap?" he groused and tried to pull her on top of him.

She laughed and twisted away, her auburn hair falling across her face. "We'll have plenty of time for that, but you know you're going to have to sleep on the couch."

He sat bolt upright. "What?"

"Appearances, Indy. We're traveling as single people and I don't want the crew talking to the other passengers about us."

"They're not going to talk about us. Besides, how are they going to know anything?"

"They'll know. They make the beds every day."

"For chrissake, Deirdre."

"Just do it for me, Indy. Please. It doesn't mean we can't have our time together."

"Brother."

"Besides, if we'd gotten married last year like we'd talked about, we wouldn't have this problem."

Indy was about to argue with her about which one of them had backed away from marriage, but stopped short. He didn't want to start the trip on a sore note.

"Let's get married then. Right here on the ship," he said offhandedly. "We'll ask the captain to marry us. He can do that, you know."

"Are you serious?"

Indy thought a moment, frowned, then made up his mind. "Yeah. Sure I am."

She jumped on the bed with him and they rolled over until they nearly tumbled to the floor. "Do you really think the captain would do it?"

"Why not?"

Deirdre covered him with kisses as his fingers busied with buttons and zippers. Their clothes fell away and their limbs tangled like vines. His mouth found her breasts, her neck, her lips. Deirdre was no longer concerned about seeing the shops before dinner or what the crew would think about the condition of the bed, and the furthest thing from Indy's mind at the moment were thoughts about Fawcett, the jungle, and the mythical lost city.

Most of the passengers were already eating by the time Indy and Deirdre arrived in the dining room, but there was no chance they would go away hungry. Indy couldn't recall seeing so much food in one place. Plentiful was not the word for it. The buffet looked as if there was enough food to serve the ship's passengers for a year. There were kettles of peeled shrimp, platters of salmon and roast pheasant, broiled chicken and grilled beef, dozens of pots of hot dishes, endless displays of vegetables and fruits as far as he could see, and finally a lavish assortment of cakes and pies.

Even though Indy wore a neatly pressed khaki safari jacket and a tie, he felt underdressed. He was one of the few men who wasn't wearing a tuxedo. But most of the passengers were on a world cruise and he'd be damned if he was going to tote a penguin suit into the jungle. Although, he thought, it would be one hell of a way to greet Colonel Fawcett at his lost city. That is, if they ever found the city and the explorer.

As they ate their dinners, they quietly discussed their marriage plans, and from time to time Indy listened to the conversation around them. A debutante in a frilly gown was twittering about sound coming to the movies and how wonderful it would be when you didn't have to strain your eyes reading the lines.

An older man with a thin mustache offered another view of the future, saying that rockets would someday be feasible transportation. "Why, just the other day I read about a man named Robert Goddard who flew a rocket a hundred eighty-three feet in two and three tenths seconds."

"It's great living in modern times," someone answered. "Just think, last week we were in Paris, today we were in New York, and next week we'll be in Rio."

All the conversation was upbeat, just like the stock market. Everyone around them seemed to be thriving, the cream of Coolidge prosperity. Despite the president's own miserly ways, the attitude was that everything was just going to keep getting better and better. The times were roaring, as the papers liked to say.

After dinner they wandered over to the ballroom where the Paul Whiteman Orchestra was playing. "Jazz, Indy. They've got jazz on the ship. Isn't it wonderful?"

"Yeah, they're real swell," he said without enthusiasm. When Indy had met Deirdre in London, she'd known little about jazz, other than it was a new type of music that had originated in America. Indy, on the other hand, had witnessed the arrival of jazz in Chicago from New Orleans. To him, the all-white band playing "symphonic jazz" was a far cry from the music he remembered in his college years. This was what his old roommate and good friend, Jack Shannon, called milquetoast jazz. The improvisional style was gone and there was nothing rhythmically interesting to what he was hearing. Real jazz was like a new language; symphonic jazz was just an interpretation. But nobody seemed to be complaining. This, after all, was what was also known as acceptable jazz.

"Let's dance, Indy. We can fox-trot, or better yet, you can show me the java that you used to do in Paris."

"Not tonight. Let's go for a walk on the deck. When we get back to New York, I'll take you to a real jazz club, and we'll dance to some low-down music."

"You promise?"

Indy took her hand and smiled as they joined the parade of fashionably dressed men and women promenading along the deck. They gazed up at the Milky Way, which swept across the sky. *Rhapsody in Blue*, Gershwin's new piece, was being piped through loudspeakers. "It's very romantic out here, Indy. I'm so glad we're together."

He led Deirdre over to the railing, squeezed her hand, leaned over, and kissed her.

"I hope this cruise goes on forever, Indy. It's so beautiful. And we're getting married. I can hardly believe it."

They gazed out to sea, lost in their thoughts.

Indy was distracted by the appearance of two men who had stopped by the railing several feet away. He studied them without seeming to do so. One was wiry with rugged features, a long nose, a narrow jaw, and sunken cheeks. His upper lip was short and made him look like he was sneering. The other man was brawny as a redwood trunk and completely bald. Both were dressed in black. Indy wouldn't have looked twice at them in a speakeasy, but on a cruise ship they looked out of place.

He turned his head toward them. Both men looked away. They were probably just off-duty crewmen, he thought. But out of curiosity, he decided to take a closer look at the pair.

"Let's go to the cabin."

"Already?"

"Why not? We can find something to do."

"Again? Indy, we're not supposed to start the honeymoon until after the marriage."

"We can have another honeymoon in Rio."

They walked in the direction of the men, passing within a few feet of them. The sharp-featured man eyed Indy. His right hand was inside his pocket and Indy wondered if it gripped a gun.

"Did you see those two?" he asked.

"What about them?"

"I don't know, but they reminded me of the *huaqueros.* Same mentality, especially the skinny one."

As they turned the corner at the end of the deck just below the bridge, they both glanced back. Neither of the men was in sight. "You're imagining things. There're no *huaqueros* on a cruise ship. No graves to rob."

They both laughed as they climbed a short flight of stairs and followed the passageway to their cabin. As Indy unlocked the door, Deirdre looked over her shoulder. "I still don't see any *hua-queros.*"

"I didn't say they were *huaqueros,*" he grumbled.

He turned on the light, and Deirdre disappeared into the bathroom. A moment later, she let out a sharp shriek.

He rushed in and found her staring at the bathroom mirror. Written on it in white lettering was a brief message: "Give up on Fawcett. Dead is dead. Go back."

"Okay, boys," Indy growled. He flung open his suitcase and dug in his clothing until he found his .455 Webley. He jammed it in his belt. "I'll be right back."

"What are you going to do?"

"I just want to have a little chat with those guys."

"Indy, you don't know it was them."

"It's a good guess."

Deirdre grabbed his arm. "Please, don't go out there. Stay here with me."

He winced. "That's my sore arm. Take it easy."

"See what I mean? You're in no condition to go looking for trouble."

"I'm not looking for trouble. I want to deliver a return message. That's all."

"What are you going to say to them?"

He paused in front of the door, his hand on the knob. "I'll tell them about their bad grammar," he said. "I think they're trying to say Fawcett is dead."

"How would they know Fawcett's dead?"

"I'd say they don't know anything."

Deirdre shook her head. "I don't understand. Why would anyone not want us to look for Fawcett?"

"It could have more to do with what Fawcett was looking for than with Fawcett himself."

There was a knock on the door. Indy pulled it open, and glimpsed two men with faces covered by black stocking caps with the eyes, noses, and mouths cut out. An instant later, he was jerked out into the passageway. One of them landed a blow to Indy's gut, then his head, then his gut again. He never had a chance. The second man struck him behind the neck and kicked his sore shoulder. Indy groaned and crumpled to the floor.

From the couch where he lay, Indy heard Deirdre talking to someone in a low voice, and then she was by his side. "The captain is here. Do you feel up to talk to him?"

Indy adjusted the ice pack, which was pressed to his forehead. "Sure."

The captain, a tall, silver-haired man, sat on a chair next to the bed and listened to Indy's account like a priest hearing the confession of a dying man—except Indy wasn't dying or confessing. He was bruised and angry and became more so as he imagined the weasel-faced man snarling at him.

"So you're fairly certain that the men you saw on the deck were the same ones who attacked you, even though they were masked," the captain said.

"The same bodies," Indy said.

"But not necessarily the same faces."

"I can't prove it."

The captain stood up and paced in front of the couch. "Let's suppose that they are the same. You said that neither of you had ever seen them before. Do you have any idea why these men might not want you to find Colonel Fawcett?"

Indy adjusted the ice pack again, and felt a trickle of water roll down his neck. A vague idea was forming, but it was still too unclear for him to express it. "None whatsoever."

"Only a couple of our friends and the man who sent us know we're here," Deirdre said. "We left on very short notice."

The captain stopped, and tilted his head, puzzling over what he'd heard. "It seems odd that you would leave for an undertaking of this magnitude on such short notice."

"I don't know what magnitude it is, but we left because there was no reason to wait around," Indy said. "And besides it's an emergency."

"I see. You're a very observant man, Mr. Jones. We have eight hundred and ninety-two passengers on board, but it's not going to be very difficult to find a two-hundred-and-twenty-pound bald man. We should have him in custody by morning, and his partner as well."

"Thanks."

"Now I'll let you rest. I'm sorry this unfortunate incident has happened on the *Mauretania*. If I can be of any service, please let me know."

"There is one thing, Captain."

"Oh, what's that?"

"Would you mind marrying Deirdre and me?"

The captain looked from one to the other. "Are you serious?"

"Oh, we're very serious," Deirdre said. "We've been thinking about it for almost a year now."

"When would you like to do it?"

Deirdre smiled. "I've thought about that, too, Captain," she said, and she told him her plan.

A week passed and the *Mauretania* was finally steaming into Guanabara Bay. Indy and Deirdre stood on the ship's bridge gazing toward shore as they waited for the captain to finish last-minute instructions to his mate. A long, curving, white strip of sand separated the city from the deep blue waters, and beyond the cluster of buildings rose dark mountains. Islands and barren rocks jutted from the sea, and at one edge of the bay stood majestic Corcovado, topped by an immense statue of Christ with outstretched arms. On the other side of the bay, the cone-shaped Sugarloaf Mountain bridged water and sky.

It had been a leisurely week, and Indy had recovered from his bruises. But all the while a tense undertone had prevailed. None of the passengers had fit Indy's description of the men, and a search of the ship by crew members had turned up neither the brawny, bald man nor his sinister-looking partner. Whoever they were, they were keeping a low profile. So low, in fact, it seemed as if they'd leaped over the side of the ship.

When the search was called off, Indy had started his own investigation. With Oron's help, he'd gotten a list of passengers who were taking all or most of their meals in their cabins: the captain's elderly mother, a retired couple, and a wheelchair-bound man who Oron said waved a cane at him and complained about something every time he entered his room.

Virtually everyone on the ship knew about the assault and the descriptions of the men, but no one had seen them. Still, he knew the pair must be here, and he kept glancing over his shoulder, expecting to see one or both of them skulking after him.

"Will you look at it, Indy," Deirdre said in a hushed voice.

"They say God created the world in six days, and on the seventh He created Rio," the captain remarked as he joined them.

"I can believe it," Deirdre said. "Look, I can see the cross on Corcovado. The bay is like a huge church and the mountain is the altar."

"I guess the ship must be our pew," Indy said, seizing on the analogy.

The captain cleared his throat. "I almost forgot. By law I'm required to have a witness. My second mate is at the helm and my first mate is sleeping after all-night duty. But maybe—"

"We've already taken care of that," Deirdre said. "Oron, our steward, will be our witness. He's waiting for you to call him."

The captain frowned at Deirdre, then addressed Indy. "But he's a *niggero.*"

"Is there some law of the sea against his being our witness?" Indy asked.

"No, but—"

"Then call him," Indy said.

A couple minutes later, Oron stood to one side as the captain paged through a leather-bound book with a well-worn silver anchor embossed on the cover. "You understand, we're going to have to make this fast. If we'd held the ceremony on the open seas, as I suggested, we could've taken our time."

"It's not the length of the ceremony that counts," Deirdre said.

"Yeah, it's the view," Indy added dryly.

"Indy," Deirdre scolded. Then she smiled up at him. She'd been the one to insist they be married as they entered the bay, and that was fine with him.

She wore a white gown and veil, which had been designed and sewn by the ship's seamstress over the past several days. Indy wore the same safari jacket he'd worn to dinner every evening. But at

Deirdre's insistence, he'd had it cleaned and had bought a new tie for the occasion.

He took Deirdre's hand. "Let's get on with it."

The captain cleared his throat again. He started reading from the marriage ceremony, but Indy barely heard a word of it. His gaze was fixed on the second mate, who had looked over his shoulder for the first time.

The man had a full head of hair, yet Indy was certain he was the burly, bald man who'd beaten him outside his cabin. Maybe he was wearing a wig. But more likely he'd been wearing a rubber skullcap.

"Do you, Henry Jones, Jr., take this woman for your lawful, wedded wife?"

Suddenly, he felt Deirdre nudge him with her elbow. He saw the captain raise his eyes from the book.

"Oh, yeah. Yes, I do."

"Do you, Deirdre Campbell, take this man to be your lawful, wedded husband?"

"I do."

"I now pronounce you man and wife."

Indy took Deirdre in his arms, and kissed her tenderly. But he opened one eye, and watched the burly man at the helm.

7

CARNIVAL

The masked ball at the Palace Hotel was one of the highlights of Carnival and attracted the cream of Rio society, who wore all sorts of exotic costumes. When Indy and Deirdre arrived at the hotel, they were told that free passes were available to the ball for all passengers from the *Mauretania*. Deirdre immediately took charge, accepting the passes and arranging for the costumes.

And here they were, their first night in Rio amid dozens of revelers, some of whom were garbed in costumes that seemed like extensions of their bodies. They wore everything from ornate, colonial outfits to fantasy attire that made them look like characters out of *Alice in Wonderland*.

Indy wore a frilly white shirt and shiny ebony boots that met the bottom of his knee-length britches. A sword hung from his belt and a black mask covered his eyes and nose. Perched on his head was a wide-brimmed felt hat with one side folded up to the crown and a long feather curving from the other side.

"Ridiculous," he murmured when he caught sight of himself in a mirrored wall as they entered the ballroom.

"Oh, you look great," Deirdre said. "Just like one of the Three Musketeers."

"Thanks. You look right out of another century yourself." She was dressed in a floor-length gown with a bustle. She wore heavy makeup and a white wig that curled high on her head and trailed down her back. In her hand she held a rhinestone-covered mask attached to a holder.

"Do you realize that not much more than a week ago we were at a museum opening in New York?"

"Too bad I didn't have this outfit then. I could have claimed I was the ghost of Columbus and mad as hell."

Deirdre didn't respond to his joke. "And we were on the verge of breaking up and now we're married." She lowered her mask and looked into his eyes. "Indy, I'm so glad I didn't get on that ship for London."

"I'm glad, too."

They wandered through the crowd toward the dance floor. "Can you just imagine what Dr. Bernard would think if he saw us now?"

"Why did you mention him?"

"You know, he's so serious. He'd never go to anything like this."

"But he might send someone else," Indy said.

"What do you mean?" she asked.

"I think Bernard is the one behind the trouble on the ship."

Deirdre nearly dropped her mask. "Dr. Bernard? No, I can't believe that."

"Listen, you don't know him very well. I don't either, but I'm starting to catch on." He told her how the professor had urged him to sign a petition condemning Brody's exhibition. "Bernard doesn't want anyone to even consider the possibility that cross-Atlantic voyages might have taken place before Columbus. He'd have egg all over his face if Fawcett proved him wrong."

"But Indy, he didn't know we were going to Brazil. It doesn't make sense."

"He must have found out."

"From who? Not from Mr. Brody."

"From Marcus's new secretary. That's who."

Deirdre looked mystified.

"Brenda Hilliard," Indy said, answering her unspoken question.

"My mother's old secretary? You're kidding."

" 'Fraid not. She worked for Bernard for several months before she moved to New York."

"Still, even if Bernard happened to see Brenda and she told him about what we were doing, do you really think he'd go to the trouble of hiring someone to threaten you and beat you up?"

"I don't know, Deirdre. It does seem sort of farfetched, but I can't think of a better suspect at the moment."

"Then tell me how Dr. Bernard could have gotten the second mate of the ship into his scheme in such a short time?"

Indy didn't have an answer. At this point, in fact, he was ready to forget about it. The *Mauretania* would be sailing tomorrow, heading down the coast of South America, and the second mate would be aboard. Indy had other things to think about, like getting to Bahia, and finding the Hotel Paraíso. Still, he couldn't shrug off the memory of the other man, the weasel-faced one with the sunken cheeks. He was still a mystery, as veiled as the masked party-goers around them.

"What are you thinking?" Deirdre asked.

Indy hitched his sword, and smiled. "Oh, I don't know. Just what a great wife I've got."

Deirdre squeezed his hand. "Did you ever think you'd get married on a boat?"

Indy spotted a table filled with hors d'oeuvres and led Deirdre toward it. "Can't say I did. But I know it was definitely a once-in-a-lifetime experience."

"You mean you'll never get married on a boat again?"

He laughed. "I mean never get married again, period."

"That's nice of you to say. If you die before me, I'll never—"

"So how are the newlyweds?" Indy turned to see a talk, dark-skinned man dressed in a pirate outfit, a mask over his eyes. "Hello, Oron."

"Guess my disguise didn't fool you," Oron said with a laugh.

"And ours didn't fool you, either."

"Mrs. Jones isn't keeping her eyes covered very well," Oron said.

"What brings you here?" Indy asked.

"Oh, just enjoying Carnival. Fun and games. By the way, Mrs. Jones, the captain's mother is here and she'd like to see you." He leaned forward and smiled. "I think she has a wedding gift for you."

"Really? Where is she?"

"Seated on the other side. You can't see her from here."

Deirdre beamed. "I'll go over and say hello, and be right back."

Just then the music changed from a waltz to an upbeat samba. Couples crammed the dance floor, and Deirdre disappeared into the crowd. "How

did the captain's mother know we'd be here?"
Indy asked.

"She's staying at the hotel, too, and asked me to
find out if you two had arranged for costumes,"
Oron answered.

"Is the captain here?"

"No, he's on the ship."

If the captain's mother had been so enfeebled
that she was confined to her cabin, what was she
doing at a masked ball and without her son? Indy
wondered.

"But Hans is here somewhere."

"Who's Hans?"

"The second mate. The big guy," Oron added,
explaining that he was wearing a pirate's outfit
with an eyepatch and a red bandana on his head.

"He's here? Where?"

"I last saw him across the dance floor." Oron
pointed in the direction that Deirdre had gone.

Indy didn't say another word. He moved
through the dancers as best he could. When he
reached the other side of the ballroom, there were
no chairs, no captain's mother, no Deirdre. He
scanned the crowd. He didn't know where to look,
or which direction to go.

"What's wrong, Mr. Jones?" Oron asked.

"Wrong?" Indy grabbed Oron by his collar.
"What do you know about this? What's going on?"

Oron held up his hands, and chortled. "Hey,
take it easy, Mr. Jones. No reason to get all upset.
It's just a little wedding game."

"A wedding game?"

"You know, steal the bride from the groom after
the wedding."

"What?" Indy gripped Oron's collar even
tighter. "Whose idea was it?"

"Well, you know word got around that there was

going to be a wedding on board. It was Mr. Frank Carino, the man in the wheelchair, who came up with the idea."

"Carino? I thought he was an old grouch."

"He got nicer by the end of the trip. And he's not so old."

"What's he look like?"

"He's thin. Not a real good-looking man."

"Rough skin? Sunken cheeks? Kind of a weasel face?"

"Oh, that's a nasty description, but you got him right."

"Let me guess, Hans is playing the game, too. Right?"

Oron nodded. Indy let go of him, realizing that they'd both been duped.

"It's no game, Oron."

"But you don't think Mr. Carino is the man you were looking for, do you?"

"One of them. Hans is the other."

"But Mr. Carino is crippled and Hans isn't bald."

"Details." Indy waved a hand. "Where did they take her?"

"I don't know. They didn't say, but they promised me they would bring her back to the hotel by midnight. Hans wouldn't do anything to harm her."

"Don't count on it." This was definitely no game with those two guys playing.

"You know, I never did like that second mate. I was surprised he would be interested in playing a joke on you. Didn't seem like his sort of fun. He's a gambler. Gambles too much."

Indy didn't have time for small talk. "We've got to find Deirdre. Where would they have taken her?"

Oron was quiet a moment. "Wait a minute. I think I know."

"Where?"

"C'mon. I'll tell you on the way."

They rushed out onto the street, not bothering to change out of their costumes. It hardly mattered. They fit right in. Everywhere Indy looked, there were people clothed in gaudy and outrageous garb, and right now a couple of thousand of them were parading down the street in front of the hotel.

"It's a *blocos carnavalescos,* a neighborhood parade," Oron said as a coterie of bare-legged dancers gyrated to the beat of a cadre of drummers. They were followed by a marching band and a series of flower-covered floats, and costumed characters who looked like they'd arrived from another planet. No, several other planets.

"Swell party," Indy said. "Which way do we go?"

"This way." They dashed into the street, dodging through the dancers, then hurried down to the corner. They turned left, then halfway down the block Oron hailed a taxi. "Pão de Açúcar," Oron told the driver.

"Sugarloaf?" Indy asked.

"That's my guess. I heard Hans say they were going to give her a view of the city. One she would never forget. That's the place for it."

Indy didn't like the sound of it. He didn't like the idea of the two men who'd pummeled him forcing Deirdre to go anywhere. The taxi had gone only a couple of blocks when it was suddenly mired in traffic as cars jammed a cross street. The driver stopped and waited patiently for the other cars to move.

"Say, can you be a little more assertive?" Indy urged. "We're in a hurry. Someone's waiting for us, and she can't wait much longer."

"You can be in a hurry if you want, but you are not going to get any place in a hurry. Not in Rio, not during Carnival," the taxi driver said.

Indy saw a break in traffic, but the driver was busy motioning with his hands and talking. "Just relax and enjoy yourself. Your friend will be waiting."

"Drive, don't talk." Indy rose up from his seat and pointed over the man's shoulder as another opening appeared. "Go. Take it."

"You are not in New York, mister."

"What does that mean?"

"We drive from the front seat, not the back."

Oron spoke in a rapid Portuguese dialect, which Indy didn't understand. Whatever he said worked. The driver abruptly shut up and sped ahead through the traffic as if it wasn't there.

Indy sat back. "What did you say to him, anyhow?"

"I told him that you are a very rich man and if he got us to Sugarloaf in five minutes, you would pay him five times the rate."

"That was nice of you." Indy tried to guess how much that was going to cost him.

Suddenly, another parade was marching in front of them, but the driver swerved in between two floats and joined the parade. People lining the street peered in at the two masked men in the back of the taxi. Oron waved. Indy adjusted his musketeer hat and wondered if he would ever see Deirdre alive again. At the corner, the driver turned and accelerated down the street and away from the parade.

They reached the base of the massive granite

cone in less than five minutes. Indy had the money ready and slapped the stack of bills into the driver's hand. He heard the man thanking him profusely as he and Oron hurried away.

"The cable cars are over here," Oron said, pointing the way.

As they rushed through the darkness, Indy drew deep breaths of salt air into his lungs. They were already high enough above the city to see the glistening waters of the bay in the moonlight, but Indy paid it no attention. He wasn't here to enjoy the view.

When they arrived at the ticket booth, Indy asked the man at the window if he'd seen two men and a woman in the past fifteen minutes. He started to describe them, but the ticket man cut him off. "Almost no one is going up the mountain tonight. Everyone is below enjoying Carnival."

"So you haven't seen them?"

"Yes, I have seen them. Usually, I wouldn't remember. Tonight, yes. They were here just five, six minutes ago."

Indy paid for a pair of passes, then gave the ticket man another bill. "How did the woman look?"

"Her face was very white."

Indy shook his head, exasperated. "That was makeup. Was she okay?"

The man thought a moment. "I heard one of them tell her not to be afraid. Some people are very frightened of the cable cars. They think the cable will break, but it never does."

"When's the next car?"

The ticket man shrugged. "When more people come. We must have at least six to go."

Indy reached into his pocket and handed the man the rest of the money he was carrying. It was probably close to what the man earned in a week. "We need a car *now*."

The money quickly disappeared from sight. "Okay. Two minutes."

"Why so long?"

"Two minutes," the man repeated. "Not so long."

They moved over to the platform and Indy paced back and forth. He could hear the beat of drums and blare of horns from the parades below. The chaotic sounds wavered eerily through the night air. He squeezed his eyes shut and the faces of the wildly costumed dancers leered at him. Carnival was a bad dream. He wanted to wake up and find himself in bed with Deirdre at his side. But this nightmare, he knew, wasn't over yet.

"At least we're looking in the right place," Oron said.

"Yeah, but what are we going to find?"

Deirdre was pressed against the window of the cable car, staring down at the city. The two men were on either side of her, and the creepy one in the pirate's outfit had a gun pressed hard in her side. She could feel his foul breath on her and she wanted to scream. But four or five other people were in the car and he'd warned her that if she said anything he would shoot.

She stared at the shimmering lights of Rio below them, and wondered where Indy was. When she couldn't find the captain's mother, the pirate had rolled up to her in a wheelchair, introduced himself as Mr. Carino, and said the old lady was waiting in the hallway. Like a fool, she'd gone with him, thinking there was something familiar about him, something she should remember. It was Indy's description, of course. He was the weasel-faced one from the ship. As soon as they were outside the ballroom another pirate appeared. This one she recognized as the second mate from the ship. Then everything Indy had said fell together.

She'd tried to run, but it was too late. Carino had bolted out of the chair and grabbed her, and his partner gagged her. No one had seemed the least bit concerned. Those who noticed just laughed. "There's Marie Antoinette," one woman had said. She was just another person in a weird costume. When they reached the cable station, Carino had taken the gag off, showed her the gun, and threatened her. But now she didn't care.

"Why don't you want us to find Fawcett?" she asked in as calm a voice she could muster.

For a moment, she didn't think he was going to answer. "I don't give a damn about Fawcett. My employer does."

"Bernard?"

Carino didn't answer.

Deirdre glanced at the burly second mate who was positioned between her and the other passengers. She didn't understand what was going on. "How did you get a job on the ship so fast?"

The second mate glanced at her, then looked away. But Carino, who seemed to be enjoying himself, answered for him. "Hans lost in poker with the wrong people when he was in port in New York. Four hundred dollars more than he could afford. He wasn't going to leave the city without a broken leg or two, but then I generously paid the debt in exchange for his services. He was just the man I was looking for."

The cable car was slowing to a stop. "I still don't understand why Bernard would go to all this trouble."

Carino took her arm and led her out of the car. "Who the hell is Bernard?"

The cable car suddenly jolted to a stop and they swung in midair high over the city. Indy glanced at Oron, who shrugged at his wordless question. He didn't know what had happened, either.

Indy imagined Carino and Hans jimmying the gears just in case they were being pursued, and here they were, trapped, unable to go forward or back or to get off. They would be here for hours, probably until morning before a maintenance crew arrived to repair the cable, and all the while Deirdre would be at the mercy of the thugs.

"Maybe it's just temporary," Oron said, hopefully. "Sometimes they stop, you know."

"No, I don't know that." Indy looked over the side, but couldn't see anything.

"Don't even think about jumping out of here," Oron said.

"Maybe the mountainside is only a few feet down."

He shook his head. "It's at least a hundred feet and it's steep. You wouldn't make it and even if you did live, you wouldn't be any better off."

Indy believed him. But there was another option. "I'm going up." Before Oron could respond, Indy climbed out the window and onto the top of the car. He reached up, grabbed the cable, and pulled himself hand over hand. He was going to get to the top one way or another. That was all there was to it.

"Indy Jones. Get your ass back down here. You can't do that."

He ignored Oron. He climbed.

He'd only gone a dozen yards or so when it dawned on him that he'd taken on a bigger challenge than he'd thought. But he hadn't thought; he'd acted. The angle was steep, and the cable was greasy. More importantly, there was no end in sight.

He looped his legs over the cable to rest and reconsider. His sword dangled from his side; his floppy hat fell off. He was no longer a dashing musketeer, but a fool hanging upside down in the dark.

Better go back.

Just then he heard a noise and felt the cable vibrate. The car was moving forward again, coming right at him. Panicking, he climbed hand over hand, his legs kicking below him as if he were running a race . . . a race he was losing.

"Jones . . . Jones . . . watch out."

Oron's yell echoed in his head. The car was right behind him, about to hit him. Shudders of fear rippled through him. He was losing his grip. It didn't matter. The race was over. He dangled from one hand, spun around, and let go.

8

SUGARLOAF

A fraction of a second after Indy let go of the cable, he collided with the front of the car. His hands slapped against the windowpane and he hung for a moment from the ledge. He could see Oron looking helplessly at him through the window. His fingers were slick with grease and scraped raw from the cable. He couldn't hold on; he slipped and fell. But his outstretched hands caught the front bumper. He dangled from the car, his legs kicking the air.

Hang on . . . hang on. If I fall, I'm dead.

He tried desperately to pull himself up onto the bumper. But just as he got one knee onto it, the unexpected happened again. The car jerked to a halt as if someone had slammed on the brakes, and he was knocked from the bumper. He twisted in midair, hoping a tree on the mountainside would break his fall, but almost instantly he was sprawled on his hands and knees against something hard and flat. He rolled over. A wooden platform. He wasn't hurt. He looked up and saw a pair of legs, and a startled man staring at him.

"Are we at the top already?" Indy asked.

The man edged around him, dumbfounded by the sight, and opened the door of the cable car. "Mr. Jones, you're alive," Oron said incredulously as he rushed from the car and helped Indy to his feet.

Indy adjusted his sword as he stood up. "I think so. Where are we?"

"Morro da Urca," the cable car operator said. "Halfway to the top."

"Why did we stop?" Indy demanded.

The operator looked blankly at him. "The cars always stop here."

"No, I mean down there, before we got here," Indy persisted.

"The cars stop when one is unloading at the top," the man said defensively. "What were you doing outside the car, anyhow?"

"Enjoying the night air," Indy answered.

"They must have just gotten there," Oron said. "C'mon. Let's go."

But Indy wanted to make sure. "Did anyone get off here a few minutes ago?"

"No, and if you're going to the top, you stay inside that car," the operator said.

"He's right about that," Oron said as the door slid closed behind them. "I've never seen such a crazy thing in my life."

"Sometime you got to take chances."

"That wasn't the time."

Indy agreed, but it didn't matter any more. The car was moving again and the dark peak of Sugarloaf was silhouetted against the sky.

* * *

Four thousand, seven hundred and forty-three miles north of Sugarloaf Mountain, Victor Bernard stared up at the clock in Grand Central Station. Eleven-fourteen P.M. and Julian Ray was a quarter of an hour late. Bernard paced back and forth like a bear trapped in a cage. His train would depart in a few minutes, and he needed to know what was going on before he left.

He tried to take his mind off the passing minutes and concentrate on what he would do in Guatemala City to get the artifacts released to him. It would require a bribe or two, but he'd be able to make up the loss, as well as a substantial profit for himself, after he sold some of the antique jewels on the international market.

Even though he needed money, the trip no longer seemed so important to him. Much more was at stake in Brazil. He looked at the clock again. *Damn it. Where the hell is Ray?*

Bernard and Julian Ray seemed an odd pair, an archaeologist and a Mafia loan shark-turned-bookmaker, but Bernard had an addiction and it didn't matter whom he associated with if the person could satisfy his uncompromising desire to gamble. When Fawcett set out on his mission in the spring of 1925, Bernard contacted the bookie to bet against Fawcett. They'd settled on a bet that gave Fawcett until May 1 to return to civilization. Ray set the odds at ten to one in favor of Fawcett's return. Bernard had tried to get Ray to specify that he must also show up with evidence of a lost city inhabited by a white-skinned race in the Amazon. But Ray just laughed, and told Bernard that was another bet with different odds.

Bernard had placed a thirty-thousand-dollar inheritance on the bet. He was counting on winning to pay off a couple of other debts to Ray. The bookie had extended his deadline to pay them to May 1. If Fawcett turned up safe, Bernard knew he would lose more than a fortune. So he'd taken precautions. He'd helped Brenda Hilliard, his former secretary, fulfill her dream to live in New York by arranging a job with Marcus Brody, who happened to be one of Fawcett's confidants. Until recently it had seemed like an unnecessary move. But now he was pleased he'd done it.

As the months passed with no word from Fawcett, the odds had shifted so that now a gambler who bet on the explorer's return would receive six dollars on every dollar bet, if he won. And because of the publicity about the Englishman's quest, betting on the side of the popular adventurer had been heavy. Bernard, though, was locked into his original odds, and now he and Ray would lose fortunes if Fawcett turned up.

Finally, with just six minutes to go before his train left, Bernard spotted the bookmaker strolling casually across the nearly deserted terminal. He was wearing a three-piece suit and a hat, and his black hair glistened with a sheen that matched his wing-tip shoes. Bernard knew he shouldn't really be meeting in public with Ray. He certainly didn't want anyone to find out about his association with the notorious underworld figure, but even more important was the mission that he'd entrusted Ray to carry out.

"Well, have you heard anything yet?" Bernard asked, forsaking any formalities with Ray.

"Calm down, Victor. The man I sent on the job is one of the best."

Ray was as suave and relaxed as ever. He made Bernard feel like an overgrown ape with an itchy ass. "I was hoping you'd know something by now."

"They're all in Rio, and everything will be taken care of. You don't want to know anything more."

"I didn't want any violence, Julian. You told me—"

"I told you I'd get the job done, and that it's better if no one gets hurt. But it's not a perfect world, my friend. Sometimes it's necessary to rough up certain individuals to convince them of your serious intentions."

"I suppose," Bernard said. "I just want to make sure that Jones doesn't do anything to throw off the odds."

The information Bernard had received from Brenda about the journal had given him a shock. What if there actually was a lost city that was inhabited? Maybe Fawcett was really onto something. As a scientist, Bernard was intrigued, but skeptical. As a gambler, Bernard knew the only thing that mattered was to keep Fawcett from reappearing before the deadline. Ray was ruthless with deadbeats, and Bernard couldn't afford to lose, not if he wanted to live.

"Don't worry about it now," Ray said. "Just enjoy your trip down to banana land."

Bernard didn't like Ray's condescending tone. At least he had a profession that in the last fifty years had become a respectable science. Ray was sharp, but he was a criminal and always would be. "There's more than bananas in Guatemala."

Ray adjusted his tie and grinned. "To each his own, Dr. Bernard. To each his own."

Bernard walked away. He should've been running if he was going to make his train. But he'd already changed his mind. He was taking a ship to Bahia, where he would find a certain pilot who owned a guava farm. He wasn't going to take any chances.

* * *

After the cable car stopped, Deirdre was quickly escorted away from the other passengers. Instead of walking over to the side of the mountain over-looking the city, they moved to the ocean side and stopped at the brink.

"What are you going to do?" Deirdre asked.

Neither man answered. Carino motioned to Hans, who took out a rope and started to tie it around her waist. Deirdre struggled and screamed for help. Instantly, Carino's gun was at her mouth. "One more word and you're dead. But if you keep your mouth shut, lady, you might just get out of this alive. You got that?"

The barrel of the gun touched her teeth; she tasted metal. She smelled gun oil. She imagined Carino squeezing the trigger and the bullet shat-tering her teeth and exploding through her brain and out the back of her head. She quit struggling and held her breath, paralyzed with fear.

As soon as Carino removed the gun, Hans tied the gag again. Then they led her along a rocky path that descended from the top of the cone. The silvery surface of the sea shimmered in the moon-light far below, but she couldn't focus on it. She couldn't focus on anything.

When they stopped, Hans slipped the rope be-neath her arms, passed the end of it through a loop, and pulled it tight. "Okay, lady, here's what's what," Carino said. "See that tree?"

All Deirdre could think of was that Carino was no doubt the one who'd written "Dead is dead" on the mirror of their cabin. Finally, she forced her eyes to focus on the tree, a scrawny juniper that grew out of the granite wall. She saw Hans loop the rope that was wrapped around her over a limb that reached out toward the sea.

"You're going to hang from that branch for a while. Now if you're real good and don't get all wild, you're going to do okay. But if you start dancing around out there like a fool, you're not going to make it. The branch won't hold you, and if it snaps, them's the breaks. If you fall, you fall. Got that? Now don't say I didn't warn you."

Carino nodded to Hans and he pulled on the rope. She was lifted off the ground. Her instinct was to struggle and pull the gag from her mouth, but she knew Carino was right about the branch. Below her, the rock wall fell in nearly a vertical drop. The rope cut into the skin under her arms. Already her ribs felt bruised. She cried into the gag as she swung out over the mountain. It didn't matter what was below her now. She just felt the pain.

"Let's get out of here," Carino said. "See ya, lady. No hard feelings, eh? And if you survive this little ordeal, you tell your new husband to find another adventure if he wants you and him to stay alive. This one's too goddamn dangerous. Got that?"

And they were gone.

Indy started talking to the cable car operator at the top of the mountain even before the car stopped. "Two men and a woman. Did you see which way they went?"

The man opened the door for them.

"The men were wearing pirate costumes and the woman a dress and wig," Oron said.

"Everyone goes to see the city lights at night," the man said. "But those three went the other way."

Oron immediately set out in the direction he

pointed. But Indy asked another question. "Are they still up here?"

The cable car operator frowned. "I haven't seen them head back down yet."

The moon shone overhead, illuminating the rocky landscape as they moved toward the bay side of the mountain. It was quiet and still, but the serenity was false. He wanted to shout Deirdre's name to let her know that he was here and to shatter the deceptive tranquility. But he held himself back.

"Mr. Jones."

Oron's voice sounded hollow and grim.

"What is it?"

The tall Negro looked like a statue of a pirate staring out to sea. It took a moment for Indy to see what he was looking at. Then he saw the body hanging motionless from the tree limb. He didn't want to believe it was Deirdre. He wanted the white wig and billowy gown to belong to a mannequin, not a real person. Not Deirdre. But then he saw her face.

"Oh, God," he gasped.

They hurried down the rocky path that passed below the tree. He moved to the edge of the precipice and saw that the rope was under her arms, not around her neck. The moon shone on her face and he saw her eyes blink, then grow wide in surprise and horror.

"She's alive," Oron said.

"We've got to get her down."

"Be careful."

Deirdre reached up and tried to pull the gag from her mouth. The branch on which she was hanging was as slender as her wrist and it was curving downward under her weight. "Don't move, sweetheart. Don't even try to take out the gag. We're going to get you down here real fast."

"How?" Oron asked.

"I knew I should've worn my whip instead of the sword," he muttered, thinking how easily he'd snap it around Deirdre's waist and pull her to him. When the branch broke, she'd be in his arms. But he didn't have his whip, so he'd have to try something else.

"Oron, you think you can hold my weight on your shoulders? I'll grab her, then you pull me back."

"I can hold your weight, but I don't know about anything after that."

"We've got to try it." The branch holding Deirdre sagged another couple of inches. "Now is definitely the time for taking a chance."

Oron nodded, then crouched down and Indy mounted his shoulders. The steward rose on his feet, and moved unsteadily toward the precipice. Indy stretched a hand toward Deirdre, who slowly reached out to him. His fingers brushed hers, but she was still out of his reach.

"Mr. Jones, I forgot to tell you something," Oron said.

"What's that?" Indy said through gritted teeth as he leaned farther forward.

"I'm afraid of heights."

Suddenly, both men were wobbling precariously. "Don't look down, Oron."

"My eyes are closed."

"Then open them." Indy swiped his hand toward Deirdre and snatched her wrist. "I got her. Move back."

"I can't. I can't move."

Indy pulled on Deirdre's arm and leaned back as far as he could. She was inches from the edge. But just then one of Oron's feet slipped and he toppled over backwards under Indy's weight. Indy's grease-slick hand slipped from Deirdre's wrist. The branch snapped. She fell, screaming into the gag.

Indy rolled over. She was gone, and his heart was ready to explode at the loss. Then he saw her hanging on the wall. He was both relieved that she was still alive, and worried that she would tumble to her death at any moment.

"Oh, God. Quick, lower me down," he hissed.

Oron's hands clamped over his ankles, and Indy crawled headfirst down the wall. His blood ran to his head, pounded in his temples, roared in his ears. He reached a hand toward Deirdre, but her fingers were still inches away.

"A little more, Oron."

"I can't go no further. That's it or we all fall."

Indy felt the sword brush against his outstretched arm. He reached up to his waist and pulled it out, sliding it through his hand inch by inch until it was out of its sheath. He lowered the hilt to Deirdre, who gripped it with both hands.

But as soon as she did, the sword started slipping through his hands. "I can't hold you," he shouted to her. He didn't know what to do.

"Mr. Jones," Oron yelled. "Hurry up!"

"I still can't reach her."

Then Deirdre solved the problem. Somehow she propped herself on the wall, grabbed the rope that was tied around her, and gripped it with her teeth. Then she slid her grip lower, repeating the process until she held the end of it with a length of branch in her hand. She hurled the rope, branch and all, up to him.

Indy snatched the branch, and found the rope. Quickly, he pulled the branch away, then slipped the noose over his arms until it was tight around his chest.

"I got her," Indy yelled. "Pull me up."

Oron didn't answer. Didn't say a word.

"Oron?"

"Sorry it has to be this way, Mr. Jones, but I've got a job to do."

"What?" He craned his head, looked up at Oron. Carino stood on one side of him, Hans on the other. They were staring down at him, and it was obvious they weren't going to help.

"Don't let go, Oron," he yelled.

"Oron's part of the game, Jones," Carino crowed. "We didn't quite plan it this way, but what works works. Right? Let him go, Oron."

"I thought we weren't going to kill anyone, Oron complained."

"Let him go or you're going with him."

Indy felt Oron's hands release him, and suddenly he was plunging down headfirst. The rope jerked Deirdre from the wall, and they tumbled downward. Death rushed at him, it's black mouth yawning wide . . .

The next thing he knew he was floating in a pale, gray light, and there was a mist below him. He heard a voice, someone talking. Calling his name.

Where was he? Who was talking? He didn't feel anything. This was his childhood image of what death was like. Or after death. A lot of mist and waiting around for someone to tell you what's going on.

Then he turned his head and saw Deirdre. Her eyes were open. She was dangling from a rope, and her gag hung around her neck. This was not part of any childhood fantasy. This was real.

"Indy?"

"Where are we?"

"My God, I thought you'd never snap out of it. Are you okay?"

It all came back to him. "How long . . . ?"

"It's dawn."

He looked up and saw that the rope that tied them together was hooked over an iron spike. "I don't believe it."

"Can you reach it?" she asked.

"Reach what?"

"The piton. We can scale the rock face to the top. Mountain climbers have done it. They put in these pitons all the way up. That's what I was hanging onto before. Remember?"

"Vaguely."

He looked over at her, amazed. "I'm glad you're so levelheaded."

"Are you kidding? As soon as I got that gag off, I started screaming for help until I was hoarse, for all the good it did."

Indy tested the rope; as soon as he did, he felt a sharp pain in his chest. He winced, but pulled up with one hand and reached the piton with the other one. The rope inched up with him and Deirdre slipped downward.

"You okay?" he called out.

"I'm on another piton. They're every couple of feet. You should be able to see them."

He looked up, trying to ignore his throbbing head and burning chest. He saw several pitons. "Okay. You ready to try it?"

"I think so."

Then he thought of something. "Should we take the rope off?"

"Oh, no, you don't. Remember. For better or worse. We make it or we don't . . . together."

"That's right. We're married."

"Almost a day now," she said.

"A helluva honeymoon," he groused.

"One we'll never forget."

He reached up and found a piton, then another.
He knew then they were going to make it.

9

HOTEL PARAÍSO

They could've been in Nigeria, Indy thought as he and Deirdre moved through the crowded outdoor market. They were in the lower city of São Salvador da Bahia de Todos os Santos. Or just Bahia, as everyone called it. It was known as the stronghold of Brazil's African culture, and that was readily apparent. The chic, fast-tempo, Latin style of Rio had been replaced with an enduring rhythmic cadence, an earthy magic that rumbled from the hearts and tongues of the people and spoke of Africa and ancient times.

A woman in a billowy cotton dress bargained for fruit in Nago, the language of the African Yorubas. Nearby, a tall man, who reminded Indy of Oron, leaned against a wall next to a stack of baskets and watched the couple walk by. A young woman sat on a stool behind a counter that was piled high with ripe mangoes as she casually nursed her young baby and rocked it in her arms.

The day after Indy and Deirdre had survived the fall from Sugarloaf, they'd taken a freighter north. It made several stops and the trip to Bahia had taken them nearly as long as their voyage from New York to Rio. But they were in no hurry and used the time to recover from their array of minor injuries.

Now that Carino and his partners had left them for dead, they were free to focus on the intent of their journey. They needed to find whoever had sent the pages from Fawcett's journal to Brody, but that was turning out to be more difficult than Indy had expected. Their only lead was the name of the hotel, and so far they hadn't even been able to find it.

When they arrived, the first person they'd asked about the hotel had looked at their luggage and laughed. Two others said they didn't know where it was. Finally, after a woman had told Deirdre to find another hotel, they did. Then they returned to the street free of luggage and resumed their hunt. Indy didn't know what they were going to do if they didn't find the Hotel Paraíso. They couldn't just turn around. It wouldn't be fair to Brody.

A crack of thunder drew his gaze skyward, where ominous purple thunderheads climbed toward what was left of the sun.

"Let's find a place to eat," he suggested.

"Good idea. I'm starving."

"How about right here?" Indy pointed to a long wooden table that was situated next to an outdoor kitchen covered by a canvas awning.

Deirdre looked doubtfully at the food being prepared by two fleshy women who wore colorful skirts and white blouses. "Here, really?"

"Why not?"

She shrugged. "Well, I suppose."

They took seats at the end of a table that was

already occupied by several others and ordered a meal of fried fish, steamed rice with coconut milk, corn on the cob, and tapioca cakes. The air was fragrant with the smells of fish and spices, manure and mud. Flies buzzed about their heads, and a stray dog was waiting patiently for leftovers.

"It's not the *Mauretania*," Deirdre said.

"Think of it as a picnic," Indy responded.

"Right. Guess I better get used to it if we're going to the jungle."

By the time the food arrived, all Indy could think about was his appetite. He quickly devoured his meal. Deirdre was less enthusiastic and tossed her tapioca cake to the dog.

A slender, brown-skinned man across from them kept glancing their way. He had large ebony eyes and curly hair and was in his early twenties. "Excuse me, my friends," he said in passable English. "You want to see the city? I have taxi. My name is Hugo." He looked over at Deirdre, and smiled broadly. "I know best shops, best prices."

"Oh, that's wonderful," she said. "Can you take us to the Hotel Paraíso?"

Hugo gazed at them with a wry look on his face. "Why do you want to go there? No tourist has ever asked me about that place."

"You know where it is?"

"Of course."

Deirdre shook her head. "Then why doesn't anyone else? We've asked at least half a dozen people today."

Hugo leaned forward. "Because they don't want to get involved. You are not from Bahia."

Indy pushed away his plate. "What's that got to do with it?"

"Well, you know, the Paraíso is not an ordinary hotel."

"Oh, you mean it's a whorehouse."

"Indy!" Deirdre said. "Not so loud."

Hugo laughed and shook his head. "You are very funny, my friend. I will take you there if you want to go. You must have questions you want answered."

"That's right. We've got questions, and we want answers," Indy said as they walked away from the table.

"Everyone who goes to Hotel Paraíso wants answers. I just didn't know tourists were asking the questions, too."

Indy and Deirdre exchanged baffled looks as they moved through the market, past stalls of fish and fruits, then pottery and baskets. Neither one of them had any idea what he was talking about.

"We're not exactly tourists," Indy said, hoping it would help. He wanted to ask Hugo more about the hotel, but he figured they'd find out soon enough.

As Indy and Deirdre followed Hugo through the crowded market to the street, two men watched from behind a stand stacked high with papayas. "It looks like they have a new friend already." Carino stepped out from behind the fruit.

"Just a driver," Oron said as they headed after the trio. "They like to latch onto the tourists."

"They're not exactly tourists," Carino answered, repeating what he'd heard Jones say as he'd passed by the fruit stand.

Carino didn't know quite what to make of either of them. He didn't know how they'd survived the fall from Sugarloaf. But when he'd stopped by their hotel just as a precaution, he'd been told the Joneses had checked out, and the clerk had sworn he'd seen them leave.

He and Oron had taken the next train to Bahia. That was where Julian Ray had said they'd go if Jones didn't heed his warning, and from this point on, Ray's orders were simple and clear: Kill them.

Oron and Carino trailed their prey through a part of the market where burros and horses were sold, and then slowed as the trio walked down a hard-packed clay road. The driver pointed to a battered Tin Lizzie, and after several efforts at cranking the starter, the engine revved up.

"This time we're going to do it right," Carino said as he watched them drive away.

"You mean you're going to do it right," Oron corrected him. "That was our agreement. I'm just your guide and interpreter. Without me, you would've never figured out what the hell the Hotel Paraíso is about."

Carino still wasn't sure he understood the place, and he didn't know how Jones was going to find anything there that would help him locate Fawcett. But it was Oron, not Jones, who was annoying him right now. It was bad enough he had to depend on him to get around this goddamn city. But now he was talking back to him.

He grabbed Oron by the arm and pressed his fingertips hard into the crook of his elbow. He liked the way the man recoiled in pain. "I'm paying you good money, and money talks. If I say kill, you kill. You got that?"

"All right," Oron muttered.

He pressed harder. "I didn't hear that."

"Yes, sir. I will."

The Hotel Paraíso was a three-story stucco building perched on the mountainside in the upper city. The front of the peach-colored hotel nearly abutted the winding street, and on the second and third floors were mahogany balconies, which afforded a view of the bay and the crowded lower city. Hugo pulled open the front door and they entered a deserted lobby. The interior walls were coated with crushed seashells and sand, and the floor was made of sun-baked ceramic tiles. On the far side of the lobby, past the check-in counter, a pair of doors opened out to a lush, overgrown courtyard.

Deirdre wandered toward the courtyard as Indy moved over to the counter. There wasn't anyone behind it waiting to register them, and the countertop was covered with a thick skin of dust. No one had checked into this place for a long time, he thought.

"Looks abandoned," Indy said, brushing off his hands.

Hugo pointed to a spiral staircase. "Follow me."

"What's upstairs?"

"The *terriero*," Hugo said, and headed up the staircase to a mezzanine. Indy thought a moment, mouthing the word which Hugo had said. Suddenly, it dawned on him. He knew where they were, and why Hugo had talked of the hotel the way he had.

He stuck his head out into the courtyard, and called to Deirdre. A large drop of rain splattered against his hat, then another.

"Deirdre?" *Now where the hell did she go?*

"Indy, over here."

"What are you doing? C'mon. Hugo's waiting for us."

In the center of the courtyard was a fountain and Deirdre was kneeling on the opposite side of it. At her feet, hidden beneath an umbrella of elephant's ear philodendrons, was a black cat and her litter. "Aren't they cute?"

"Yeah." Indy paused at her side, and looked around uneasily. "They probably use them for sacrifices."

"What?"

"This is a candomblé temple."

"What's candomblé?"

"Let's get out of the rain." He touched her elbow, helping her up, then clasped her hand tightly as they moved away. "It's the old Yoruba religion, which was brought here by slaves, and mixed with Catholicism."

"Mixed how?"

"They worship the Catholic saints, and for every saint there's a Yoruba god with the same characteristics." They stepped back into the lobby.

"What's it got to do with cats?" she whispered, hurrying after him.

"Maybe nothing. I think they prefer chickens and sheep."

"They kill them for sacrifices? That's horrible."

"Why? You Scots are slaughtering sheep all the time. We go more for cows in the States."

"That's different."

"Is it? Sacrifices are usually quick and relatively painless. It's probably not a bad way to die."

She made a face. "You've got such a strange sense of humor."

"Hugo?" Indy called out as they climbed the staircase. They moved along the mezzanine, then turned down a dark hallway. "Swell, no sign of him."

"Where do we go now?" Deirdre asked.

"Maybe into the cauldron."

She grabbed his arm. "Don't say things like that. Maybe we should get out of here."

"This is where we're supposed to go. It's our only lead."

"I know, but—"

"Indy. In here."

Hugo was holding open a door.

Deirdre took Indy's arm. "You sure about this?"

He shrugged. "Let's take a look."

The size of the room surprised him. It was long and narrow, a dozen feet wide and several times that in length. The interior walls of three or four hotel rooms had been removed to form a single room. Lightning flashed in a window directly across from the door, and for a moment Indy was blinded by the glare. Hugo closed the door and motioned them to follow him. At the far end of the room was an altar, a table covered by a white cloth and cluttered with icons. To one side of the altar was a rocking chair, and on the opposite side was a wooden table with a bench on each side.

They stopped several feet short of the altar. Hugo walked over to another door, and rapped on it three times. It opened, and after an exchange of a few words, he entered the room and the door closed after him.

"Well, here we are," Deirdre said. "Now what?"

"I guess we wait." Indy moved a few steps closer to the altar. On it were statues of Catholic saints, Indians with headdresses, and Negro slaves. There was an empty wine bottle, a red-and-black woven basket, vases of flowers, and bowls of herbs. Candles filled the empty spaces on the altar, but only one was lit. Next to it was a pewter cup with coins and bills in it.

"Indy, look on the floor underneath the altar," Deirdre said tensely.

At first, all he saw was a plate of rotting fruit. Then he spotted the bowl near a leg of the table; it was half-filled with blood. "It's an offering."

"Oh. Wonderful, just wonderful."

"Probably chicken blood." *Let's hope.*

The door where Hugo had disappeared opened, and an aged Negro woman entered the room. She was tall and gaunt and dressed in a loose white dress that reached her ankles. Her feet were bare. She looked like a skeleton covered with dry skin the color of mahogany, and could have been fifty or eighty. Her short, natty hair was like a patch of snow.

She was followed into the room by a man who looked to be in his thirties. He was tall, slender, and supple, and moved with the ease of a dancer. But what Indy noticed was his shock of red hair, his tanned skin, and his pale blue eyes. Indy knew that some whites in Brazil were involved in the old African rituals which pervaded the country, but he was surprised that the man looked so much like what Fawcett considered the archetypal resident of his lost city. Was it merely coincidence?

The man set a corked bottle on the end of the table. "Your driver is waiting outside," he said without looking at Indy.

"Good." Indy refused to be intimidated. If they wanted him to leave, they'd have to do better than that. Then the old woman moved in front of Indy and Deirdre.

"My name is Julia. I am the *babalorixá*. What do you want?"

"What did she call herself?" Deirdre whispered.

"She's the temple priestess," Indy quickly answered. Then he introduced himself and Deirdre. "I have a question. All I want to know is—"

Julia waved a hand, cutting him off. She studied Indy's rugged features for a moment. "You have come a long way, and you have something important to you on your mind, something you want to ask me, and you think I am the only one who can answer."

That didn't take much to figure, Indy thought. "You're right. But I'm not here for any sorcery. I just want to find out about the journal. Fawcett's journal. Do you know anything about it?"

"Please sit," she said, pointing at the bench. "It is not yet time to ask your question."

Indy remained standing. "I think it's a fine time."

The younger man stepped forward, but the *babalorixá* motioned him back. "Joaquin will answer you when he is ready," the old woman said firmly.

Indy turned to the red-haired man. "Are you Joaquin?"

"My name is Amergin, Julia's assistant. Joaquin is not here yet."

Indy was getting impatient, but maybe there was hope. "Does Joaquin have the journal?"

"I know nothing about it," Julia answered. "Joaquin is the son of Xango."

Of course, Indy thought. Joaquin was not an ordinary person, but a trance personality. He was vaguely familiar with the name Xango as one of the Yoruba pantheon of gods.

"Who is Xango?" Deirdre asked.

Julia looked at her as if seeing her for the first time. Then she smiled as if accepting her presence. "He is the patron of fire, thunder, and lightning. He brings victory over enemies and all difficulties. We also see him in Saint Barbara. They are the same."

"Oh. That's interesting," Deirdre said tentatively.

While Deirdre was the brightest student Indy had ever had, she was not well traveled and knew little of myths besides those of the Greeks, the Celts, and the Norse. She was lost and puzzled about what was going on, and he didn't blame her for her unease. Among the Yorubas, myth wasn't just stories, it was the reality they lived.

He realized that nothing was going to come of his effort to cajole Julia. Besides, it didn't matter how he got his information, as long as he got it. "I'll ask Joaquin then." He sat down on the edge of the bench with Deirdre, took off his hat, and set it next to him. Without another word Julia walked over to the rocking chair and slumped into it, as if the effort of talking to them had drained her of strength.

Amergin stepped forward and firmly told Indy a price. Indy quickly computed the exchange rate in his head and realized it was hardly more than the cost of a couple of beers in New York. Indy paid him, and Amergin placed the bills in the pewter cup on the altar.

Julia stared straight ahead and rocked in her chair. Her head slowly nodded and she spoke Nago in a singsong voice. Amergin stood to one side and joined her in the recitation. Indy had no idea what they were saying, but it was obvious that it was some sort of invocation to Xango and other Yoruba deities.

Gradually, the *babalorixá*'s motions became more animated and her voice grew in strength. Amergin lit a cigar and handed it to her. She took several puffs, and continued muttering as the assistant shook a copper rattle. Lightning flashed followed by a low, sinister rumbling that seemed to surround them. Julia's body shuddered. Spittle dribbled from her mouth. The cigar fell to the floor.

"What's wrong with her?" Deirdre whispered.

"Trance," Indy said under his breath.

Julia dropped down to one knee. It looked as if she were reaching for the cigar, which had rolled a couple of feet away. Then, she rapped on the floor with her knuckles and snapped her fingers.

"Now what's she doing?" Deirdre said.

Indy shook his head. "Don't know."

Amergin scooped up the cigar and moved over next to them. "Joaquin is here," he announced. "He was a slave who lived in the early part of the last century. He had a pet snake. He's calling him now."

"Swell." Of all the pets that Joaquin could have, why a snake? At least he didn't have to look at it, Indy thought.

Joaquin was on his feet now and pacing about. He was looking at his arms and body and smiling. "Ah . . . the physical. Again I ride my horse." His voice was stronger and deeper than Julia's. He walked about the room with the nimble step of a young man.

Amergin relit the cigar, puffing on it, then handed it to him. "The horse is what he calls Julia," he said to them.

"Did he smoke cigars in his . . . his other life?" Deirdre asked.

"The smoke cleanses and protects. It allows him to take over his horse without injuring her," Amergin explained. "No harm can come to Julia while Joaquin is here."

Indy doubted that, but kept his thoughts to himself.

Joaquin, meanwhile, sucked on the maduro and smoke billowed around him. He paced back and forth, his face animated, his eyes like vivid points of light. Then he stopped abruptly and ground out the burning coal on the inside of his forearm.

Sparks and ashes drifted to the floor; he threw the cigar to one side.

He moved over to the table and grabbed the bottle of wine. He pulled out the cork, then held the half-full bottle to his mouth and drained it. Some of the wine splashed over his chin and ran down his neck, but most was swallowed in three or four gulps.

Carelessly, he smashed the bottle on the floor, and shards of glass skidded across the terra-cotta tiles. Lightning flashed, and for seconds the room was lit in a stroboscopic glow so that Joaquin seemed to flicker like a character in the movies Indy had seen as a child. Joaquin's bare feet stomped on the broken glass. If he felt any pain, he didn't show it. A sharp clap of thunder applauded the spectacle.

Suddenly, Joaquin spun on his heels and pointed at Indy. "Who are you?" he asked in Portuguese.

"Tell him," Amergin said.

Indy reintroduced himself and Deirdre.

"Why do you call me here?"

"I want to know about Colonel Fawcett."

Joaquin thrust his hips back and forth in an erotic matter. He laughed. "That's your man. Full of energy for the women. He knows nothing else. He cares for nothing, nothing but the act."

As prophecy went, the old woman, or rather Joaquin, was off to a poor start, Indy thought. Fawcett was eccentric. But he was also sixty and a proper Englishman. But maybe Indy could turn Joaquin on track. "The journal. Tell me about the journal."

Joaquin ignored him, and instead bent down and looked into Deirdre's face. She pulled back from him. He pointed at her. "You will travel the astral planes. Soon."

"What did she . . . I mean he say?" she asked.
"He's jabbering."

Now Joaquin moved over to Indy and pulled
him to his feet. He placed a hand on the side of his
head where he'd bumped it on the fall atop Sugarloaf. There was still a lump under his thick hair and
Joaquin was feeling it.

"You are in danger. Serious danger. You need
protection." He glanced at Amergin and snapped
his fingers.

The assistant moved carefully across the glass-
strewn floor to the altar, where he pulled a bou-
quet of white flowers from a vase. Joaquin
snatched them from his hand. He took the flowers
by the stems and brushed them up and down Indy's body, murmuring an invocation in Yoruba. A
snowstorm of petals fluttered through the air,
blanketing the floor.

He tossed the battered stems and crushed flowers aside, then turned Indy around until they were
back to back. Before Indy knew what was happening, Joaquin had linked his arms under Indy's
elbows and lifted him onto his back as if he
weighed no more than a bulky pillow. They spun
around three times, then Joaquin deposited him
on the floor.

Amergin was immediately by Indy's side helping him to his feet. "The cleansing is for your spirit,
to purify and protect you from both visible and
invisible assailants," he explained. "One is as real
as the other."

Indy tottered, still dizzy. He still hadn't learned
a damn thing about the journal, but he was
amazed by the strength of the old woman's body.
Joaquin told Indy to sit down. "The danger comes
from more than one place. Beware of the secret
enemy."

Great. Just what he needed to hear. "What we're here for is the journal," Indy said, trying to sound in control. "Fawcett's journal. Do you know where it is?"

"You are here because the daughter of Oya has called you."

"I don't know what you're talking about. I'm here about the journal. Fawcett's journal."

"The daughter of Oya can help you."

Now they were getting somewhere. "How do I find her?"

"She will find you."

"Can we find Colonel Fawcett?" Deirdre asked.

Joaquin paced back and forth in front of them. With every few steps, broken glass crunched under his feet. "The writing you seek will guide you to the ancient land of Orun, but it will not be enough." His voice was hoarse and his words were spoken harshly. "Oya will help, but . . ." He shook his head. ". . . so many enemies surround you. You need great protection. Even then there is no certainty that you will survive to see the land of Orun."

He moved over to the front of the altar. He spoke Nago in a raspy whisper as he lifted the top from the woven basket, and reached into it.

"Better not be a snake," Indy muttered. Joaquin pulled out his hand, but Indy couldn't see what it held. He moved back over to Indy, a red necklace dangling from his hand. "Wear this *colar*," he said, draping the necklace over Indy's head. "It is consecrated to Xango, and will protect you as long as you wear it."

Joaquin stared at him until Indy wondered what he was looking at. "The son of Exu can open and close doors, but he is cunning and tries to control the doorways for his own purposes."

Indy was baffled by this latest revelation. "Who is he?"

Joaquin grimaced and moved his arms awkwardly as if he'd forgotten how to use them. "No more questions; no more answers. Now I abandon my horse. Tell her not to worry. We will soon travel together, and no longer as rider and horse."

Amergin helped Joaquin back to the rocking chair. He slumped forward, holding his hands to his face. After a few moments, Julia looked up. She seemed confused as if she'd just awakened from a nap and didn't know where she was. "I am old," Julia said softly. "Joaquin can't ride me much longer, even with his protection."

"He said not to worry," Amergin told her.

Deirdre knelt down in front of Julia and examined her feet. "Indy, look at this. I can't believe it. Her feet aren't cut."

Indy took a look. Deirdre was right. Julia, or rather Joaquin, had walked repeatedly over broken glass, but none of it had pierced her skin. Tough skin, he thought. Then he noticed the ash on the inside of Julia's forearm. He touched it with a finger. "Does it hurt?"

Julia shook her head.

Indy brushed off the ash. The skin wasn't burned or even red. When he questioned Julia about what happened, she didn't seem to remember any of it. He didn't know what to think.

"I hope I have answered your questions," she said.

Indy felt even more confused than when they'd arrived, but he knew the old woman couldn't help them. He thanked her and they headed on their way. As they reached the mezzanine, he glimpsed movement below, a figure more shadow than substance, a ghostlike image that darted across the lobby and into the courtyard. "Did you see that?"

"See what?" Deirdre asked.

"I thought I saw someone."

When they reached the bottom of the stairs, they looked around the lobby and walked into the courtyard. The rain had stopped, and droplets glittered on the dark green foliage. The spray from the fountain shimmered in the sunbeams. Indy followed the path leading to the fountain, and peered closely into the shrubbery, where he spotted the kittens and mother cat under their leafy covering. He crossed the courtyard to an old wing of the hotel. There were four doors, all secured with rusty padlocks.

"I don't see anyone," Deirdre said.

"Neither do I. But I'm sure I saw someone."

"Who do you think it was?" Deirdre asked.

Only one thought came to mind. "I'd guess it was the daughter of Oya."

10

VEILING

"Did you see anyone leave the hotel just before we came out?" Indy asked as they approached Hugo, who was waiting by his taxi.

The driver shook his head. "No one went in or out, not while I was here."

"You know anything about this *candomblé*?" Deirdre asked.

"Everyone who lives in Bahia knows something about *candomblé*. It's in the blood and in the air, they say."

"Do you know anyone called the daughter of Oya?" she asked.

Hugo laughed. "Sure I do."

"You do?"

"In *candomblé* everyone is the son or daughter of one of the gods." He frowned, trying to explain. "It's how you are, you know. How you look at things."

"It's the way a person orients himself in the religion and to the outside world," Indy explained. "The gods are their protectors and guides."

"Yes, that's it."

Deirdre looked confused. "So you're saying that there's more than one daughter of Oya?"

"More than one?" Hugo laughed again. "Oya has many hundreds of daughters in Bahia."

"Let's get going," Indy said. Just as he opened the back door of the taxi for Deirdre, Hugo tapped him on the shoulder. "Now someone is coming out."

Amergin approached them, carrying Indy's hat. "It is very rare that we see foreigners here, and I'm curious about what you think of your experience."

"She was amazing," Deirdre said. "No burns, no cuts, no injuries at all."

Amergin smiled. "Xango protects."

"I thought it was Joaquin who was doing the protecting," Indy said, putting his hat back on.

"Xango works through Joaquin. Sometimes the gods mount their horses themselves and speak. Other times the god works through a man or a woman of power who has passed on to the next world, but who likes to return to this one."

"Who is Exu?"

"A powerful *orixá*. He's a messenger who guards the gate to the *orixás*. He can open and close doors of opportunity."

That was a lot of help, Indy thought. "What about Oya?"

"She is the patroness of justice. According to legend, she gave the power of fire and lightning to Xango. She was also his concubine."

"What do you know about the land of Orun?"

Amergin considered the question. "Orun is the sun god. He's not a very popular one among the followers of *candomblé*."

"More popular in his own land, I suppose." Indy

studied Amergin closely, wondering if he was telling them everything he knew. "I'm a bit surprised to see a white man involved in *candomblé*."

"You are in Brazil, my friend. This is a land where the races are not as separated as in North America. There is much for the whites to learn from the old African ways."

"In the United States, whites are learning from their music, not their religion."

"Here the music and the religion are one."

"So what do you know about Fawcett's journal, Amergin?"

Amergin looked back toward the building. "You will have it soon. Trust the daughter of Oya."

"Who is she?" Indy asked.

"Patience," Amergin said and walked off.

Only someone from Ceiba, a master of the veils, would have spotted Rae-la in the courtyard. Everyone else would have seen only the lush tropical growth. If they looked closer, they might have noticed the separate plants, their leaves and flowers. But they probably wouldn't have seen the vague shadows of each plant or been able to define an individual shadow, even if they were looking for it. That's why they wouldn't have noticed Rae-la.

Amergin, however, easily deciphered the shadows and found Rae-la crouched down next to the kittens. He'd seen her in the same spot when he'd watched Jones in the courtyard from the window of the *terreiro*. Jones had looked right at her, but had seen only the garden and the cats. She was veiled, of course, and to the untrained eye she was virtually invisible.

But then Amergin had grown up under the eye of Bel. In Ceiba, the art of the veils was a skill as basic and necessary as reading and writing was among Brazil's educated populace. Once you could define a plant's shadow amid other shadows or a shadow on a cloudy day, you had penetrated the first veil, and could learn to veil objects and eventually yourself. And those were just the lower levels of the veiling art. While some of the more adept *babalorixás*, like Julia, were as skilled as the moderately advanced veil masters, in the months Amergin had studied the Yoruba magic in Bahia, he had never discovered anyone with the abilities of a six-fold veil master like himself.

"What do you think?" Rae-la asked as she petted one of the kittens. "Will they give up if they don't get the journal?"

"They're not ready to give up yet, but I don't think they'll go looking for Fawcett without it." To someone watching, it would've looked as if he were talking to the cats, and the cats were answering.

"That's good." She stepped onto the walkway and the veiling dropped away. "Thank you. I've been worried you would go back on your word."

He placed his hands on the flare of her hips. "I had hoped you would trust me more by now."

She leaned over the fountain, dipped her hand into the water, and picked up a fallen leaf. "You know if Fawcett is held much longer, more outsiders will come to look for him and we'll have the same problem over again."

He took her hand and led her around the fountain. "But if you were caught helping him escape, you know what the penalty would be."

Her back stiffened. "I still don't think you are completely with me."

Amergin embraced her from behind, crossing his arms under her breasts, resting his chin on her shoulder. Their relationship had been tense ever

since Rae-la decided that it was wrong to lure outsiders to the city. Like it or not, that was their
assignment, he'd told her, and that was why the
journal pages had been sent to Fawcett's friend in
New York. But that tack hadn't worked, and it had
taken all his effort to persuade her not to leave him
and return to Ceiba on her own.

"Of course I'm with you. Things can still be good
with us again, you know. Come up to my room."

She pulled away from him. "I have to go. I need
to be alone . . . to think."

"When will you be back?"

She shook her long mane of chestnut hair as she
glided gracefully through the courtyard. "I don't
know, Amergin. I don't know."

Amergin followed her into the lobby and
watched her close the door behind her. Lost in
thought, he climbed the steps to the mezzanine.
Without hesitating, he walked to Rae-la's room.
She'd locked the door, but that wouldn't stop
him. He was a master at opening and closing doors
of all sorts. He held the knob, and concentrated.
He slowly turned it. The door opened. He walked
onto the balcony, which overlooked the lower city
and the bay, and glimpsed Rae-la as she walked
down the winding street.

Amergin loved Rae-la, and yes, she had a point
about the rightness of holding outsiders against
their wills. But there were greater responsibilities.
He was a member of the council of orbs, after all,
and he fully understood why outsiders were
needed. Any other course would only lead to the
city's inevitable discovery and destruction.

He turned around and surveyed the room. She
could hide the journal from any outsider, but not
from him. He looked underneath the bed, and
lifted the mattress. He checked the drawers of the

dresser. In one drawer were the dresses he'd bought Rae-la when she'd arrived. The others were empty. None of them hid the journal. He pulled the dresser away from the wall. The floor looked as barren as the empty drawers, but he knew better. He could see through any veil.

Amergin brushed a mote of dust from the cover, and tapped the book against his palm. He smiled, thinking how excited Jones would be. But Joaquin had been right. The journal itself wouldn't help Jones get into the city. He'd need help, and he'd be back looking for it. If Jones wanted to find Fawcett, Amergin would help him. What Jones didn't know was that Amergin was the secret enemy, the son of Exu, as Joaquin had put it, the one guarding the gate to the immortal gods.

They were in the back of the taxi, returning to their hotel room in the lower city. Indy held Deirdre's hand lightly in his, loving its shape, its coolness. "I hope we don't have to wait long."

"Me, neither, but there's not much else we can do." She leaned over and bussed him on the cheek. "We'll just have to relax and enjoy ourselves."

When Hugo pulled up to their hotel, he asked if they wanted him to wait. "I don't want to keep you from your business," Indy said.

"Why don't you come back in a couple of hours after we're rested? We can go around to those shops you mentioned," Deirdre suggested.

"Here's what I'll do. I'll wait for business right here. Maybe I get it, maybe I don't. But if I do, I'll still be back in two hours."

As they climbed the stairs to their hotel room, Indy considered their options if they didn't get the journal. They could return to New York empty-handed, or they could follow Fawcett's route to the area where he disappeared. Neither option appealed to him, and he'd already said he wouldn't do the latter. The journal was definitely worth waiting for.

"Look at that," Deirdre said as they reached the third floor. A note was tacked to their door.

Indy pulled it off and held it up in the dim light. " 'Come at nine. Alone. Bar de Luxo. I have the journal for you,' " he read. "It's signed with the Eye of Bel symbol and an ogham letter D."

"Well, the daughter of Oya didn't keep us waiting long at all," Deirdre said.

Indy frowned at the note. "Either she made a mistake, or she's not literate in ogham."

Deirdre looked over his shoulder. "What's wrong with it?"

"The cross-bars are drawn on the wrong side of the vertical line for the letter D."

"How did she even know we were here? That's what I want to know," Deirdre said.

"Beats me. Maybe she's been watching us since we got off the freighter. Who knows? Guess I'll find out tonight."

"I want to go, too."

"The note says to come alone. Let's not chance losing the journal because we didn't follow directions."

She gave him a look that said she didn't like it, but that she wouldn't argue about it.

He slid his arms around her waist. "Don't worry. I won't leave you for an Amazon."

"Promise?"

"Promise." He lifted her off her feet and carried her to the bed. "We've got plenty of time before I have to leave."

She pulled the beads over his head as he unbuttoned her blouse, and dropped them on the bedside table. "You don't need any protection from me."

"You may need it from me, though."

She smiled. "I'm not worried. Not at all."

At eight-thirty, Indy found Hugo lounging next to his taxi. "Take me to the Bar de Luxo."

Hugo leaped to his feet. "The Bar de Luxo? I know a much better place where all the foreigners go. The waiters all wear bow ties and white coats. You will see. Your lady will like it."

"My lady's not going," Indy said. "Take me to the de Luxo."

Hugo wrinkled his nose. "It's not such a nice place."

"I still want to go there."

Hugo shrugged and walked around the taxi. As they drove off, Indy wondered why the woman would choose a bar, any bar, to give him the journal. Maybe the daughter of Oya likes to share a shot of whiskey once in a while. More likely she had someone protecting her who would be in the bar, watching. But why would she consider him a threat?

Indy turned his thoughts to the future. Once he had the journal, and had learned as much as he could from this daughter of Oya, it would be time to get moving. He'd wired the pilot, Larry Fletcher, the night they'd arrived in Rio, and told him to expect them in Bahia in a few days. He was looking forward to flying in an amphibious plane, and hoped everything would go well so they could be on their way tomorrow. "Hugo, do you think you can take us to a farm outside the city tomorrow if I give you directions?"

"A farm. Of course. You're going to leave Bahia so soon?"

"There's a man with an airplane out there."

"You mean Captain Fletcher."

"You know who he is?"

"Of course. He landed his plane here in the bay, and everyone went down to see it. Are you going to fly in the airplane to Rio?"

"No, to the interior. Mato Grosso."

"You are missionaries?"

"Not exactly."

"Not exactly tourists, not exactly missionaries," Hugo said. "The missionaries go to the jungle to save the naked savages from everlasting damnation. But you know, the Indians never knew they were damned until the missionaries came to save them."

"I'm not a missionary."

Hugo glanced back at him.

"I know only of two other reasons to go to the jungle. To look for gold and to look for lost cities, like Colonel Fawcett."

Indy tensed with alertness. "You know about Colonel Fawcett?"

"Of course. He is famous."

"Do you think he found his lost city?"

He shook his head. "He will not find it."

"Why do you say that?"

Hugo straightened his shoulders. "My mother is a Caraja Indian. I was born in the jungle. We know about the city he is looking for from the old stories."

"And what do the old stories say?" Indy asked with growing curiosity.

"That you could be in the city, and wouldn't know it."

"I thought you had Indian blood in you. What else do the stories say about the city?"

"There is one the mothers tell the young children. If they wander away into the jungle, the red-haired people from the invisible city will catch them and take them away."

Indy nodded. "How long have you been living in Bahia?"

"Since I was fourteen years, when I came here to find my father."

Hugo slowed and came to a stop in the middle of the street in a shabby neighborhood that looked far off the tourist route. He yelled at someone on the wooden sidewalk. "Bar de Luxo?"

The man pointed and shouted directions. Hugo waved, and drove on. "It's not a place I go, you know. I don't like to leave my taxi in this neighborhood."

"You won't have to. I want you to wait outside for me."

The Bar de Luxo was a dark place that smelled of beer. A thick layer of sawdust and wood shavings covered the floor. There were no tables, just a bar where a dozen or so men stood. Indy joined them and ordered a shot of rum. When it arrived, he told the bartender he was waiting to meet a woman here.

"No women allowed here. They cause too much trouble," the bartender said and walked away.

"Swell. No women," he muttered. A few feet away one of the patrons was urinating in the sawdust. No one seemed to care. It wasn't hard to see why Hugo didn't include the place on his list of recommended bars.

"Now you know why they have sawdust on the floor," someone said to him. "They just sweep it out the door."

Indy recognized the deep voice. "Hello, Oron. Nice place to meet you. What can I do for you?"

"I should be asking you that," Oron said. "I'm a steward, you know."

"Well, at least your sense of humor hasn't changed. But I lost mine in Rio," Indy said, and jabbed Oron in the gut. He folded over, stunned by the unexpected blow. Indy followed it with a punch to his jaw and Oron fell back into the urine-stained sawdust. He spat out bits of debris, started to rise, then slipped on a sodden clump of sawdust.

It didn't matter. A revolver was aimed at Indy's head. "Fun's fun, Jones. But fun's over," Carino said with a wide grin. "Hate to spill blood all over this fine floor, but I don't have much choice. I've got a job to finish off."

A foot slashed the air, and the gun flew out of Carino's hand and landed behind the bar. Indy collared Carino, and looked up in amazement at Hugo. "Did you do that?"

Oron, on his feet again, rushed Indy. But Hugo's leg jutted out, tripping him, and he crashed into the bar. He started to rise again, but the heel of Hugo's foot crashed into his forehead, and Oron slumped to the floor.

"You're pretty good with that foot," Indy said. Carino was trying to wriggle out of Indy's grip, but Indy grabbed a handful of Carino's hair and jerked. "Who put you up this?"

No answer.

Indy jerked his head up and smacked Carino's nose into the edge of the bar.

"Who?"

"Ray. Julian Ray," he rasped with a distinct nasal twang.

"Who is he?"

No answer.

Indy jerked back his head again. Carino's nose

was bleeding and looked misshapen. "I guess you want me to flatten your nose some more."

"No. Don't. He's a bookie. Odds are against Fawcett showing up now. I'm supposed to make sure you don't find him."

"How did you know about the Eye of Bel?"

"What?"

"You know, the eye you drew on your note to get me to come to this stinking place."

"Some goddamn professor. Big gambler."

It took Indy a moment, then it all fell together. "So Bernard was a gambler. He nearly laughed. "Well, I guess I'm not going to get the journal from you. Am I?"

Carino spat at him.

Indy clenched his fist and was about to smash the thug in the mouth when several soldiers burst into the bar. He let go of Carino, who immediately threw a punch. Indy blocked it, and countered with a punch of his own, which connected with Carino's nose. Then something struck Indy in the back of the head, and he sank to the floor.

11

FAWCETT'S JOURNAL

The room was dark when Deirdre awoke. She'd heard something, like the sound of a door closing. She sat up and listened, suddenly awake and alert.

How long have I been asleep?

She turned on a bedside light when she didn't hear anything further. She'd taken off her shoes and lain on the bed after Indy had left. It was almost midnight. She'd slept three hours.

Where was he? Was he still at the bar with that woman? *I knew I should've gone with him.* Then she saw it. A ragged-looking notebook lay on the corner of the bed. She reached for it and flipped through several pages. It was the same handwriting as on the pages that Indy had shown her. It was Fawcett's journal.

Indy had gotten it, and brought it back. But why did he leave again? The daughter of Oya. That was why. He was going somewhere with her. This wasn't fair, not at all. They'd just gotten married. *Damn him.*

She swung her legs over the side of the bed and

stood up. She didn't even care about Fawcett's journal. She wanted Indy back in this room, and right now.

She walked over to the door and opened it. She heard voices on the landing and moved down the hallway. A mulatto man was arguing on the landing with a wide-girthed Negro woman whose hair was wrapped in a white turban. She was gesturing toward the man, who held a bottle of wine, and stopped when she saw Deirdre. They both peered at her from the dimly lit landing.

"Excuse me. Did you see a man walk past here, a white man wearing a hat?"

"No English." The man gulped from the bottle.

The woman snapped at him again, and the man said something back to her. Deirdre's Portuguese was minimal and she didn't understand what they'd said. She was about to retreat to the room when the woman turned to her.

"No, *senhora.* No man has walked past here. Not for fifteen, twenty minutes."

"Is there another way downstairs?"

"The other door is locked at night. I tell them they shouldn't do that. What if there was a fire? But they do it for the safety. You understand?"

Deirdre nodded. *"Muito obrigada."* She walked away, puzzled. She was sure she'd heard the door closing.

Back in the room, she considered what she should do. If Indy had returned and left again without waking her, he probably had a good reason for it. Maybe he was hungry, and had come up to the room for her. When he'd found her sleeping, he'd gone out to eat by himself, not thinking that she would wake up as he left. That must be it.

She picked up the journal and sat down on the edge of the bed. She opened the cover, and saw that several pages were torn out. No doubt they'd been sent to Marcus Brody. She began reading the first entry.

20 August, 1925

When we left the mission, I had planned to take daily notes. After all, this is the most important leg of my journey, the one which will cap all of my efforts and make worthwhile all of the hardships that I and others have endured these past months. That, however, has been an impossible goal. There is little time for contemplation. We are either moving through the wilderness or doing what is necessary to survive another day in the jungle. Finally, after dark, when there are a few moments to gather one's thoughts by the camp fire, I am usually exhausted and fall asleep before I can muster the energy to take out pen and paper.

Another reason I have written so little is that early on I realized that I would not be able to provide explicit directions to the city. The rivers are the only landmarks and even those are now of questionable value. So numerous are the branches and tributaries that a map of the region would look like a spider's web.

I have chosen to pick up the pen at this time because tomorrow morning, after six days of paddling upriver, we will reach the Rio San Francisco and Maria insists we must abandon the canoe and continue our journey on foot. Walters is distinctly uneasy about the idea. He says the region north of the Rio Tocantins and east of the Rio San Francisco is known as a place inhabited by hostile Indians. He has never gone looking for potential converts anywhere near this territory.

I've done my best to quiet Walters. I knew he joined us because of a curiosity about the tribe Maria came from, and I think because of a certain attachment he feels toward her. It was his opinion that Maria must have been lost or stolen from her white parents as an infant and raised among Indians with no knowledge of her heritage. The missionaries believed the same thing. But I'm convinced missionaries of the time would have heard about the missing child. So few whites venture here that such a terrible event would be well known.

For their part, neither Walters nor the missionaries accepted my belief that she might be from a tribe of whites, though they admitted hearing of such a legend. The missionaries, however, were sure that a white tribe would know of Christianity and would therefore have contacted at least one of the missions by now.

Walters has his own views on the subject. He says whites are not savages and therefore are incapable of living for extended periods in the jungle unless they do so in a civilised fashion, and if that were the case, he would know of them.

I didn't argue with the missionaries, but at odd moments I've tried to explain to Walters that these whites would have come to the jungle more than two thousand years ago in search of the survivors of the lost continent of Atlantis. There is no doubt that they would have adapted to the jungle every bit as well as the Indians. My efforts are directed at preparing him for what we will encounter, but I suspect they are falling on deaf ears. Maria listens during these chats, but adds nothing. I'm not sure how much she comprehends. Her English is still limited. But no matter what language I use, when I quiz her about her home she offers very little, only

*promises that she will tell me about it later when
we are closer.*

Deirdre looked up from the notebook. "C'mon,
Indy. Hurry up."

Restless now, she paced the room, the notebook
tucked under her arm. She stopped by the bedside
table and gazed at the red and black beads that the
babalorixá had given Indy. She fingered them a
moment, and recalled Joaquin's warning to Indy
about the dangers that surrounded him. She made
a fist and squeezed the string of beads, hoping that
the forgotten talisman wasn't an omen.

She considered searching the nearby pubs for
him. But she didn't like the idea of going out alone
at night. She didn't know this city, and the pubs
here weren't like the British ones, which wel-
comed everyone, including wives and grandpar-
ents and children. She glanced at the clock again.
The pubs in her hometown of Whithorn, Scotland
would've been closed for more than two hours.

She decided she'd read one more entry and if
Indy wasn't back by then, she'd find a taxi and
search the streets.

24 August

*Now the river is far behind us, and we can no
longer supplement our modest supplies of rice,
flour, and sugar by netting fish. We're forced to
hunt every afternoon, a chore which Walters
readily assumes. From dawn to late afternoon, we
walk and sometimes run. Maria moves barefoot so
swiftly through the jungle that Walters and I have
difficulty keeping up with her. I have not encountered anyone during my months in the Amazon*

who seems so at ease in the jungle. That includes the guides I hired during the first stretch of the journey. I am truly amazed by her.

But these past two days, Maria has been acting oddly. Whenever we stop at a clearing to rest or eat, she appears ill-at-ease. She is constantly alert, watching, and I swear she sees things that Walters and I are blind to. At first, I thought that we were nearing her home and she was anxious about bringing visitors. Now I realise her concern is about the hostile Indians Walters had mentioned. But so far we've seen none of them.

I have repeatedly attempted to talk with Maria about the city, but she still has little to say, and what she does say makes little sense. I've started to categorise her comments into those which are logical and understandable, and those which are not. The latter might seem to be mere rubbish in this modern age of science, but instead I'm labeling them as "jungle lore."

She contributed a couple more tidbits to my collection of lore this evening at dinner. First, she answered my prodding about the location of the city by saying that it can only be found by those with trained eyes. "I guess we will see," I answered, but she didn't laugh at my attempt at humour.

Neither did Walters. He told me to stop badgering her, that we'd find her tribe soon enough. I don't think he likes me talking to Maria. He seems jealous and protective of her, as if she were his woman. I don't like his attitude, and am concerned that his belligerence will continue to escalate. But now it's time for bed.

Deirdre closed the journal. She wondered if Indy had read any of the entries. She couldn't

imagine him dropping off the journal without
bothering to read it. She looked at the clock again.
She'd waited long enough. She was going to look
for him. She tucked the notebook in her shoulder
bag, and headed down the dingy hall.

Fifty years ago, the Hotel Europa must have
been charming. Now it was only tired-looking,
with well-worn carpeting and walls in need of
paint. Deirdre and Indy had selected the hotel
simply because it was the first one they'd found
after realizing they weren't going to stay at the
Hotel Paraíso. As long as she was with Indy, Deirdre didn't mind the place. But right now it gave
her the creeps.

The woman with the turban was behind the re-
ception desk. Deirdre asked for a taxi. The woman
frowned at her. "You going out at this hour looking
for your man?"

"I don't know if it's any of your business, but yes,
I am," Deirdre answered.

At that moment, the door to the hotel opened,
and the woman pointed. "There's your taxi
driver."

Deirdre turned and saw Hugo walking toward
her. "What happened? Where is he?"

She listened to Hugo's story as the woman in the
turban leaned over the counter, and nodded as if
to say she expected as much.

"I can't believe it," Deirdre said. "He's in jail?"

"They don't allow no brawling," the woman
said.

Deirdre ignored her. "Let's go get him."

Hugo shook his head. "It won't do any good."

"Why not?"

"Not until morning when the captain arrives."

"They never let them out until morning," the

woman behind the counter added, knowingly. "And it's going cost you. You better believe it."

If only they had just left Rio and returned to New York, instead of coming here, Deirdre thought. After what had happened on Sugarloaf, it was crazy to try to go on. But Indy was as stubborn in his own way as she was in hers. He wouldn't be intimidated.

"What did the other guys look like?"

Hugo described them. Carino and Oron. No doubt about it. Deirdre's mind raced through the events of the evening. The two thugs must have left the note. That was why the ogham letter was written wrong. But then who had delivered the notebook to her room while she slept?

"You say they were arrested too?"

"All three. You better get some sleep now. I'll be back at seven, and we'll get Indy then," Hugo said.

When he showed up at a quarter to seven, Deirdre had barely slept an hour or two as she'd waited for morning. She couldn't stop wondering if Indy was hurt and what was happening to him. She and Hugo arrived at the jail only to begin waiting all over again. Every few minutes Deirdre asked how much longer it would be, and each time the over-weight policeman behind the desk said soon.

She was fed up with the treatment. She opened her shoulder bag and dug through it until she found her money. She counted it, certain she'd have to pay off somebody. Maybe that was what the fat cop at the desk was waiting for. Standing up, she approached the man again, and set a modest sum on the desk. "Maybe you could check to see how soon the captain will be ready. That's for your time," she said, pointing to the bills.

"Take your money. You'll need it later," he said, brusquely dismissing her.

"You don't really know when he'll see me, do you?" she said accusingly.

"Madam, please sit down. If you don't stop bothering me, the captain may not be able to see you at all today. Do you understand?"

She returned to the hard bench. As she put the money back in the shoulder bag, she felt the notebook. She might as well read the journal and stay calm, she thought.

26 August

My concerns about Walters, unfortunately, are coming to pass. He is infatuated with Maria. She is a drug and he needs numerous injections each day. I can understand, of course, how Maria can affect a man in the jungle. Almost every time we reach a stream, she slips out of her clothes and bathes, making no attempt to hide herself. Yet, there is nothing lewd in her behaviour. She is simply an innocent creature of the jungle. I've tried to act the part of a gentleman, but must confess my gaze has wandered. There is no denying that her slender, tanned body is something to behold.

Walters watches her constantly now, and talks with her at every opportunity. He's obviously trying to impress her. He seems to think that telling her about his escapades with women will make her more receptive to him. She takes it all in stride, responding to most of his stories with a smile. Yet, she remains distinctly aloof, an attitude which I'm sure infuriates Walters and also drives him on.

I can tell by his attitude toward me that he is planning something. Outwardly, he is still acting civil and doing everything that is expected of him. But he offers nothing extra and rarely speaks to me now unless I address him first. He is acting as if Maria is his partner and I am the outsider. This is the problem with a woman and two men in the jungle.

27 August

Matters are quickly coming to a head with Walters. He is increasingly protective of Maria and sullen toward me. It is a preposterous situation.

We are taking a short lunch break. Maria has gone off on one of her solo walks, and Walters went after her. I know he wants to be alone with Maria more than anything.

I can hear him calling her now. The fool seems to have forgotten his own concerns about this region. I suppose I should have ordered him to stop, but I don't think he would have paid me any heed. Earlier, he told me that if I wanted game for dinner tonight, I had better hunt for it myself. No doubt to give him more . . .

28 August

I cut short my last entry as I heard a piercing cry from beyond the forest wall. I instantly recognized it as human. I started off in the direction my companions had taken, but hadn't gone ten yards when suddenly Maria burst through the jungle, a wild look in her eyes.

She spoke concisely: "Walters is dead. We must leave now."

I wanted to see the body, but Maria insisted we flee. Our lives were in grave danger. When someone tells me I'll be killed if I go in a particular direction, I listen. We grabbed our packs, and raced away.

I'm still mulling over what happened next. Maybe by writing about it, I'll comprehend it. We'd barely been running longer than a minute when Maria ordered me to stop. I looked around. At first I didn't see them because they blended so well with the forest. But there they were, not more than a dozen yards away. Painted savages with whiskers like a leopard's. They were armed with blowguns and spears.

We were trapped. As good as dead, I figured.

Then Maria wasn't there any longer. How had she gotten away? She'd somehow escaped, leaving me to cope with the painted brutes. I didn't even have time to think about it, because the Indians were stirring, talking excitedly among themselves. Then they dropped away into the jungle, and I was alone.

I had no idea what had happened. Had my appearance sent the savages fleeing? I knew from experience that a civilised man could be as strange and frightening to a primitive as they were to us.

"We are safe. They won't bother us."

I spun around to see Maria. "Good God, woman. You startled me. Where did you go?"

"Nowhere."

"Nowhere?"

"I was right here, veiled."

I asked her to explain what she meant, but she said there was no time now. We moved on, and spoke little until we stopped by a stream. I wasn't up to hunting and was glad that the fish were plentiful and easily netted. We ate well, and to my surprise, Maria sipped a little of the rum with me, and she became talkative. She explained that the Indians had done them a favour by killing Wal-

ters. His behaviour would not have been tolerated
by her people and it would have endangered my
own life.

She took a stick and drew a vertical line in the
dirt, then added two short horizontal bars which
extended from the left side of the line. She said
that in her written language, it represented the
city. I was almost certain the script she was talking
about was ogham. However, the letter she had
drawn was not a Z, but a D. I had committed the
alphabet to memory and drew another letter. Her
name for the letter was different from the one I
had learned, but she had recognised it. Then she
confirmed my greatest hope. She said she was
happy that I knew ogham. The people of the city
were indeed descendants of ancient Celtic druids.

29 August

Another day of tedious travel. Thankfully much
of the trek was through relatively open land with
little underbrush. But Maria has picked up the
pace. She is anxious, and says we are getting close.
She also says that the mountains are visible in the
distance above the treetops. I can't see them yet,
and told her I thought she was seeing clouds. "You
are seeing clouds; I see mountains," she said.
"Such is the way things are with us."

The letter D in ogham stands for defense and
the defeat of all enemies. When I mentioned this to
Maria last night, she nodded and said that it also
represented the most sacred of trees, the ceiba, and
in fact Ceiba was what the city was actually
called.

From my study of ogham, I know that the tree
representing the letter D is an oak. But there are no

oaks here. A significant point, since the ceiba is similar to the oak in that it is a tree of great strength. I asked Maria if the ogham alphabet was still used for divination or prophecy, as was the practice of the ancient druids. She answered with an obscure comment, saying that the practice of divination was one of the seven veils.

That led to a long discussion, which I will attempt to summarise. How much of what I'm now going to describe about the place she calls Ceiba is myth and how much fact is yet to be seen. I'm not convinced that Maria can distinguish the two. However, I do believe—

"Madam, excuse me," the desk cop said. "The captain is now ready to see you."

Deirdre slapped the cover of the journal closed. "Finally."

12

THE ORBS

Amergin stopped in the open doorway of Rae-la's room. He saw her standing on the balcony gazing out toward the lower city.

"Rae-la?"

She moved her head, acknowledging him, but she didn't turn.

"What's wrong?"

"You took the notebook didn't you?"

"Jones has it now."

She turned, a look of astonishment on her face. "You gave it to him? Why?"

"Because we're going back to the city and releasing Fawcett."

"What?"

He told her his plan. "We'll get in, get Fawcett out, and he'll fly back with Jones before anyone knows what happened."

"Amergin, this is more than I could have hoped for, and we'll get there so quickly. How did you find out about the airplane?"

"Their taxi driver. He's been keeping an eye out for foreigners asking about the hotel."

"Very clever." She embraced him, then kissed him lightly on the mouth. "I'm sorry I doubted you."

He held her by the shoulders at arm's length. "You realize what this means, though? We must admit to releasing Fawcett and face the consequences."

Rae-la wrinkled her nose. "Couldn't we make it look like he escaped on his own?"

"You know it would be impossible to escape without help. Our arrival will give us away. We've got to admit it."

She looked up at him, worry skewing her features. "But you could lose your position on the council."

"I know." He took her hands in his. "But I'm willing to give it all up."

"Just for me?"

He noticed the suspicious look in her eye that said she doubted him. He had to be careful how he answered. "Because I know you're right, and if I lose everything, I'll still have you."

"But if they exiled us and veiled our memories of everything we know of Ceiba, we would mean nothing to each other."

"I don't think they would inflict the ultimate punishment."

"Why not?"

Suspicious again. "Because I'm on the council, and because we will veil Fawcett's memory. That will be taken into consideration." He smiled. "Who knows, maybe they'll even decide we did the right thing."

She squeezed his hand. "Let's go find Jones right now."

"Don't worry. He'll be back."

* * *

Footsteps echoed in the hallway as Indy lay on his back in the jail cell. They were growing louder, coming nearer. He rubbed the sleep from his eyes, and the two lights burning dimly from the ceiling merged into one. He raised his head from the wooden bench, wincing at the pain in the back of his neck.

A soldier unlocked the door and pulled him to his feet. He was led down the hall past other cells to an office where an army captain was seated behind a desk. The man's black hair was slicked back. His eyes were dark, and his mustache looked as if it had been drawn with a fountain pen. His nose turned up at the end, leaving an impression of arrogance. He pointed to a chair, then looked down at Indy's passport.

"Henry Jones, Jr., professor of archaeology, resident of London, England, and barroom bowler," he said in heavily accented English.

Indy sat down and rubbed the back of his neck. "That's barroom brawler. But no, that's not what I am. Not usually."

"What are you doing in Brazil?"

"I'm a tourist."

The captain raised his eyebrows. "Not on an archaeology expedition."

"No, just a holiday." A busman's holiday, he thought, but he wasn't going to get into his search for Fawcett and the lost city, not with this guy.

The officer tapped a pencil against his desktop. "And why were you fighting, Dr. Jones?"

Indy had to think a moment. "Something one of them said to me. I can't even remember what it was."

"Why were you in that bar? That's no place for tourists."

"I was in the neighborhood and wanted a drink."

The captain nodded. He seemed to be buying the story. "Did the men want to rob you?"

"I don't know. I didn't give them a chance."

"That was either brave or very stupid. One of them had a gun, you know."

Indy shrugged. "He didn't have it for long."

"I like you, Jones. But I'm confused about one thing."

"What's that?"

The officer stared hard at him; his upturned nose twitched. Then he unfolded a piece of paper and pressed it against his desk. Indy leaned forward and recognized the note he'd found on the hotel door. He'd stuck it in his pocket with his passport.

"What is this about a journal and who were you going to meet?"

"Oh, that. You see I lost my journal or someone stole it. I went there to get it."

"Why didn't you say that before?"

He'd wanted to keep things simple, but now he was backed into a corner. He looked for a way out. "I forgot about it, you know, because of everything that happened."

The captain scowled at him and was silent for almost a minute. He twisted his pencil between his fingers, then dropped it on his desk.

"Dr. Jones, your story leaves me with more questions than answers. I don't know what you are doing in Bahia, and at this point I don't really care. If your beautiful wife was not so concerned about you I might keep you here until I found out. But I am going to let you go."

"Thank you."

"My advice to you is to get out of Bahia. If you

are caught in any more trouble here, I will lock you up for a long time. Do you understand?"

Indy nodded.

"I hope you do." The captain dismissed Indy with a flick of his hand. "Your wife has paid your fine."

Indy quickly left the office and found his way to the waiting room in the front of the building. Deirdre leaped to her feet. "Indy, are you okay?"

"I've got a sore neck, and a couple bruises. About normal for the way things have been going."

Deirdre examined a bruise on his forearm. "It's all black and blue."

"Ouch. Don't press it like that. Let's get out of here. How did you find me, anyhow?"

"You can thank Hugo for that. He followed you in his taxi, then came and told me what happened," she said as they walked outside.

Indy glanced over at the driver. "How come they didn't arrest you?"

"I blended in with the crowd."

"I think we'd better change hotels." Indy opened the back door of the taxi for Deirdre. "It was Carino and Oron, and they'll probably bribe their way out before long."

"I'm way ahead of you," Deirdre answered. "We're already checked out, and I've got a surprise for you."

He wasn't sure he wanted to hear about any surprises just now. "What is it?"

Deirdre reached into her shoulder bag and pulled out a notebook. "Ta-da. Colonel Fawcett's journal."

"What? Let me see that. Where did you get this from?"

She told him where she'd found it. "The daughter of Oya must be shy. She didn't wait to even say hello to me."

Indy paged through it. "Doesn't sound like she was so shy about breaking into the room."

"Do you want me to take you to the Hotel Paraíso?" Hugo asked. "Maybe you can stay there."

"No," Deirdre said. "That's the last place I'd want to stay. They'd probably drain our blood while we were sleeping."

Indy looked up from the journal. It was time to find Larry Fletcher. "Take us to the guava farm I told you about."

Hugo shrugged. "Suit yourself."

"And make sure our friends from the bar aren't following us."

"Don't worry," Hugo answered. "We'll know if we are followed. There aren't many cars where we're going."

Indy started reading the journal, but it didn't take long before he realized they were going to need a guide. The journal was strong on color, but weak on directions. "Hugo, how far are we from the Hotel Paraíso?"

He stepped on the brakes. "I can be there in a few minutes."

"Good. Take us there, but don't hurry."

"Do you think we'll find the woman there?" Deirdre asked.

"My guess is that the daughter of Oya is not only waiting for us, but that she needs our help as much as we need hers," he said, returning to the journal.

After reading for a couple of minutes, Indy shook his head. "Walters. Nice guy."

Deirdre leaned over and saw how far he'd read. "Keep reading. You'll see what happens to him."

"Too bad, I'll miss him," Indy said sarcastically when he read of the rummy's demise. He read on.

The passage about the alphabet caught his attention, and he quickly moved on to the August 29 entry, where he learned the actual name of the city. After a few paragraphs, Fawcett picked up his discussion of the seven veils. While he questioned whether Maria could tell the difference between myth and fact, Fawcett thought that whatever he learned about the veils would help him understand the social structure of the city.

From what I gather, veiling is supposedly an ability to make objects and people look like shadows or, for all practical purposes, become invisible. It seems the society is divided into seven levels or veils, and one's social status is directly related to the veiling ability one has achieved. The first five veils, Maria tells me, deal with nothing but making people and things invisible.

In all my years of exploring the hidden corners of the world, I have never heard of such an outlandish means of achieving social and political power. I don't doubt the validity of the structure, but whether the abilities professed are real or imagined is another matter. Maria explained that the teaching of the veils begins at age four and can continue throughout one's life. Most of the residents of Ceiba never pass beyond the third or fourth veils; these are the craftsmen, farmers, and menial workers.

As I understand it, those at the first level learn to pick out shadows not visible through normal sight. Once they've achieved this skill, they advance a level and learn how to veil small objects. At the third level, they learn to veil themselves, and even others who are willing subjects. After that it gets a bit confusing. Those who have mastered the upper four veils belong to clubs of sorts, called orbs. The Outer and the Inner Orbs are associated with the fourth and fifth veils, while the sixth and seventh levels are known as the Higher and Eternal Orbs.

But they're not what I would call social clubs. The initiates of the fourth veil know all the basic skills well enough to teach them to those less advanced. Many reach this level and are involved in occupations other than teaching, but those who wish to go on to higher levels must teach for at least two years while preparing to advance to the next orb.

Those of the Inner Orb or fifth level possess another skill, a quite incredible one. They supposedly spend several hours a week in a meditative state during which time they maintain the Over Veil, which blankets the entire city and even the surrounding mountains. To outsiders like myself, only the jungle remains visible, while to those inside Ceiba everything remains the same, as if there were no Over Veil at all. The masters of the Inner Orb are well respected and are trained as warriors even though, I'm told, there is little internal or external conflict requiring physical combat. Rather than warriors, they are known as guardians.

Maria explained that the gods have created certain veils themselves, and that the two highest levels of veil masters are involved in removing them at certain times. Those who have mastered the sixth veil are priests, philosophers, and healers. They are capable of removing the veil between the present and the future through the use of the sacred alphabet. Further, they consider sickness to be a veil, which can be lifted, but only with the coop-eration of the one afflicted.

While Maria was willing to talk at length about the Higher Orb, she refused to say much of anything about the seventh veil and the related Eter-nal Orb. About the only thing she would reveal was that most of the residents of the city aren't even certain that the masters of the seventh veil exist. That comment, of course, provoked my curi-osity. It almost seems as if they are mythical be-ings, but Maria remained unwilling to say anything further. I'm hoping that once I'm in the city, I will have plenty of opportunities to converse with those of the Higher and Eternal Orbs, and learn of their ways.

When I asked if the members of the top two orbs were the rulers, she shook her head. She explained that Ceiba was governed by the Council of Orbs, which is exactly what it sounds like, a council made up of representatives from the orbs. I asked if the members were elected, and she told me that they were, but not by ballots. She said they were chosen in their dreams. Yes, more jungle lore. I hope I'll be able to sort it all out before long.

Maria interrupted my writing a few moments ago to say that she is almost certain we will reach the city tomorrow. She added that from this point on I was to address her by her real name, Rae-la.

The taxi wound up the hill and Indy recognized the street. They were nearing the Hotel Paraíso. "Keep driving around for a bit," he told Hugo.

"This is fascinating, Indy," said Deirdre, who was reading over his shoulder.

"It's definitely another world," he replied, and they returned to the journal.

30 August

Maria, or rather Rae-la, has disappeared. I've taken several short forays into the surrounding jungle in search of her, but to no avail.

Once I thought I detected someone following me. I called out her name, but no one answered. I turned around and spotted an Indian boy. He stared at me a moment, then vanished into the forest. I started after him, hoping he would give me directions to the city, but after a short distance I thought better of it. I didn't need the complications of encountering an Indian tribe that might be hostile.

As I returned to the small clearing where I'd last seen Rae-la, I came across a path and followed it to a river. To my surprise there was a rope bridge crossing it, and on the other side was a massive ceiba tree. Could this be the entrance to the city? I wondered. I crossed the bridge, a perilous feat in itself, then I walked for nearly an hour moving in the direction of the late afternoon sun. Rae-la had indicated that the city lay to the west.

The light of day was waning and I was worried that I was hopelessly lost when, before me, rising from the jungle, was a mountain. Its rocky, precipitous walls ascended several hundred feet and its peak was not a peak at all, but a flat top like a mesa. Then I saw something else. On top of it was a structure like a watchtower. It looked as if there was a light burning in it; no, it was probably just a rock structure, and the light was simply a ray from the setting sun glinting off the surface.

Nevertheless, I rushed anxiously ahead. As I moved closer, I noticed the shadows of other mountains. These were mountains, not clouds. I had found the Snoring Mountains. I was sure of it now. But the distance was greater than I'd expected. Then I saw something else. The wall of the bluff was covered with an array of twinkling lights. It was a beautiful sight. But I had no idea what the lights were.

The jungle blocked my view for several minutes, and when finally I arrived at another opening in the forest, I couldn't find the mountains. I couldn't find any of them. It was as if I had never seen them. The lights, the bluff, the watchtower. All of it gone. I can't explain it.

I decided to stop right there for the night. I was tired and out of breath. I needed a drink, and was glad there was still rum left in my pack. Walters, bless his soul, had been kind enough to die before he'd drunk it all.

For the past couple of hours now, I've been sipping regularly on the rum.

An odd thought occurred to me. What if Rae-la's talk of veils is actually true, and I have indeed arrived in Ceiba? It's an eerie thought, especially now as I sit in the dark by my fire. I want to believe that I'm alone, and that I'm not being observed by strangers whom I cannot even see. Do the veils also muffle sound? Rae-la never said.

But now I'm acting as if all this is real. It's crazy how one's imagination can take over with the onset of darkness. This begins when we are children, imagining creatures lurking in the shadows, and for many of us it continues into adulthood. All my life I have hoped to dispel the darkness and shed light on the mysterious and unknown, and here I am huddled in fear.

Another thought. What if I am going crazy? The jungle can do strange things to people. Maybe the water is different here and affects the mind.

*Maybe it's just the rum. What if there is no Rae-la?
Could I have imagined her and everything she
told me? Maybe I've been wandering out of my
head for days, and everything that has happened
is all just bloody nonsense.*

*No. I refuse to believe that. I met her at the
mission. I'm certain of it. She helped heal me. She
is real. She must be.*

*Better not think any longer. These wild
thoughts hurl my imagination in dangerous directions. It shows how much I've been affected by the
jungle, by Rae-la, by the rum, by all of it. I'm
going to finish the bottle. Then to sleep. Blessed
sleep.*

Indy shut the journal and looked up. "Let's get
there, Hugo."

"It's right around the corner," the driver answered.

Deirdre shook her head. "What do you think?"

"Too much rum."

"Maybe," she said. "Don't you think you should
finish it before you go in there?" The taxi pulled up
to the hotel.

"It'll have to wait." Indy handed the journal
back to her. "It's time to find the daughter of
Oya."

"It's Rae-la, isn't it?"

"That's my guess, and I'd say our friend
Amergin is her partner."

13

RAE-LA

Indy approached the hotel alone. The lobby was as empty as the last time he had been there. The place gave him the creeps. It was a ghost hotel, inhabited by spirits and gods called down by the old *babalorixá*. He hoped he didn't have to see her or Joaquin again.

He started for the staircase, and that was when he saw the phantom standing halfway up the stairs watching him. She was slender, attractive, and otherworldly, and it took a moment before Indy was certain that he was seeing a beautiful woman and not the ghost of one.

"Hello, Indy."

"Rae-la?"

She nodded, smiled, and descended the stairs. It was odd to see her in person after reading about her in the journal. It was like meeting a character from a novel. "Fawcett thought the people of D had red hair and blue eyes," he said.

"Some do."

She stopped a few feet from him, and Indy could

see why Fawcett and Walters reacted to her the way they did. As far as jungle guides went, she would be as appealing as they came. Her skin was bronze and flawless, her eyes green and penetrating. Her chestnut hair reached to the middle of her back.

"Please call the city Ceiba. D is only the written form, as you should know if you've read Colonel Fawcett's journal."

Indy smiled, and took a step closer to her. She was taller than Deirdre, and a few years older. "I guess you sent the journal pages to Marcus Brody and delivered the rest of it to our hotel room last night."

"No. That was me," a voice boomed from behind him.

Indy spun around and saw Amergin standing by the counter ten feet from him. "Where did you come from?"

Amergin didn't answer. He was probably trying to show him that the veils were real, but Indy knew he could've been hiding behind the counter.

"What do you want?" Indy asked.

"Maybe I should ask you that question, but I think our goals are the same. We know about the airplane. We'll show you the way to Ceiba, then you can take Fawcett home."

It sounded too pat, too good to be true, and too much like a setup. "Why are you so interested in helping Fawcett?"

"Because it's a mistake to hold him against his will," Rae-la answered.

Indy wasn't quite ready to jump into anything with these two, but he knew he had time. He would take them to the guava farm and finish the journal en route. Then he'd make up his mind. "How long will it take you to get ready?"

"A few minutes," Amergin said.

Rae-la nodded in agreement.

"I'll be waiting," Indy said and turned away.

Back at the taxi, Indy quickly explained the situation to Deirdre. She glanced apprehensively toward the hotel.

"You'd better read the rest of this journal right away," she said, handing it to him.

"That's exactly what I had in mind."

1 September

Midmorning. I awakened today with a hangover. But there was little time to think about that. My God, I found myself lying in a bed. I'm in a room with peach-coloured walls. A real room, not a hut. At last, I have finally made it! I'm in the city now, waiting for their leaders, the ones from the Higher Orb or Eternal Orb or whatever, to arrive with a formal greeting. I don't like the fact that my door is locked from the outside, but I suppose they want to orient me to the city before I go walking around on my own.

Early afternoon. It didn't take me long to figure out what must have happened. I had obviously overindulged with the rum, and at some point Rae-la arrived with others from the city. They must have thought I was ill, or maybe they're not familiar with the sight of someone in a drunken stupor. I suppose they put me on a stretcher and carried me into the city.

I'm fascinated with my recollection of the mountain with the lights and the watchtower. I saw it, then lost it, almost as if it blinked on and off. I'm very anxious to see the city, but it seems they have decided to give me extra time to repair myself.

The room has two windows, vertical slits several inches wide and about a yard high. I can't see anything of the city through the windows, only clouds. Clouds above, clouds below. Yet, the clouds seem distant, not at all like fog. Why is there nothing between? There is no glass or screen of any sort on the windows, but there are no insects in the room. The windows are too narrow for me to slip out. Otherwise, I would have done so by now.

Evening. I suspect I'm in some sort of quarantine. I've been given two meals today, both delivered through a slot in the door. The food, I must say, was delicious. The second meal was baked fish and a tuber type of vegetable that was somewhat similar to a sweet potato.

I want to talk to someone. I've pounded on the door and yelled, but no one responds. Where is Rae-la? Why hasn't she come to see me, to tell me what's going on?

2 September

Still in the room. I'm thoroughly disappointed in the people of Ceiba. I plan to file a formal complaint about my treatment as soon as I can talk with someone. I'm going to demand that I be allowed to move about freely, or at least in a less restricted manner.

My activities have been confined to examining the room in detail. There is no furniture except a simple wood table, two chairs, and the bed, which I've discovered doubles as a couch when the wood frame is adjusted. There are no decorations on the walls save for a simple painted inscription. It con-

*sists of a vertical line with an X crossing its center.
I believe it is an ogham symbol representing the
letters CH. Each of these letters has meanings beyond the alphabetic denotation. But I've forgotten
what this one means.*

*Mainly I'm bored. If this city were a part of the
known world, I would demand to see my ambassa-
dor. Unfortunately, Ceiba has no relations with
the British empire. In fact, the empire doesn't
know it exists.*

Indy pondered the ogham letter, which Fawcett
had scrawled in the journal. It was related to druid
groves and referred to a sacred place, a place
where everything that appears hidden is ultimately understood. It was a reassuring sign, even
though Fawcett didn't understand it. He just
hoped that it was true.

"They're coming," Deirdre said.

Indy looked up from the journal and saw
Amergin and Rae-la heading toward the taxi. They
took seats in the front with Hugo, and after the
usual greeting and introductions, they drove off. A
look passed between Amergin and Hugo, and he
had the distinct impression the two already knew
each other.

Deirdre made a few attempts at conversation,
asking questions about the Paraíso Hotel. But neither Amergin nor Rae-la had much to say. Finally,
the monotonous rumble of the engine took over as
the conversation lapsed. That was fine with Indy.
He was anxious to finish the journal, and the fewer
the interruptions, the better.

3 September

Rae-la finally visited me. She was accompanied by a man named Amergin. Although she greeted me in a friendly way, she deferred to Amergin when I questioned her about the reason I was being treated like a prisoner. He responded that I was fortunate to be here at all, and that it hadn't yet been determined how I would be dealt with. But a decision was coming soon.

As if to clarify the predicament, he explained that those in the higher echelon of the society, the so-called orbs, are quite familiar with the outside world, but have no interest in becoming a part of it. Indeed, Ceiba's very existence is predicated on its separateness. He said that exposure to the outside would cause decay and demoralisation within.

Amergin was surprisingly open with information, which was odd because it seemed to contradict what he was saying about the need to keep the city isolated. The entire range of mountains was veiled because the Ceibans, as he called them, lived not only in the city but throughout the mountains, where many were farmers and hunters. Altogether, there were more than fifteen thousand Ceibans.

Also found in these mountains are the ruins of other cities that were long abandoned even before the Ceibans arrived. Their legends said the past inhabitants of those cities were their ancestors, long separated by an ancient disaster of a great magnitude. This I found particularly interesting, as it fit well with what I had already surmised. The Ceibans were certain that those before them were invaded and overrun, and they knew that they too

*would be destroyed unless they devised methods
of protection. That was when the high priests, then
known as druids, began teaching the secret of veiling.*

*Indeed, the society seems geared toward remain-
ing invisible, at least in spirit. Although I am
fascinated by their belief system, I doubt that it
will stand up to close inspection. No doubt a pla-
toon of armed soldiers could easily capture the city
in half a day, and once the residents realised that
they are indeed as visible as anyone else, they
would panic. The very fiber of their society would
crumble.*

*It's sad, but generally accepted now, that the
cost of advancing civilisation always results in the
decline and disappearance of those societies less
capable of handling change. If not I, someone else
will expose Ceiba. It's inevitable. In ten years, Ceiba will probably be just another exotic outpost of
civilisation with a curious cultural background.
My sincere hope is that those who survive the
changes will be able to explain their legends so we
can learn more of the fantastic history of these
people.*

*There is just one thing to add here. What I said
about meeting Amergin and Rae-la is somewhat
spurious. I took these notes after awakening from
a nap. It seems I've dreamed up this Amergin person. I'm still waiting to talk to Rae-la or anyone.
Yet, I am puzzled by the vividness of the dream,
and its curious contents.*

The bumpy road made it difficult to read, and
Fawcett's handwriting was not the easiest to deci-
pher. But the tale he was telling compensated for
it. Indy continued reading and finished the journal
before they arrived at the farm.

6 September

Late last night, a hand shook me from my sleep. I started, leaping up from bed. It was Rae-la. I demanded to know what she was doing in my room in the middle of the night. When I finally calmed down, I could tell that she was distressed.

She said I would be held indefinitely, to serve as some sort of breeder, of all things. She said she didn't have time to explain, but said she wanted to help me. She will be leaving soon for Bahia and she wants to take my journal with her and send it to someone who can help me.

My first response was that it would take too long. I asked her why she couldn't simply help me escape. She answered that she would be exiled, and that she could not spend the rest of her life away from Ceiba.

In the end I agreed. She's taking the journal and sending a few pages to Marcus Brody in New York. I already tore out the ones I wanted her to send. Marcus is one of the few friends of mine who accepted the possibility that the city might actually exist. He will understand and get help. Hopefully, it won't be long. I will be waiting.

In the morning, I awoke and remembered another dream about Rae-la. After a few minutes, the details came back to me as I've recorded. But before I began this entry, I turned to the front of the journal. Several pages were indeed torn from it. I'm at a loss, but fear these people are attempting to drive me mad.

14

GUAVA FARM

The farm wasn't exactly what Indy expected. He'd imagined long neat rows of fruit trees arcing over rolling hills, a neat ranch house, and a yard with buildings for tractors and farmhands. What he saw, when Hugo turned into the farmyard some twenty miles outside of Bahia, was a decrepit shack, and a cluster of barren-looking trees with leaves that drooped under the hot summer sun.

"You must have made a wrong turn somewhere," Indy said. "This couldn't be it."

"I followed your directions very closely, and those are guava trees," Hugo responded.

Outside the shack a dog was sleeping in the dirt, and it didn't even raise its head as the taxi rolled to a stop a few feet from the door. Nearby was a horse-drawn wagon with no horse and a broken wheel.

No one moved from the taxi and no one emerged from the shack. "Indy, are you sure your directions were right?" Deirdre asked.

"I'll go find out right now." Indy got out, kicked

an empty whiskey bottle out of his path, and then pounded on the door. "Fletcher, you there?" When there was no answer, he pounded again.

The others had gotten out of the car and were waiting for him. Deirdre leaned against the car and fanned herself. "Maybe we won't be flying after all."

"We'll see," Indy said and moved around the side of the house. Hugo followed him.

To the rear of the shack was a garbage heap with several chickens pecking on its outskirts. Beyond the yard was a wall of tall trees that served as a windbreak, and between the trunks, Indy saw the glistening surface of a lake.

"Indy, over here."

Hugo was peering through the trees toward the lake when Indy joined him. Tied to a buoy, fifty feet from shore, was a shiny silver trimotor airliner equipped with pontoons. "Well, I'll be damned," Indy whispered.

A rowboat bobbed between the pontoons, and a man wearing a cap with a long bill was seated in it, painting the underside of one of the wings. He'd stopped his work, and was peering at them. "Hold your horses, gentlemen. I'll be right with you."

"I'll go tell the others," Hugo said, and he hurried off.

"You must be Jones," Fletcher called to him as he rowed to shore. "I've been expecting you."

The rowboat touched shore, and Fletcher hopped out. The two men shook hands and exchanged greetings. Fletcher's face was burned a deep reddish-brown, and showed a three-day growth of beard. He had a square jaw, blue eyes, and a friendly smile. He looked to be in his late forties, and Indy guessed he'd already done more living than most people do in their entire lives.

"Nice plane," Indy said.

"Thanks. It's a Fokker F-VII trimotor. The Brazilian government is going to start an airline with flights between Rio and Bahia. They bought three of these equipped with pontoons so I can land in the bays."

"What are you doing with it?"

"They hired me right out of the English Flying Club as their chief pilot," Fletcher said. "They gave me this farm as an incentive to come over here." He laughed, and shook his head. "Don't know what I was thinking. I don't give a damn about farming, and I'd never seen a guava. But here I am."

Indy liked the man. "You must have quite a bit of flying experience."

"Well, I flew around the world in '24. I was on the crew of the two Douglas World Cruisers that circled the globe together in one-hundred and seventy-four days."

"Really?" Indy couldn't help being a bit awed. Pilots, after all, were the heroes of the day, and Fletcher sounded like one of the best.

"By the way, did you see your friend? He's been getting worried you weren't going to show up."

"Who are you talking about?"

"What's his name, you know. Damn, the guy's been here two days. I should remember his name."

Fletcher was distracted as the other three arrived, and his eyes darted among them. Indy quickly introduced them, and was about to ask Fletcher to explain what he was saying when Deirdre spoke up.

"Is the plane big enough for all of us?"

"Well, if it isn't a Scottish lass. Welcome to Brazil.

This plane has plenty of space. It's the finest trimotor passenger plane ever made."

"I've never been in an airplane," Rae-la said in accented English.

"Well, don't you worry, sweetheart. You'll be in good hands with me."

Who would be waiting here for him? Indy wondered as Fletcher rattled on about his flight experience. It couldn't be Carino or Oron. Neither of them could've been waiting here for two days.

"You can fly us into the Amazon?" Amergin asked.

"Would love to," Fletcher said without any hesitation. "I'm bored to death. The way these bureaucrats are taking their time, hell, it'll be six months before we get our first flight off the ground. I mean off the water."

"Do you know about Colonel Fawcett?" Deirdre asked.

"Of course. I hope I can help you find him. We'll all be famous."

"Where's this friend of mine?" Indy asked.

"He's around here, somewhere. I'm sure he'll be along."

"What friend?" Deirdre looked mystified.

"English bloke, like myself, but more of a thinker than me. Brody, that's it. You know, the man who sent you down here."

"Marcus? What the hell is he doing here?"

Fletcher was staring past Indy. "Now who the devil is this coming?"

"I've got a gun in his back, Jones. Don't try anything."

Indy spun around to see Carino. His weasel face peered over Hugo's shoulder. Following by a few steps was Oron. "I thought you lost your gun," Indy said.

"I bought it back from the cops," Carino snickered. "You know, they're very accommodating when the money is right."

"What do you want?" Deirdre yelled.

"We're going for an airplane ride," Carino said. "All of us."

"Who are these guys, Jones?" Fletcher said under his breath.

"More friends."

Oron walked up to Indy, and yanked the whip from his belt. "If you don't mind, sir," he said in his best steward voice. "I'll need this to tie you up, since we weren't expecting a party." He wrapped the whip a couple times around Indy, then tied it behind his back. "That should hold you just fine, sir. If you need anything else, you just let me know."

"Don't worry. I will."

"Cut the crap, Oron," Carino said. "Tie the rest of them."

"Where are you taking us?" Deirdre demanded.

"Like I said, for an airplane ride. Then we're going to see how well you fly on your own." Carino guffawed, his lips pulling back from his teeth with predatory glee.

Indy watched Oron tie Amergin's and Rae-la's hands behind their backs. If they could vanish, why didn't they? he wondered. Maybe Fawcett's doubts were right. Maybe the vanishing act was just some sort of gimmick to keep superstitious people in line.

After Oron tied Deirdre, he moved over to Fletcher. "Don't tie him, you idiot," Carino snapped. "He's got to fly the plane."

"Well, Frank, I just thought—"

"Don't think, and don't call me Frank. I'm Mr.

Carino. You got that? Now put the luggage in the boat."

"What about him?" Oron asked, nodding toward Hugo.

"Let him go," Indy said. "He's a taxi driver. He's got nothing to do with us."

"Don't be stupid, Jones. He's working for your buddy here," he said, nodding toward Amergin. "I saw them together at that phoney hotel before you arrived."

"It's true," Hugo said. "But Amergin promised me he and Rae-la weren't going to do anything bad to you. They just wanted to know what you were up to."

"Well, nobody likes traitors," Carino said, and without hesitating, he shot Hugo in the back of the head. The driver slumped to the ground, dead.

Victor Bernard stood near the edge of the trees and watched as Julian Ray's thug shot the taxi driver, and Deirdre screamed. Unnecessary violence. He wasn't pleased, but he was glad to see that things were finally coming to a head.

It seemed as if it had taken him forever to get to Bahia, and he'd been worried that he was too late. He'd come directly to the farm after spending less than an hour in the city. He'd told Fletcher he was Brody and he was here to meet Jones. Fletcher hadn't seemed surprised. He said he'd received a cable Jones sent from Rio more than a week ago, and he was expecting him any day.

Now it was time to act. Bernard stepped out from the trees and strode toward the shore.

"I'd shoot you too, Jones, but I want you and your pretty wife to finish what you started on Sugarloaf," Carino said. "And this time when you fall, you fall."

Indy stared into the barrel of the gun that was pointed at his nose. He knew Carino would fire it if he tried anything, and without the use of his hands his chances weren't good.

"Oh, Christ, here's Brody," Fletcher muttered. "Fine time to show up."

Carino turned. At that moment, Indy might have kicked the gun from his hand. But he was too surprised by the sight of Victor Bernard.

"My God, Doctor Ber—" Deirdre began.

"Don't point that thing at me," Bernard barked at Carino.

"Who the hell are you?" Carino snarled.

"I'm the man who hired you. That's who."

"Don't give me that. I know who you are, Brody. You sent Jones down here and got him the pilot."

"I'm not Brody. I'm with Julian Ray."

Carino laughed. "I doubt that." He turned back to Indy and put the gun to his temple. "Who is he?"

"Brody."

"You son of a bitch, Jones." Bernard tried to reason with Carino. "Don't you see what he's doing? He's trying to divide us."

"Tie him up, Oron. He's going with us."

Bernard shoved Oron away, but Carino lurched forward and slammed the butt of his gun across his face, rendering him unconscious.

Carino waved his gun at Oron and Fletcher. "Carry him into the boat."

A minute later, all eight of them were crowded into the rowboat. Oron and Fletcher took the paddles and rowed out to the trimotor, while Carino remained aft with the gun aimed at their backs. They boarded the plane, loading Bernard like a piece of luggage. Carino kept an eye on Fletcher as the pilot released the plane from the buoys and prepared to take off. Oron, meanwhile, brandished a vicious-looking knife and guarded the two couples, who were still tied up.

"Guess you don't want us to get hurt," Indy remarked when Carino ordered Oron to buckle everyone's seat belt.

"I don't want you bouncing off the ceiling when we take off, Jones. You'll get your chance to test your wings soon enough."

Finally, the plane's engine revved to life and they taxied down to the end of the kidney-shaped lake. Indy was strapped in the front seat with Deirdre behind him. Amergin and Rae-la were across the aisle. Behind her was Bernard, who was still unconscious. Under different conditions, Indy would have been looking forward to the flight. He'd traveled by air from London to Paris and back, but this was the first time he'd been in a plane with pontoons or flown over a rain forest.

The trimotor's engine rose in pitch to a high whine as they accelerated across the lake. Indy craned his neck, looking out the window. He saw the row of trees between the shack and the lakeshore rushing toward them. For a moment, he didn't think they were going to make it. Carino, who was still in the cockpit, shouted in alarm. Then, with less than ten yards of water left, the plane lifted. Its nose rose in a steep climb and barely cleared the top limbs of the trees.

"That was damn close," Indy said. All the while he worked to loosen the knot in the whip.

When they leveled off, Carino stepped back into the cabin. He held a bloody handkerchief to his forehead with one hand, and wielded the gun in the other.

"What happened?" Oron asked from the rear of the cabin.

"What do you think? I hit my head when the clown jumped over those trees."

"Now what?" Oron asked.

"Get Mrs. Jones. Ladies first."

"No," Indy said. "Me first."

"You shut up," Oron said.

"If he wants to die first, let him," Carino said. "The quicker we're through with you, Jones, the better."

As Oron unbuckled the seat belt, Indy made one last effort to loosen the whip, but it was still bound tightly around him. Oron jerked him to his feet, and pulled him by the whip over to the door. The knot rubbed against Indy's fingers and he furtively worked to loosen it.

"Now, the door," Carino ordered.

Oron gripped the handle, and turned it. To Oron's surprise, the door swung out, nearly pulling him with it. He let go and grabbed a rail next to the door. He glared accusingly at Carino. "Why didn't you tell me that was going to happen?"

"You're not on a boat, Oron. You're two thousand feet above the ground and flying at over one hundred and fifty miles an hour. What did you expect? Now get him out of here."

Even without Oron's assistance, Indy felt the suction of the air pulling him forward. "Indy, no!" Deirdre yelled.

He looked up at her, thinking it was his last look. The rope was looser, but still bound him. He'd never get his hands free in time. Then he noticed something. Or rather the lack of it.

Amergin's seat was empty.

"Hey, you're missing someone," Indy yelled above the howl of the wind.

Oron turned his head, gaping in amazement. In that instant, he relaxed his grip on the rail. Indy butted him in the gut with his head and drove him screaming through the open door. But now Indy tottered in the doorway. If his hands had been free, he would've caught the rail. He glimpsed the ground far below him and felt himself being sucked out. Then his feet slipped out from under him and he was gone.

Deirdre was desperate. She struggled to get free of the seat belt. Carino was raving. He seemed more concerned about the whereabouts of Amergin than his lost companion.

"He's gone," he stammered. "Gone is gone. There's no place he could hide."

As Carino moved up the aisle, he suddenly stumbled and fell as if an invisible leg tripped him. The door to the cockpit was still open, and Fletcher, who had watched what was going on, didn't miss seeing Carino fall. Without a second thought, he rolled the plane clockwise and Carino slid toward the open door. He clawed at the floor, but he was losing ground.

"Help, help me," he called out.

Then Fletcher jerked the plane a few more degrees and Carino lost his grip and shot out the door and into space.

Luck was with Indy.

His leg had hit the strut between the wing and frame of the plane, and he was hooked by his knee. He hung upside down, his heart pounding in his mouth. But he knew he couldn't hang for long. The rush of wind threatened to rip him free at any moment. The knot had loosened and he frantically worked the whip over his shoulders. He gasped for breath. Despite all the air, he could hardly breathe.

The roller coaster ride seemed endless, but finally Indy's hands were free. He gripped the strut with both hands and the whip in his teeth. The plane tilted downward on its side, and he wrapped his arms tightly around the strut. A body flashed past him and he heard a yell. *Carino. Good riddance.*

The plane leveled off. Indy gasped for breath, and pulled himself up the strut toward the wing until he was peering into the doorway. Someone had to see him. They had to realize he was out here.

All he could see was the railing on the inside of the door, but it gave him an idea. He took the whip from his mouth, found the grip, and hurled it toward the doorway, aiming for the railing. The wind was too strong, though, and it flung the whip back in his face.

"Never was any good going upwind," he muttered.

He tried again with the same result. That was when he saw Fletcher's face in the cockpit window, staring at him.

Tears were running down Deirdre's cheeks when Fletcher rushed from the cockpit and unlatched her seat belt. "What are you doing? Who's flying the plane?"

"No one. Give me your hands. Indy's out on the strut."

She could hardly believe what she was hearing. "He's alive? My God, land the plane. Fast."

Fletcher slashed at the rope on her wrists with a sharp blade. "It'll take too long." The bindings popped; her hands were free. "The buoy rope. It's behind the last seat. Get it."

As Deirdre jumped from her seat, the plane hit a pocket of turbulent air and slipped into a roll. She stumbled, struck her head against the side of a seat, and was knocked to the floor.

She felt as though she might pass out, but she fought it, and ignored the pain. The plane leveled out. *Fletcher must be back in the cockpit. It's going to be okay. Indy's still alive.*

She reached the last seat. *Where's the rope, damn it? Where?* Then she spotted a black metal box, and pulled open the top. She grabbed the rope and stood up. Feeling woozy, she nevertheless struggled toward the front of the plane. As she grabbed the railing, she saw Indy. She couldn't believe it. He was only six or seven feet away, his whip dangling from his mouth.

"Tie the rope to the rail," Fletcher yelled.

She knotted the end, hoping it would hold. She didn't need any further directions. Indy was watching her; he knew exactly what she was doing. She fed the rope out the door and it slid along the frame of the plane. Indy reached for it, but it was too far away. She reeled it back in and this time tossed it out a few feet.

He grabbed it.

Indy didn't hesitate. He pulled himself hand over hand toward the door. Stretched out parallel to the plane, he fought the wind, which threatened to tear him loose and toss him a mile. He reached the door and felt Deirdre grab his arm. The next thing he knew, he was on the floor of the cabin.

"You made it. You're alive."

He looked up, panting. "Thanks for the rope."

"You're lucky." Indy's head snapped around at the sound of Amergin's voice. He wasn't gone after all. He was still in his seat, his hands tied behind him, his seat belt fastened.

15

JUNGLE LORE

A deep green carpet spread out below them, laced with silvery spider webs of rivers, tributaries, and streams. The jungle looked impenetrable, alien, and ready to swallow anything that stepped into its domain. Indy found it hard to imagine that ancient explorers had traipsed through the jungle with expectations of finding a city.

He had an excellent view of the terrain, because he was at the controls. Fletcher had been giving him flying lessons, and Indy was spelling him for short periods. He hadn't taken off or landed yet, but he could maintain straight and level flight and follow a course. They had landed three times at jungle outposts on rivers for refueling, and last night had slept in hammocks under thatched huts in Cuiabá, the last outpost before the Great Unknown. Indy was surprised by the availability of fuel, but Fletcher had explained that air transportation for commercial purposes was developing faster in Latin America than in the United States because of the lack of roads and the rugged territory. Already missionaries were relying on airplanes to fly supplies to the interior.

Today was the third day since their departure from the guava farm, and the deadly confrontation with Carino and Oron. Indy had found plenty of time to mull over what had happened that first day. He figured that Brody's secretary must have unwittingly told Bernard about Fletcher and the amphibious plane, just as she'd told him about the journal and the rest of Indy's plans. Bernard had passed on the information to someone named Ray, who'd hired Carino, and the thug had known that the guava farm was his last chance to make good on his assignment to keep Indy from searching for Fawcett.

Carino hadn't expected Bernard, didn't even know who he was. Indy's initial intent was to drop Bernard off at their first stop and let him fend for himself. But the longer he thought about it, the more he liked another idea. Bernard, more than anyone he could think of, would make the best impression on the world if he returned from South America with news that an ancient Celtic-based civilization existed deep in the Amazon. Sure, he would get much of the credit, but he would also be forced to make a one-hundred-and-eighty-degree turnaround in his position on pre-Columbian journeys to the Americas. Indy, for his part, would be content with rescuing Fawcett, the one who would ultimately be known for making the incredible discovery.

As they flew deeper into the jungle, Indy's thoughts turned to Fawcett, his journal, and what he knew about the explorer's past. He was intrigued by the colonel, because he was both a man of action and a mystic. Fawcett had served several years as an officer with the Royal Artillery in Ceylon, where he studied Buddhism and spent his leave time following the clues in a cryptic map as he searched futilely for the buried treasure of the Kandyan kings. He'd also made several expeditions to South America in the early years of the century. Then, after serving in the war, he'd returned to Brazil. In 1920 he embarked on his first quest for the lost city, which he thought was called Z.

Fawcett failed, but his hopes were hardly dimmed, because while in Rio de Janeiro he came across Manuscript No. 512 in the National Library. The document was the record of a Portuguese expedition that set out in 1743 for the Amazon, in search of ancient gold and silver mines supposedly discovered more than a century earlier by a soldier of fortune.

According to the explorers' report, they came upon a rugged range of mountains in the heart of the wild central plateau, where they discovered an immense stone city, apparently totally abandoned. The expedition found hieroglyphs resembling Celtic ogham inscribed on some of the stone monuments. Fawcett was uplifted by the report, and vowed to return for a second attempt to find the city.

"I'd better take over," Fletcher said, joining Indy in the cockpit. "We should be approaching the mountain range at any moment."

"I don't see any mountains yet," Indy said, turning over the controls. The Serra do Roncador, or the Snoring Mountains, were supposedly situated between the Araguaia and the Xingú rivers. They'd passed over the Araguaia half an hour ago; Indy could see the Xingú off the port side.

"I'm not really surprised. These charts are rough guesses at best."

Indy glanced back into the passenger compartment and saw Amergin moving toward the cockpit. "How's Bernard doing?"

Fletcher shrugged. "The same. Subdued."

"Very close now," Amergin said, pushing his head through the door of the cockpit.

"How can you tell?" Indy asked. "It all looks the same."

"Not to me. I feel the pull of the trees."

Tugs from trees and disappearing acts were the sort of thing that Fawcett had lumped together in his journal as jungle lore, the product of a primitive environment, nonscientific reasoning, or maybe just too much sun. While Fawcett seemed to regard Rae-la's jungle lore with skepticism, Indy knew that the adventurer was also intrigued by it. After all, if Fawcett had believed the stories of the lost city were nonsense, he wouldn't have spent so much time searching for it.

Like Fawcett's, Indy's opinion on the mystical realms of ancient cultures was guarded. It wasn't something he talked about, but it was always lurking in the back of his mind. After all, he had seen and experienced a few things himself that were not easily dismissed. If he was to accept what happened to him a year ago at Stonehenge as real, then he would have to say that he had seen and spoken to none other a personage than Merlin the magician. If not jungle lore, it was his stone lore.

"Look there," Amergin said. "Do you see that tributary leading from the river? Follow it. You will see a lake in five minutes to the right of the river. You land there."

"Fawcett didn't say anything about a lake," Indy said.

"He didn't see it."

Amergin had said little about how they would

enter the city without being seen. Every time Indy or Deirdre had brought up the subject, Amergin's response was that he would explain when the time was right. Amergin, in fact, was short on explanations of anything related to himself or Ceiba. When Deirdre had asked what had happened to him at the beginning of the flight, he'd simply told her to read Fawcett's diary, as if that would explain everything.

"I still don't see any mountains," Fletcher said.

"Don't worry about it," Amergin answered.

Indy knew that they were supposed to believe they were veiled from sight. "Let us know if we're going to crash into any mountains," he said, just to be on the safe side.

"We're not going over the mountains."

"But won't we be seen from the city when we land?" Indy asked, trying again to prod more information from Amergin.

"We are still too far away."

Indy spotted the lake, but he also saw something else: a clearing several hundred yards from the shore, with an array of round, thatched roofs. "What's that?"

"An Indian village."

"I guessed that. Who are they?"

"We call them the Morcegos, but we don't have anything to do with them."

The name of the tribe meant bat in Portuguese, and Indy immediately recalled his confrontation with the Mayan bat god and his real-life counterparts. "Bat people?"

"They like to hunt at night, and paint themselves to look like bats."

"They sound like a friendly bunch."

Amergin shrugged. "They're cannibals."

"Oh, swell. We're going to land right in their

territory. I suppose by tonight they'll be hungry and hunting."

"They won't come near us," Amergin assured him. "They'll think we're an evil spirit from the sky."

"Do they know about Ceiba?"

"Very little. They won't cross the river because they think the land is enchanted."

"From what Fawcett wrote about it, I'd say they're right," Indy said.

Amergin ignored the comment. "We once traded with them, but they have very little for us. Besides, they're busy with their wars."

"What wars?" Fletcher asked as he circled the lake.

"Battling neighboring tribes. But as I said, we have no reason to fear them."

Indy peered at the shoreline of the lake, but couldn't see anyone watching them. "That's good to know. But I'm still looking forward to getting to Ceiba."

"That won't be possible." Amergin spoke in a brusque voice.

"What do you mean?"

"You four will stay by the lake. Rae-la and I will enter the city during the night and get Fawcett. Then we will all return to Bahia. We'll leave before dawn tomorrow. That is the only way we can do it."

"But can't one of us go?" Indy wanted to be the one, of course. But he knew who should go. "Take Bernard with you."

"We'll see," Amergin said.

"I'm going down," Fletcher said. "Get in your seats."

"Can I see how you bring it down?" Indy asked.

Fletcher jerked his thumb toward the seat next

to him. They came in low over the lake. The smooth, lapis surface looked like a vast runway.

"The trick is to avoid coming in too steeply," Fletcher explained. "On land, you can bounce a couple of times on the tarmac if you come down too sharply, but on water it's a different story."

"So what happens?" Indy asked as the lake loomed below them.

"You flip over. Hang on. Here we go."

They dipped down; Indy's stomach lurched into his throat. They touched the water with a slight jolt, then skidded like a duck landing on webbed feet. Water sprayed on either side of them.

"Nice landing," Indy said, relieved that they were still upright.

Amergin came forward again and told Fletcher where to go ashore. It was halfway around the lake from the Morcegos, but Indy wished it was much further away. Fletcher taxied the plane to within twenty feet of shore, and turned off the engine. They leaped into the water one at a time and waded ashore. As Indy and Fletcher tied down the plane, the others set out in search of a sheltered spot to set up camp.

Indy wondered if Amergin was going to allow Bernard to go with them. He'd be disappointed if Amergin refused, but he'd be even more disappointed if he and Rae-la never returned with Fawcett. Indy decided that whether Bernard went along or not, he would follow them to Ceiba just to make sure they kept their promise. Besides, he hadn't come all this way to stop a few miles short of what could be the most historically and archaeologically significant city in the Americas. He wanted to take a look for himself, even if it was just a quick one.

* * *

Amergin moved quickly into the forest as the others set up camp. It wasn't long before he realized the Morcegos were nearby. They had seen the airplane and were moving toward the lake to investigate. He called out a greeting to them in their language. They couldn't see him, and thought he was a spirit, as they always did. He told them about the people who had arrived in the water-bird and explained how they should react to them.

The Morcegos had a name for Amergin. He was the spirit of woods, and he didn't mind the title. As he spoke, he moved from tree to tree because some of the warriors were nearly able to see through the veil and probably would succeed if he stood in one place. He completed his instructions, and demanded that the warriors leave an offering of fresh meat. They argued among themselves, but then one of the men stepped forward with a fresh kill of three rabbits and laid them on the ground.

Amergin would've preferred more food, but he knew it was a sacrifice for the Morcegos to give up as much as they had. He told them that their offering would bring them good fortune, but they must make sure they did what he said, or the spirits from the invisible city would haunt them.

"Where's Amergin?" Deirdre asked when she realized she hadn't seen him for awhile.

"Maybe he's right here watching us," Indy said as he dropped a load of firewood. "This disappearing act seems like a good way of getting out of work."

Deirdre noticed Rae-la watching Indy, and wondered what she was thinking. The woman made her uneasy. Deirdre's efforts to talk with her had been met either with short replies that didn't encourage conversation, or with icy stares. Rae-la had hardly spoken to any of them since they'd left Bahia. But she was always watching them, especially Indy, and Deirdre didn't like it one bit.

"Watch what you say," Deirdre whispered to Indy.

"Amergin hasn't deserted us," Rae-la said. "He's hunting for our dinner."

A few minutes later, Rae-la's words proved true. Amergin marched into camp bearing the carcasses of three rabbits. He dropped them at Deirdre's feet. "Skin them for us. You think too much."

Deirdre looked uncertainly at the furry heap, then back at Amergin. But he'd already turned away. To her surprise, Rae-la offered to help her.

"Let's go. We'll do it together."

Deirdre nodded. It was the most Rae-la had said to her. But that wasn't the only surprising thing: Rae-la had spoken in a language that sounded like Gaelic. Deirdre was baffled for a moment, but then it all made sense. If the people of Ceiba were Celtic in origin, and isolated, why wouldn't they speak a form of Gaelic?

They carried the carcasses away from the camp, and Deirdre didn't waste any time picking up the conversation in Gaelic. "So are the people of your city really druids?"

"We are not druids or Celts anymore, just as the Brazilians are not Portuguese. Yet, in many ways we are closer to our druid past after more than twenty-two centuries than the Brazilians are to Portugal after just three centuries."

Even though it wasn't the same dialect she spoke, Deirdre could understand her. "How did you know I spoke Gaelic?"

"I guessed. I can see the Celtic blood in you, and hear it in your accent."

"My mother always spoke Gaelic to me as a child. I'm glad I learned it."

"Languages are important to the people of Ceiba. We teach our children in Greek and Latin, and of course they learn Portuguese."

"In Fawcett's journal, he said that your English wasn't good, but you seem to speak it very well."

"At that time, it was best that I spoke it as I did. It made me more interesting and primitive to Fawcett and the priest at the mission."

"But why do you learn languages if you are so isolated from the rest of the world?"

Rae-la laughed as she stepped carefully over a dead branch. "The rest of the world is isolated from us, but we are not isolated from it. Our people have always traveled. It is a part of our nature. But we have traveled more than ever in the last fifty years, and gained much from it."

They stopped near a stream, where Rae-la set down the rabbits. Handing Deirdre a knife, she picked up one of the carcasses and showed her what to do with it. As they skinned and gutted the rabbits, Deirdre tried to take her mind off what she was doing by prodding Rae-la with more questions.

"What do you do at Ceiba?"

"What do you mean?"

"Do you have a job?"

"Oh, you want to know who I am. I am a healer and teacher."

"Really? What do you teach?"

"About trees."

"Trees?" Deirdre laughed, but she saw that Rae-la was serious. She recalled that trees played a significant role in the teachings of the ancient druids.

"Our communion with trees is all-important."

"My mother was an archaeologist who knew a great deal about the Celts. I know that each of the letters of the ogham alphabet is associated with a tree and also a deity. But you don't have the same trees here in the Amazon. There are no oak or ash or birch trees."

"No, but there are many others that are comparable, and serve the same purposes. For instance, the oak is now the ceiba tree. The ash is the mahogany, hazel is the Brazil nut, and the apple is the cashew."

"Why is the city named after the ceiba tree?"

"The ceiba is associated with the Mother Earth goddess Anu, who nurtures us. The tree itself is like a strong door guarding our world."

"What about the god Bel? Where does he fit?"

"He is the male counterpart to Anu. He is our guardian and protector. In the ancient days, Bel was associated with the laurel, but now it is the clove tree. He is linked to the sun, fire, and healing. He is special, because there is no letter which can represent him. He is the guardian of the seventh veil and the Eternal Orb."

In all the talk of trees and gods, Deirdre had forgotten about the veils. She recalled now what Fawcett had written. "Why are children taught about the veils?"

"Because it is the most important thing they learn. Veiling is survival."

Rae-la peeled the hide down over the hind legs of the rabbit she was working on. She laid the skinned carcass on a bed of leaves, then went to work on the last rabbit.

"Aren't you missed from your classes when you leave the city?"

"No. There are more important things for me to

do now. I am one of those who was designated to bring new blood into the city."

Deirdre remembered Fawcett's words about being chosen as a breeder, and suddenly felt uneasy. "Why do you need new blood?"

"Because we have been too isolated. Something is happening to our blood. We are losing our power to veil, and when that fails we are lost."

"Are you part Indian?"

"My mother was a Morcego. She was brought to the city when she was a child. But we do not take Morcegos any longer. We need others."

"That's why you brought Fawcett to Ceiba."

"Yes. But I didn't know the council would make him a prisoner."

"Why are they doing it?"

"Because of a prophecy."

Deirdre wiped the blood from her hands as she finished skinning her rabbit. Rae-la was almost done with the third one. "What prophecy is that?"

Rae-la didn't answer for a minute as she worked on the rabbit. Then she laid it down with the other two and looked around. Deirdre wondered if she was going to answer her question.

"Over here." Rae-la walked up to a sapling. She took hold of a slender branch with both hands, muttered something under her breath as if she were addressing the tree, then snapped it. She moved over to another, repeated the procedure, then found a third tree. When she had three branches of a similar length, she led Deirdre back to the carcasses. Rae-la handed one of the branches to Deirdre and told her to remove the bark and sharpen the ends.

As they carved the branches, Rae-la finally answered her question. "Every nineteen years when the sun and the moon align in the sky, an important prophecy is made by the oldest member of the Higher Orb. The last one was given by Tuatha shortly before his death several years ago. He had always opposed allowing any outsiders into the city, even children. But at the end of his life Tuatha became concerned about the future of Ceiba, and everyone awaited his prophecy. As the heavens aligned, he drew chips of bark inscribed with the sacred letters from a basket, and he read them."

"What did they say?" Deirdre asked.

"He said many things, but the most important words were these: 'Outsiders seek to destroy us, but outsiders must save us from destroying ourselves.'"

Deirdre nodded. "That sounds like a double-edged sword."

"We know we must deal with outsiders, but we must do so with care."

"Is that why the council decided to keep Colonel Fawcett a prisoner?"

"Now you understand. We all hoped that Colonel Fawcett would be a willing participant. There are many beautiful women in Ceiba, and I thought that eventually he would decide to stay with us. But he was never even given a chance."

"So if we went to the city with you, we would also be in danger."

"You could not enter the city without being detected, even with our help. You would be discovered immediately and captured."

Deirdre grimaced as Rae-la rammed one of the sharpened sticks through one end of a carcass and out the other. Rae-la picked up a second carcass and pointed to the last one. Deirdre knew she was supposed to join in the staking. She picked up a carcass and worked the stick through it.

"Do you think that Amergin will take Dr. Bernard with him?"

"Do you wish not to see him again?"

"We would like him to see the city so Colonel Fawcett is not the only one to attest that it exists."

Rae-la staked the last carcass with a quick thrust. "The council would not allow it. Fawcett's memories of Ceiba will be swept clean. He will not know what happened to him."

"What about his journal?"

"It won't help his memory. He'll think he had just lost his mind for a while, and will be happy he recovered it."

"I see." Deirdre knew she sounded disappointed, and did nothing to hide it.

"I know you and Indy would like to see the city," Rae-la said as they headed back to camp. "I wish I could show it to you. If you are thinking of following us, please don't."

"What would happen?"

"Either you would not find the city, or, worse, you would be captured, and neither you nor Colonel Fawcett would ever be seen again."

"Would we be made breeders?" Deirdre asked as they headed back to camp.

"You would be required to share Indy with other women, and you would be forced to lie with other men and bear their children."

16

BAT PEOPLE

Three rabbits for six people didn't amount to much for Indy's appetite, but fortunately for him Deirdre hardly touched her portion of the rabbit they shared. Still, he wasn't exactly full when he were finished. Fletcher had contributed a couple of cans of corn to the meal and coffee, which was now steaming above the fire.

Indy poured himself a cup, sat back, and stared into the fire as the others finished their meal. As was nearly always the case, he was the first to finish eating. He could remember his mother shaking her head and saying that he must be inhaling his food, the way it disappeared from his plate. Yet, his hunger for travel and adventure had always surpassed his desire for the comforts of home and a full stomach, and that was why he was here right now.

He looked over at Deirdre, who was still busy with her bowl of corn. When she'd returned with the skinned rabbits, he could tell that she had something to tell him, so he had asked her to help him find some more wood for the fire. He'd been pleasantly surprised to learn that Rae-la spoke Gaelic. He'd assumed that the inhabitants of Ceiba had adopted Portuguese as their language, since Amergin and Rae-la spoke it so well.

Deirdre had told him about the "blood problem," the prophecy, and Rae-la's warning. He realized now that his interest in seeing the city would greatly endanger their chances of getting out. If he were alone, he'd probably follow them. But he had Deirdre to think about.

He didn't like the idea of staying here with the Morcegos so nearby, either. At least he had his Webley with him. He'd taken it out of his bag after the incident in the airplane and had kept it holstered, mainly as a warning for Bernard. But Bernard had been acting like a tranquilized bear ever since he'd taken the blow on the head.

Fletcher refilled Indy's cup of coffee, then passed a cup to Bernard and poured a third for himself. The others said they didn't want any.

"Amergin, do you mind if I ask you a question about the orbs?" Indy asked.

Amergin looked up at him. "We don't speak of such matters lightly."

Indy wasn't put off. "I found what Colonel Fawcett said about the veils and the orbs very interesting, but there was nothing about the seventh veil. What is it, anyhow?"

Amergin stared into the fire.

"Well, if you won't tell me that, what about the people who are in the Eternal Orb? What are they like?"

"They are the ancients," Rae-la said quietly.

"The ancients? You mean old people?"

He laughed. "Not the way you think of old people. They are different."

"Do you see them and talk to them?"

"Sometimes," Rae-la said, "but only with a sincere purpose."

"Do they make the laws?" Indy asked.

"No," Rae-la said just as Amergin answered affirmatively.

"It's complicated," Amergin said. "They do not make decisions or tell anyone what to do. They are not directly represented on the Council of Orbs. Yet, they are directing us in everything."

Whatever the Eternal Orb was, it was more than could be comprehended with a brief description. Indy could see why Rae-la had said little to Fawcett about it when she explained the orbs.

"You're talking about predestination," Bernard said, speaking for the first time since they'd landed.

"Not the way you understand it," Amergin responded. "We have free will, but we also have a design we are following without really knowing it."

"If you knew it, it probably wouldn't be any fun any more," Indy said.

"Who said life is fun, Jones?" Bernard scoffed.

"What is it then, Dr. Bernard? I'd like to hear your thoughts, since you haven't had much to say lately."

"Life is a gamble. That's what it is."

"And you're going to lose your bet, because Fawcett's going to make it out alive."

Amergin abruptly stood up and took Rae-la by the hand. "It's time for us to leave."

"How long will it take you to get there?" Indy asked.

"The mountains are nearer than you think. We will reach them in three hours, and the city an hour later."

"There is a trail that begins not far from here," Rae-la said. "And we will move rapidly."

"Take him with you," Indy said, nodding toward Bernard. He knew if Bernard never saw Ceiba, he'd never believe it existed. Indy also knew that Bernard might never get out of the city, and it didn't bother him. He wouldn't miss him, not for even a fraction of a second.

"No," Rae-la said firmly.

"So we'll never know," Deirdre said. "It seems hardly fair."

"Life is rarely fair," Bernard replied.

"We'll be back by daybreak, and Fawcett will be with us," Rae-la said.

"We'll be waiting right here," Fletcher said. "The plane will be ready. We've got just enough fuel to make it to Cuiabá."

With that, Rae-la and Amergin turned and moved off into the forest. Pale beams of moonlight filtered through the dark canopy of jungle, illuminating their way, but within a few feet of the camp, the pair was lost from sight.

Indy finished his coffee as Deirdre gathered the dishes and pots to wash in the lake. "I'll go down with you," he said, and he picked up Bernard's cup, which lay on the ground. "Keep an eye on him," he told Fletcher as the pilot handed him his cup.

"Where the hell do you think I'll go, Jones?" Bernard asked. "You think I'll chase after those two and their so-called city? It's probably just an Indian village with a few oddballs who think they're druids. That's why they don't want you to see the place."

"Why are they releasing Fawcett?"

"Wake up, Jones. They're probably holding him

for a ransom." Bernard pulled off his boots as he prepared for bed. "They'll show up tomorrow with some sort of demand from their so-called council. They'll send you away with an empty promise, and expect you to come back with whatever they want."

"You haven't read Fawcett's journal," Deirdre said.

"Neither has Fawcett. They probably wrote it themselves. I doubt if they even have Fawcett. They've made up the whole damn thing because they knew they could get something out of it. No doubt they threw in a few good words about their ancestors from Atlantis. That's a favorite of their type."

Indy noticed how Bernard was escalating his dire commentary with every sentence. He cut him off. "It's Fawcett's handwriting. Brody was sure of it."

"I wouldn't count on Marcus Brody to be sure about anything," Bernard snorted. "But even if it was Fawcett's handwriting, it only means these phoney druids are forcing him to write it."

"Let's go, Indy. I don't want to listen to him any longer," Deirdre said.

Indy started to walk away, but he wasn't going to let Bernard get the last word on the matter. Not this time. They weren't in Tikal. He glanced over his shoulder. "You want to bet on it?"

Deirdre hooked her arm through his. "Don't let him get to you. When we get back to Bahia, we should report him to the police."

"Yeah, right. And how are we going to prove anything? Hell, if that captain sees me, he'll lock me up and throw away the key."

"Then we'll wait until we get back to New

York," Deirdre said as they stepped out onto the beach. The moonlight glistened on the water and the dark shadow of the plane on the still water looked like some phantom craft from the future.

"They're not going to investigate murders that took place in Brazil. It would be Bernard's word against ours. Anyhow, we can't even prove that Bernard was the one who was behind the whole thing. And if we make accusations against Julian Ray, he'll send some Mafia creeps after us."

Deirdre scrubbed the plates with sand and water. "So what do you think's going to happen?"

Indy crouched down at the water's edge and rinsed out the cups. "Oh, I'd say that if Fawcett remembers anything, Bernard's going to deny it. He'll definitely fire me, and do everything he can to make sure I'll never teach again. I might be able to sweep the floor in an archaeology department somewhere, but not at the University of London."

Deirdre laid down the plates and silverware, and hugged him. "It's not going to be that bad. I'll stand up for you. I'm sure Marcus Brody will back you up. He'll help you find another job."

"Don't count on it. If Bernard has his way, Marcus is going to lose his job, too, if he hasn't already."

A piercing scream shredded the silence. "That sounded like it came from the camp," Indy said. "C'mon."

Then another cry cut through the night.

"Fletcher," Indy hissed, as he pulled the Webley from his holster.

They scrambled through the forest to the camp and were almost to the clearing when Indy stumbled over a root. Deirdre slammed into him, and they both hit the ground. As he picked her up, his eyes darted around uneasily. The jungle now seemed alive and hostile. They rushed ahead.

The fire was burning low and nothing looked any different, except that Fletcher and Bernard were nowhere in sight. Then he heard a moaning sound.

"Indy, look."

Fletcher stood on the edge of the camp, leaning against a tree. He raised a hand, tottered, and flopped forward to the ground before they could reach him. His back was a pincushion of darts. His body shuddered for a few seconds, then he was still.

Indy pulled one out, and examined the tip. "Poison."

"Is he . . ."

"He's gone."

"Oh, God."

They stood up, slowly looked around. Indy walked over to where Bernard had been seated. His boots were where he'd left them, but there was no sign of him.

"Indy," Deirdre whispered. "They're still here. I can feel them."

Something zipped past Indy's ear. He jerked his head, and saw an arrow sticking in the tree next to him.

He fired several rounds into the jungle. Voices cried out in surprise. "Run for the plane," he yelled, and they both dashed out of the camp. He didn't know what he would do when they got to the plane, but there was no other place to go.

But as they reached the edge of the forest, several figures dressed in loincloths stood at the edge of the lake, examining the plates and pots and silverware. In the moonlight, their painted bodies seemed almost luminous. Then Indy saw the body lying in the sand nearby. It was Bernard. He was almost certain of it.

Indy reloaded the revolver and considered their options. They could wait and watch, and probably be discovered. He could fire on the warriors, but others might show up, and he and Deirdre were no match for an entire tribe. Then he knew what they had to do.

"Let's look for the trail that Rae-la mentioned. We're better off in Ceiba than here."

She didn't argue.

They moved as quietly as possible away from the edge of the forest. The farther they got, the faster they ran. Branches snapped in Indy's face, low hanging vines lashed out at him, and roots conspired to snare his feet.

They'd covered nearly a mile of jungle, cutting back and forth, searching for the trail, when they reached a clearing. Nearby were several pieces of thatching that looked man-made.

"Which way?" Deirdre asked, gasping for breath.

"Good question." Indy took a couple of steps toward a square of thatch when suddenly the end of it tipped up, and he was staring at an Indian warrior. The Morcego yelled, and the ground literally quaked as thatched pieces lifted off the ground, revealing painted warriors with blowguns and spears.

Indy spun around. Several men blocked their escape route. He and Deirdre were surrounded. As the Indians climbed from the holes, they moved closer, their weapons raised. Their faces were painted black with large, tear-shaped white eyes. Bat eyes, Indy thought. The Webley was in his belt, and maybe he could scare them off as he'd done the others. Slowly, he reached for the gun, but just as he touched the grip, one of the Indians stepped forward and shouted at him.

"No!"

Indy's hands hovered over the gun. "No?"

"Don't be foolish."

"You speak Portuguese," Indy said.

The Morcego was an older man with wrinkled skin and piercing eyes. Probably the chief. "You frightened our enemy. We were waiting for their attack."

"You mean those weren't Morcegos who killed the others?"

The chief shook his head.

Indy remembered what Amergin had said about the Morcegos fearing airplanes. "Did you see us arrive?"

"You came with the winged god to stop our war." The chief said something to his warriors and they lowered their weapons.

"Now you will have peace," Indy said, hoping he was saying the right thing.

He tried to think what to do next. It was too dangerous to go back to the camp, and there was no point in staying with the Morcegos. While they were safe for the moment, the Morcegos could change their minds about them at any time. Sticking with their plans to go to Ceiba seemed the only alternative. He just hoped that the Morcegos could put them on the right path.

"But we must visit the people who live in the mountains. In Ceiba."

"The evil place."

"Have you been there?"

"No. In the old time, the evil ones came in the night and stole our children. The warriors who went looking for them never returned."

"We will talk to them about that. But we want you to show us the way."

The chief waved a hand. "Follow the path to the river. Beyond it lies the evil city."

"Take us to the path," Indy commanded.

The chief said something to the men near him. "They will take you as far as the river."

"Where did you learn Portuguese?" Deirdre's Portuguese was clumsy, but she made herself understood.

"From my father and from his father. My grandfather was held captive for many years by the evil ones, who forced him to mate with their women. Finally, he escaped and returned to his people."

"If there are others still held, we will try to free them," Deirdre said.

The chief swept a hand around him. "Evil spirits protect the city, and they can listen to our words."

"Did you hear that?" Deirdre whispered as they followed the warriors into the jungle. "They were talking about the veiling, but they think it's evil spirits."

"Maybe it is," Indy responded. "Evil spirits are about as believable as veiled druids."

Deirdre and Indy headed into the forest, moving quickly, following the warriors, who seemed to glide over the rugged terrain. Indy was already thinking ahead. With Fletcher dead, their escape would be by land rather than air, unless he flew the plane himself. He was confident he could fly the plane; it was taking off and landing it that he wasn't so sure about.

In a few minutes, they reached a wide trail, and the warriors picked up the pace. Indy's ankle was slightly sprained from his fall and he was having difficulty keeping up with the Morcegos. There was no choice but to keep moving. The quicker they reached Ceiba, the better. From time to time, the Indians would stop and wait for them, but as soon as they caught up, the warriors would start moving again.

Finally, after walking for what seemed like half the night, the trail ended at a riverbank that rose nearly a hundred feet on either side. Indy figured it was the same tributary that they'd followed from the air until they'd veered toward the lake. The water rippled and splashed over the rocks, glistening in the moonlight. One of the Morcegos pointed downstream at a rope bridge that crossed the river. He recalled the rope bridge that Fawcett had mentioned, and he knew they were on the right path.

When the Morcegos made no effort to cross the bridge, Indy gestured toward it. The warriors firmly shook their heads, and took a step back. "I think we're on our own from here," he said. He started to thank the Morcegos for their help, but they'd already vanished into the forest.

"Indy, look at the huge tree on the other side," Deirdre said as she moved along the cliff to the rope bridge. "It's the ceiba. The same one Fawcett wrote about."

"The doorway," Indy said.

He grabbed the hemp handrail and stepped out onto the bridge. "Are you with me?"

"Right behind you. I don't like this very much. I can barely see these ropes," she complained.

"Yeah, but they're close together."

"It's still scary."

"Just think of it as an ordinary bridge, and you won't have any trouble."

Indy had no sooner made the remark when his

foot slid off one of the ropes and he lunged for the handrail. The bridge swayed and Deirdre wobbled on one foot. Then her other foot slipped off the rope and she hung from the rail by one hand.

"Indy!"

"Hang on. I'm coming." Indy worked his way over to her, grabbed her around the waist, and pulled her up until she was standing again.

"I bet there're piranhas down there just waiting for a midnight snack," she said.

"You okay?"

"Fine. Let's just get across."

Indy moved ahead, stepping gingerly from rope to rope. Finally, he made it to the other side, reached back, and took Deirdre's hand.

"Take a look at this." He stepped toward the Ceiba. The tree was incredibly sturdy, with branches that grew at ninety-degree angles and formed perfect crosses. But it wasn't the branches which interested Indy right now.

"What is it?"

He pointed to the trunk. On it was carved the ogham symbol for the letter D. "Duir," he said, pronouncing it in Gaelic.

"That's right," Deirdre said.

"It means strength, solidity, and protection in both Gaelic and Sanskrit. It's where the English word 'door' came from." He knocked on it.

Deirdre laughed. "You think it'll open?"

"Druids used to rap their knuckles on oak wood for protection."

"Knock on wood," she said, and did the same. "Rae-la told me they harvest the pods and make clothes from the fiber inside."

Indy tugged on his hat. "We better get moving."

"How much farther? My feet are killing me."

"You heard Rae-la. It's at least another hour. That is, if we find it."

"Oh, God. I don't know if I can walk another hour."

As it turned out, Deirdre didn't have to walk, but she wished she did.

17

Into Ceiba

"Indy?"

That was the only word Deirdre could utter. Behind him stood several men with long wooden spears. They were tall and muscular and looked nothing like the Morcegos. Their pale blue eyes stared intently at them.

Indy turned, and after a moment's hesitation greeted the men in Portuguese. They didn't respond.

Deirdre had barely recovered from the confrontation with the Morcegos, and now they were face to face with a bunch of men who for all the world looked like white-skinned Indians armed with primitive weapons.

Finally, her mind started working. They speak Gaelic like Rae-la, she thought, and greeted them in the language. She did her best to sound relaxed. "We're waiting for a friend. We won't be bothering you. We'll just wait here by the stream."

If they understood, they didn't let on.

She noticed the men's eyes shift toward the dark

jungle across the river. She followed their gaze, but saw nothing. Suddenly, one of the men hurled his spear. It shot through the air like a bullet with hardly any arch, crossing the river and vanishing.

A cry of pain rang out from the dense undergrowth just as a second spear was cast in the same direction. Another piercing wail followed and Deirdre gasped as she saw one of the Morcego guides stumble out from the forest with the shaft of the spear sticking through his chest and out his back. He dropped to his knees and tumbled down the bank of the river. A frightful moan issued from the darkness, and then another spear whistled across the river. A choking sound cut through the night, then there was silence.

"Swell bunch," Indy said, and reached for his revolver. Immediately, a spear knocked it from his hand. He and Deirdre were prodded in the stomach and legs, forced away from the river. Then, abruptly, they were shoved into a wooden cage, and the door was slammed shut.

Deirdre had the feeling they were going to join Colonel Fawcett whether they liked it or not.

Rae-la gazed up at the twinkling lights on the mountainside; they looked like a thousand lightning bugs against the black sky. Then she raised her eyes to the flickering glimmer high above all the others and smiled. The glow emanated from the eternal flame in the watchtower overlooking the city.

Seeing the familiar lights made her painfully aware of how much she missed the city when she was away. It was a world of its own, a world that was here on earth, but not of it. What the rest of the world called magic was accepted as normal, and for century after century this magic had been practiced to shield Ceiba from the rest of the world.

"I can hardly believe we're back," she said softly. The return trip had seemed short, but it had also made her aware of the dangers that airplane travel would create in years to come if the Ceibans' ability to veil the city continued to weaken. Suddenly, they were no longer separated from the rest of the world by vast stretches of jungle that took weeks and months to cross. Now it was days, and soon it would probably be hours.

"Don't think too much about it, not if you're planning on leaving tonight," Amergin said.

They moved on, picking up speed. The city was originally built on the flat mountaintop, but over the centuries the south face of the mountain had been honeycombed in a vast network of habitats. Some families resided in as many as a dozen interconnected rooms, while single people usually lived in one chamber. Two sets of stairways climbed the south face, and open corridors ran parallel beneath each row of dwellings, with short stairways leading up to the individual residences. Each corridor was numbered, and each dwelling labeled with an ogham letter.

Although a mechanized pulley system was used to raise cargo up the mountainside, there were no elevators. The machines of the city were run on generators charged by energy harnessed from a waterfall in the river below the city. A spring that percolated at the top of the mountain allowed for running water, and a sewage system that carried away waste along underground ducts built centuries ago.

Rae-la and Amergin climbed the stairs with a sense of confidence that they wouldn't be noticed. They were both masters of the veil art. Only if they encountered one of the others from the higher orb would they be seen, and the likelihood of that was not great. Just as they were about to reach the corridor where Fawcett was being held, Amergin touched Rae-la's shoulder and motioned her to the side. They blended in with the wall, and a few moments later four men from the security force rushed past them. They were talking among themselves, moving as if something important was happening.

"I don't like it," Rae-la said. "Something's going on."

"You go on and talk to Fawcett. I'll find out what it's about, and join you in a few minutes."

She hurried on, moving quickly down the corridor until she reached the room assigned to the Englishman. It was designated by koad, the ogham letter for CH. She tapped at the door, and a moment later it opened.

"Rae-la . . . what a surprise." Fawcett's thick mustache turned up at the ends as he grinned, and the wrinkles around his gleaming eyes deepened. "Back from Bahia so soon?"

"I've got good news."

"Sit down and tell me about it. Tea?"

"There's no time for tea," she said and told him about Indy and Deirdre, and their journey. "They're waiting for you now by the Morcego lake."

"So you were actually successful in contacting dear old Marcus, who promptly sent a pair of emissaries," Fawcett said. "Very interesting. I'd like to meet your new friends, and see how things are in the old world. Do you think they could come in for a few days?"

She was surprised how blandly Fawcett seemed to take the news. It was as if he didn't care or understand that help had arrived, and that she was willing to assist his escape. What had they done to him? Where was his spirit?

"Colonel Fawcett, I've come to get you out of here. Amergin and I are going back to Bahia on the airplane with the Joneses, and we want to take you with us tonight."

"Out of the question. I have no interest in leaving Ceiba. This is my life now."

She stared into his unblinking eyes. *Look what they've done to him.* "But you have another life, a wife and family and friends."

Fawcett was quiet a moment. "I've given all that plenty of thought. Every day for months, I plotted ways to get out of here and return to my old life. Then one day, not long after you left, I realized I had everything I needed, and more. There was no reason to fight it any longer. I was not going back, and once I came to that conclusion I was free and alive and happy. Happier than I've ever been. In fact, do you know—"

They both turned to the door as they heard a rap. Rae-la was about to veil herself when the door burst open and Amergin stepped inside. "They've got two of the outsiders. The fools tried to follow us."

Indy clutched the wicker rails of the cage as he and Deirdre were carted along. From the angle of the cage, he knew they were climbing. But he hadn't seen any mountains from the lake or from the air. Had they been veiled, or had they just been out of sight?

Even now the darkness around them seemed unnaturally thick. Maybe the moon had gone down, or the jungle canopy had become impregnable. It was as if he'd just come out of a brightly lit room and his eyes still hadn't adjusted to the darkness.

"What do you see out there?" he asked Deirdre.

"Nothing. I think we're surrounded by a veil," she answered.

"I don't like veils. I can tell you that right now. I like seeing where I'm going." Indy tried to find a comfortable position. The steep angle and the continual bouncing and rocking made it impossible to sit in one spot for long without jarring some part of his body.

He couldn't help recalling a similar cage in the hands of modern-day druids led by Deirdre's half-brother, Adrian Powell. Deirdre had been imprisoned in it at Stonehenge, and had barely escaped a sacrificial death.

"Indy?"

"Yeah."

"You remember what I told you about my conversation with Rae-la."

He moved closer to her. "What about it?"

"Do you think they would force me to . . . you know?"

"No. They won't, and don't worry about it. Don't even think about it." He wondered if his voice gave away his uncertainty.

"If you're forced to have sex with beautiful women, will you promise me that you won't enjoy it, and that you won't fall in love with any of them?"

Indy laughed. "Don't worry. I don't enjoy much of anything that's forced on me."

"Would you fight it, though, even if the woman was really beautiful?"

"Deirdre, let's just see what happens."

"I knew it. You'd like it. I could never . . . it

would be horrible. But I think it's different for men."

He took her hand. "It won't come to that. I promise."

Several times over the next two hours, the cage was lowered to the ground only to be lifted again, and the jostling was renewed with a surge of vigor that probably meant a new crew was carrying the cage. From time to time, Indy heard voices, but they sounded muffled and distant. Finally, they were lowered to a flat surface.

This time no one picked them up. The voices grew fainter until he couldn't hear them. He lifted his head; he felt groggy and battered. The darkness around them was still complete.

"They're gone." Indy moved toward Deirdre on his hands and knees. "You okay?"

She arched her back, tilted her neck from side to side, and stretched her legs and arms. "I think so. I'm just sore."

"I wonder how long they're going to leave us here?" Indy had no sooner spoken than the cage started to rise. This time, though, it kept rising. They swayed from side to side, but there were no jolts. "We must be on a platform. We're being lifted by ropes. I can see them now."

"I hope they don't drop us."

He counted the seconds, guessing that they were rising at least two feet a second. From the smoothness of the ascent it seemed that a machine was lifting them.

"Fifty-eight . . . fifty-nine . . . sixty . . . One . . . two . . ."

Deirdre caught on to what he was doing and joined the count. Another minute passed, then a third. About fifteen seconds later, the cage came to a stop. It rocked back and forth, then lowered several inches and came to a rest. "We went up at least five hundred feet," Deirdre said.

"I'd guess closer to eight or nine."

Indy heard voices again, and could see shadowy forms moving outside the cage. Now the cage rocked to one side and was lifted again. This time they were carried on a level surface along a faintly lit corridor with a low wall on one side that looked out into blackness.

They turned, and were carried up a short flight of steps. Then they were lowered to the ground, and the gate was opened. Indy was yanked out; he had no time to get his bearings. He struggled, and his hat was knocked from his head as he was shoved into a room. Deirdre was pushed into the room after him, and the door slammed shut. He grabbed the door handle, and pulled.

"Locked."

Rae-la balanced a bowl of water in her hands as she climbed the seventy-seven steps leading to the top of the watchtower. She had come here many times in her life when she had a problem and needed counseling. And now was one of those times. It was an hour before dawn, and she needed to know how she would resolve the serious matter facing her.

After Amergin had arrived with the news that Indy and Deirdre had been captured, he'd told her that they must make their presence known. At dawn, the council would gather, and Rae-la and Amergin would report that they had brought the outsiders here as new blood. And, of course, Rae-la was not to say a word about trying to help Fawcett escape.

She was confused; she didn't know what to do. So she had come here, the place where those from the orbs discussed their predicaments with the gods. But this wasn't an ordinary problem. She had to address Bel himself, the high god of Ceiba, who was called upon only in dire situations.

When she reached the circular room at the top of the watchtower, she set her bowl of water on the floor, then walked around the great cauldron where the eternal flame burned. She took five red candles from the bag she carried, placed them around the cauldron, and lit each one. She returned to where her bowl lay, and stared into the flame until her vision blurred and the flame multiplied.

"Oh, mighty Sun of power, sun of gold, protector of Ceiba, the city which is not a city, in the mountains which are not mountains, hear my words of supplication," she began. "I give honor to you and call upon you in your ancient names, both known and unknown."

She dipped her fingers in the bowl and shook them, splattering the water first on herself, then on the cauldron. "I consecrate this circle so that you may manifest and guide me in this time of great need. I implore you to answer my call; I await you."

Something was wrong here, Deirdre thought, and yet the feeling was familiar to her, as if it were rekindling a memory she'd pushed away.

An ovoid light was glowing from an alcove, and Indy was examining something on the wall near it. "You see this?" He pointed at a vertical line with a curlicue extending from its right side. "It's the ogham letter phagos, or PH. It relates to ancient knowledge."

But Deirdre's attention was already distracted by a table. She couldn't believe what lay on top of it. "Indy, there's your gun, and my god, a newspaper."

"What?" Indy snatched up the revolver and put it back in his holster, and stared at the paper. "Hey, the London *Times*. Must come with the room. What's the date?"

"April fourth. That was less than a week ago."

"They've got damn good delivery service here. How d'you figure that?"

"No, look at the year—'27. Next year!"

"What? This must be some sort of joke." He picked up the paper and scanned the front page. His eyes immediately fixed on a headline near the top of the page. " 'Expedition to Seek Missing Explorer,' " he said, and started reading the article.

" 'Did Colonel Fawcett find his missing city? That's the question the members of a newly formed search party are asking themselves as they prepare to leave London in search of the famed missing explorer, who disappeared two years ago in the Amazon.' "

He shook his head. "I don't get it."

"Something's wrong here, Indy. Can't you feel it? It reminds me . . ." She didn't finish the sentence. They weren't alone in the room.

"It's just a lesson for you in the ways of Ceiba," Amergin said.

He was standing near the door, but she hadn't heard it open or close. In his hand was Indy's fedora. He moved toward them and offered Indy the hat.

Indy snatched it from Amergin's hand and tossed it toward the bed. It slid underneath the frame and out of sight. "What's going on here?"

"Dreaming takes many forms, Professor Jones. You are now experiencing one of the most ancient and advanced practices."

"What are you talking about?"

"You are both asleep and dreaming the same dream, a dream where the present and the future intermingle."

Deirdre knew he was right. This was a dream.

"Maybe you're dreaming, but I'm not," Indy said. "But just out of curiosity, what's your point?"

"I'm showing you that others are coming, and that's only the beginning. We must prepare for them by strengthening the Over Veil. That is why you were taken here. We need you, both of you. You will be part of the future of Ceiba."

"You were lying to us," Indy said, accusingly. "You were never going to help Fawcett escape."

"Rae-la and I are a team. Our job is to bring outsiders here. You answered our call."

"Why are you hiding from the rest of the world?" Deirdre asked.

"Because we know what would happen. We in Ceiba have a better understanding of the earth and its forces than you do. But your modern world is filled with superstitions about ancient ways, and instead of learning from us, you would destroy us as evil, just as your ancestors did when they encountered the Indian world."

"Maybe you're right. But that doesn't mean you can turn us into baby-making machines," Deirdre said.

Indy's hand crept toward the holstered revolver. He shifted to one side, blocking Amergin's view of the weapon. "If you wanted us here, why didn't you lead us yourself into the city?"

"I wanted to show Rae-la what fools you are. I didn't need to force you here. You came on your own, in spite of our warnings."

Indy pulled the gun and aimed it at Amergin. "This is no dream, fellow. But it's going to be a nightmare if you don't get us out of here right now."

Amergin didn't act a bit surprised. "That won't do you any good."

Indy snapped open the cylinder. "It's loaded." He fired a shot into the air. "And the gun is working just fine."

"Then shoot me, Jones," Amergin challenged. "You can't hurt me. It's a dream."

"Don't, Indy." *The gun must be some sort of test,* she thought.

Indy aimed the gun at Amergin's chest. "Open the door now or I'll shoot."

Amergin moved toward him. "Give it to me. You don't want to do that."

The gun fired. Amergin's body jolted; he clasped his hands over his heart and blood spurted between his fingers.

"God, Indy. You shot him."

18

DREAM TIME

Rae-la sensed the presence of Bel more than she saw him, but she knew he was there beyond the eternal flame. Bel, the protector of Ceiba, the ancient guide, had answered her call. She told him what had happened, and that she felt the outsiders must not be held here against their wills. How could he help her?

Rae-la didn't know whether she heard Bel's answer in her head or if the words were being spoken aloud. It didn't matter.

"Before the outsiders can leave, a wrong must be righted, a spell dispersed. Mix betony, laurel, vervain, and woodruff and burn it before the one who must be cleansed."

She thanked Bel for his help, and when she sensed he was no longer present, she quickly descended the steps of the tower. She knew what she must do.

The sound of gunfire rang in Deirdre's ears as she blinked open her eyes. She was in bed, facing a wall covered with wood shingles. She rolled over onto her back. Log beams crossed a ceiling twelve feet over her head. She turned the other way and winced as she felt the bruises on her back and sides. Then she saw Indy asleep next to her.

She sat up, and slowly swung her legs over the side of the bed. It was still dark outside, and a soft light glowed from one wall. She had no idea what time it was, but she had to talk to Indy. She shook him awake, and he squinted up at her.

"Where am I?"

"In Ceiba."

He rubbed his face. "Oh, yeah. God, am I sore. That damn cage."

"Right, the cage. But what happened after that, when we got here?"

He sat up, scratched his head. "After that? We were dumped in this room. We looked around, lay down, and I guess we fell asleep."

"What did we talk about?"

He thought a moment. "We were wondering what happened to Amergin and Rae-la. Then I said something like I hoped they delivered the London *Times* in the morning. But you didn't answer. You were already asleep."

"Do you remember seeing a newspaper on the table?"

"Here?"

She told him about what she recalled.

He laughed. "You had a dream. That's all. Amergin even said it was a dream."

"That's it. You see, it wasn't an ordinary dream."

"It sounds like typical dream nonsense to me. They'd never leave my gun on the table, and they don't have newspapers from next year here. I guarantee that. You just heard me mention the *Times* and you dreamed it."

"Maybe," she conceded. "Are you sure you don't remember?"

"Positive. Think about it. You know I was suspicious about Amergin so you saw me kill him. Besides, if I shot him, where's the gun and where's the body, or at least the blood?"

She shook her head. "I don't know. I can't answer those questions. But you know what it was like, Indy? Just like what happened to me with Adrian. It was the same feeling. Like being awake, but everything was sort of eerie and ominous."

When she met Adrian Powell, Deirdre didn't know he was her half-brother. He was only a handsome young member of the British Parliament, and a friend of her mother's. Adrian had taken an interest in her, but it didn't feel right to her and she'd broken off the relationship. Adrian didn't leave her alone, though; he'd become obsessed with her. She eventually found out not only that he was her half-brother, but that he was the leader of an order of druids. Twice he had appeared to her under strange circumstances, and the experiences had been both dreamlike, yet real.

Indy pulled on his clothes. "Except in those dreams, or whatever they were, I was never with you."

"So, what do you mean?"

"I mean I don't remember shooting Amergin. It was a dream. Your dream."

Indy walked into the bathroom adjoining the room as Deirdre got out of bed. Her slacks were soiled and tattered, but she had no other choices this morning. She wouldn't mind fresh clothing, but she would gladly do without it if she could avoid a lifetime of outfits made from the fiber of ceiba pods.

She walked over to the door and tried the handle. As she expected, it was still locked. She moved over to one of the windows, which were merely vertical slits. There was a faint hint of dawn, the darkness fading to gray. But all she could see was a great emptiness, as if there was nothing out there at all. The windows and the nonexistent view reminded her of the room Fawcett had described in his journal. Where was the colonel right now? she wondered.

Fawcett was sleeping when Rae-la quietly entered his room. She had interpreted Bel's words to mean that she must rid him of the spell that had been cast upon him. She had quickly gathered the herbs from her supplies, and now mixed them in the incense burner, which she set near Fawcett's head.

Vervain was sometimes called the enchanter's herb and was used in many rites, including those of purification. Woodruff helped change the course of one's life and bring victory. Laurel counteracted negativity and was closely associated with Bel, and betony was a sacred druid herb used to expel bad influences.

She lit the mixture, and as it burned, she lifted an empty bowl above her head offering it to Bel and Anu, his female counterpart. Then she lowered it to her chest and silently called for the spell to be removed from Fawcett. She turned the bowl upside down, and shook it.

"I offer the contents of this bowl and ask that in return you protect this man as long as he is in the territory of enchantment."

"Well, they've got running water, hot and cold," Indy said as he walked back into the room. "Beats that place we stayed in Bahia."

"Don't you feel, though, that something's not quite right?" Deirdre asked.

There were a lot of things that weren't right, but he knew what she meant. The water, for instance, seemed different here, as though it weren't really water. It sparkled too much; it seemed too perfect.

"What do you think it means?"

Deirdre started to answer when a knock on the door silenced her. Indy's first instinct was to open it, but he knew it was locked. "Who is it?"

The door opened and a sturdy, gray-haired man with a thick mustache and leathery skin entered the room.

"Dr. Jones, I presume . . . and Mrs. Jones. Jack Fawcett here." He pumped Indy's hand.

"Colonel Fawcett," Indy stammered. "Is that really you?"

"Of course."

"You're actually here. You can't imagine what a time we've had."

"Oh, yes, I most certainly can, Jones. It's not an easy place to find, and once you're here it's not so easy to understand, or leave for that matter."

"What going on, Colonel Fawcett? Are you all right? Are you a prisoner?" Deirdre asked.

"Those are all good questions, but let me ask you one. Have you had any visitors since you've been here?"

"Yes. Amergin," Deirdre answered.

"I think she was dreaming," Indy said with a laugh. "I didn't see him."

"Yes, well, the trick to understanding this city is to know that sometimes when you're dreaming you're more awake than normal, if that makes any sense."

Indy wondered what the hell he was talking about. The colonel reminded him of his father, at least when the old man was in a good mood. Fawcett wore baggy pants and a loose-fitting shirt with a V neck and voluminous pockets. The cloth was fawn-colored and looked as if it was made of unrefined cotton, but with a glossy tinge to the material.

"I don't think I understand at all," Indy said.

Fawcett waved a hand. "Well, don't worry about it. You'll figure it out soon enough."

"Why don't you just tell us?" Indy persisted.

"Okay. Do you recall what I wrote in my journal about seeing the city after Rae-la had disappeared? That was a dream."

"What's your point?" Indy asked.

"My point, Jones, is that these people perform many of their functions in the dream state."

"But did Indy really kill Amergin?" Deirdre asked.

"No. You can't kill a dreamer, but they still consider it an offensive act."

"But I don't even remember doing it. I was sleeping," Indy protested.

"Of course you were. Now before we go any further, let's be civilized and have a cup of tea. They don't have any Earl Grey here, but they do have a pleasant herbal concoction. Let me go see what I can turn up."

"Wait. Don't worry about the tea." The door slammed shut just an instant before Indy grabbed it. He shook the handle and pounded on the door. "Damn it. I don't want tea; I want answers."

As Rae-la finished the ritual of cleansing and protection, she sat down in the chair in the corner of Fawcett's room. The burning incense curled around her, making her drowsy. She hadn't slept at all, and her exhaustion was catching up with her all at once. She closed her eyes. She needed to sleep and to dream. It was time.

"My dear, your tea's getting cold."

Fawcett, she thought. He was seated at a wooden table in a grove of trees. "I've been working on you," she said, approaching him.

"So I've noticed. I feel as if a cloud has lifted from my head. I'll be leaving soon, you know."

"I hope so," Rae-la said. "I'll do my best to get the council to release the three of you immediately."

"I wouldn't count on the council."

She sipped her tea, and noticed there was an extra cup on the table. "Why three cups?"

"I was going to take two of them to the Joneses, until you came along. While you were doing your mumbo jumbo, I dropped in on them for a quick visit."

"Oh, what happened?"

Fawcett set down his cup. "It seems your friend, Amergin, visited them, and Jones shot him."

"What?" She knew that Indy couldn't hurt Amergin while dreaming, but if Indy had a gun, it meant that Amergin had made it available and provoked the incident. Suddenly, she understood everything. She'd been a fool.

"But it seems Jones couldn't remember any of it," Fawcett said. "So I gave Deirdre a suggestion that she wouldn't remember me. That way Jones should get the hint."

The colonel was learning fast about the ways of Ceiba, but Rae-la didn't approve of his technique. "That's only going to confuse them."

"Well, I guess you'll have to straighten things out."

"I was just on my way to see them. It's time to take them to the council meeting."

"Good God. You're going to subject them to that nightmare?"

"I have no choice." She set down her tea, closed her eyes, and considered how she would proceed. Immediately, she saw the ogham letter AE, represented by a rectangle divided into nine parts and attached to the right side of a vertical line. Mor was the only ogham letter that was not represented by a tree. Instead, it indicated the sea, and travel. Travel by water. She realized what she must do, and explained it to Fawcett.

"Take it easy, Indy. What's wrong with you? Who're you yelling at?"

He turned from the door. "Fawcett. Who do you think? The king of England?"

"Fawcett? What are you talking about?"

"I'm talking about the famous Colonel Percy Harrison Fawcett. You know, the man who just walked out of this room to get us tea."

She looked oddly at him. "Don't play games, Indy. Not this morning."

"Are you telling me Fawcett wasn't standing here in this room a minute ago talking to us?"

"No one's been here, except us. You walked out of the bathroom and started banging on the door and yelling that you didn't want tea, you wanted answers."

"Did you hear someone knock at the door?"

She shook her head.

He pointed at the floor in front of the door. "Look, fresh tracks."

She bent down and touched them. "I don't know how they got here, unless someone came in before we woke up. Or else . . ."

"Or else what?"

She stood up. "Maybe we're still sleeping, and we just dreamed that we woke up."

"Don't start on that again. Look here." Indy pinched his arm. "It hurts; I feel it." He rapped his knuckles on the table. "It's a real table." He propped his eyes wide open. "See, I'm awake."

"In these sorts of dreams things can seem real and it seems like you're awake, but you're not."

Indy sat down at the table with a heavy sigh. He'd never imagined that Ceiba was going to be so confusing. And they hadn't even been out of their room yet. "If this is a dream, I'll eat my hat. If I still had my hat."

"You do. It's under the bed."

"What makes you think so?"

"You threw it under there after Amergin gave it back to you."

"Now I'll prove you were dreaming." He bent down, and patted his hand under the bed. "See, no . . ."

He felt the brim, then the crown of a hat. His hat. He picked it up, and brushed it off as he stood up. "Well, I don't remember putting it there."

"Now do you believe me?"

"What exactly am I supposed to believe, Deirdre? That's the question. That this is all a dream or that it's all real?"

"Both, I think."

19

THE COUNCIL OF ORBS

Indy heard a tap on the door. "That's Fawcett.
Come on in, Colonel."

It wasn't Fawcett, but Rae-la.

She stood in the pale light beyond the door.
"Hello, Indy."

He had an urge to rush past her, but decided
against it. "What's going to happen to us?"

"I warned you not to come here, but you came
anyhow."

"You don't understand," Deirdre said. "We
didn't know what to do." She explained what happened at the camp.

As Rae-la listened, Indy saw that she wore a
loose-fitting, light gray dress and sandals. The material of her dress looked somewhat coarse, but
with a silvery glint like the outfit that Fawcett had
been wearing. He detected a hint of surprise in
Rae-la's expression when Deirdre finished the
story.

"I don't know what other tribe would attack the
Morcegos," she said. "They're greatly feared in

the region because the other tribes believe that they are protected by the invisible city."

"I didn't see what they looked like," Indy said, "but we both saw their handiwork."

"I'm sorry about what happened. But it was still wrong for you to come into our region. There is no way you could have entered the city undetected or even found it if the guardians hadn't taken you. The fact that they did is not a good sign."

Indy didn't trust her any more than he did Amergin. "Where's Fawcett?"

Rae-la shook her mane of dark hair. "I can't talk about him now. We have other things to do. You're going before the Council of Orbs. They want to meet you."

She opened the door and led them out into a courtyard that was shrouded with tropical plants. Indy looked up and saw that fifteen feet above them was a rock ceiling. "Are we in a cave?"

"Not really a cave," Rae-la said.

They moved through the courtyard and down a short flight of stairs. As he walked, the young archaeologist felt a peculiar sensation that he couldn't quite place. He felt lighter than normal, and he seemed to move with a grace that was usually absent in his stride. At the bottom of the stairs they reached a wide, cobbled corridor with a low wall on the far side, the one he'd seen when they'd arrived. Beyond the wall in the dim pre-dawn light was a sight that made him stop and stare. Far below, the jungle was a dark green carpet, and directly across from them a massive shadow formed a peak and behind it was another.

"Mountains," Deirdre whispered.

"I see them," he answered.

"Where are we?" Deirdre asked in a louder voice. "Is this Ceiba?"

"Of course it is," Rae-la answered.

"But we're on the side of a mountain."

"Yes. And now we're going to the top."

At the end of the corridor they reached a long stairway, and climbed higher. Stone walls loomed on either side of them, but were interrupted by more corridors traversing the side of the mountain. Finally, the stairs ended at a blank wall. Rae-la touched it lightly, and the rock face revolved on its central axis.

"Nifty," Indy said.

They entered a tunnel that was at least fifty feet wide from wall to wall. It smelled dank and ancient and wound upward at a gentle slope.

"Does the council meet on the mountaintop?" he asked.

"Yes. All of our workshops, classrooms, markets, and meeting places are there. We only live on the wall."

"Where do you get your food?" They hadn't eaten since the rabbit last night, but oddly Indy didn't feel a bit hungry.

"It's all grown in the valleys," Rae-la said. "We don't import any food, or any outside products for that matter."

After they'd walked a couple of hundred yards, the tunnel ended abruptly at a thick wooden door. Rae-la opened it, and they climbed a stairway to what at first appeared to be an immense garden. But as they followed one of the paths, Indy noticed that the garden was actually a plaza surrounded by tiered buildings, which seemed to grow out of the greenery. Indy had no idea what the altitude was, but the temperature was more moderate than it had been in the jungle surrounding the lake. It was neither hot nor cool. But it wasn't only the climate that seemed somehow exceptional. It was the air itself. Everything appeared to possess a certain vibrancy. Colors were deeper, brighter; the air literally sparkled.

They walked toward the center of the square, which was dominated by a huge ceiba tree heavy with pods, many of which had burst open like ripened cotton balls. A couple of dozen men and women dressed in robes milled near the tree as if they were drawn to it by some magnetic force. *Robed like druids,* he thought.

Rae-la stopped near the edge of the clearing that surrounded the ceiba. "We will wait here until the council is ready." She nodded toward the group around the tree.

"What are these buildings?" Deirdre asked.

"That's our library over there." Rae-la pointed to the nearest building. "Classes are held in that one. And the one on the other side is the public house where the council and the orbs gather."

Indy didn't notice any signal being given, but suddenly all the robed figures pulled their cowls over their heads. They surrounded the tree, linked arms, and bowed their heads. Indy saw that some of the robes were pale blue, others light gray like Rae-la's, and still others green. Then, again with no apparent signal, they began to chant. It was the same refrain over and over again. The chanting filled the plaza, and Indy was surprised by how well the sound was amplified. He imagined a person could speak from the center without raising his voice and someone in a far corner could hear him.

He glanced at Deirdre to see if she could understand what was being said. She nodded and whispered her translation in his ear.

> "Keep us strong; keep us secure.
> Cure what ails; strengthen our veil.
> Our ancestors survived the flood;
> Now we must enrich our blood.
> Cure what ails; strengthen our veil.

Swell, Indy thought. He knew what they meant by enriching their blood. He liked women and sex just fine, but these guys had another thing coming if they thought he was going to spend his days like a retired race horse put out to stud.

The chanting went on for a couple of minutes, then stopped as abruptly as it had begun. The cowled figures marched single file across the plaza and up the steps of the public house.

Rae-la signaled them to follow her, and they headed toward the building. Indy looked around and wondered what the chances were of escaping. But he had no idea which way led to the outside, and he knew they wouldn't get very far before they were caught.

"Unless you disapprove, I will speak for both of you before the council."

"What are you going to say?" he asked.

"I will do my best to see that you are allowed to leave. We have a history here of freedom and it should be extended to you."

Indy didn't know whether to believe Rae-la or not. "What if we don't like what you are saying?"

"Then you can object, or speak yourself. But I would not recommend it. It would be like defending yourself in one of your own courts where you are not familiar with all the procedures."

"Are we on trial?" he asked as they climbed the steps toward the door of the building where the robed council members had disappeared.

"It's not a trial, but a ruling that will be made on your future."

"That sounds like we're in big trouble," Deirdre said.

"You are, as you say, skating on thin ice, and neither of you has yet realized what is under the ice. But you will very soon."

At the top of the steps, they passed through an arched doorway and entered a foyer that resembled a greenhouse. Trees rose thirty feet toward a skylight. Low shrubs and flowers surrounded a fountain and pool. The trio moved quickly into a hallway, and Indy noticed the intricately carved cornices and richly paneled walls. Even though trees were considered sacred, woodworking was obviously an acceptable craft.

Rae-la nodded toward a door and they stepped into a circular room. The first thing Indy saw was a huge Eye of Bel, painted on the wall opposite the entrance, staring down at him. Next to it was an ogham inscription. Filling the center of the room was a round, wooden table, large enough to seat all of the council members. The members were taking their seats now as Rae-la motioned Indy and Deirdre toward a gallery with several rows of chairs backed up against the wall below the Eye of Bel.

The council members peered curiously in their direction. A few were of mixed blood, but the vast majority were clearly of Celtic descent with tanned skin, light hair, and pale blue eyes. Then Indy spotted Amergin, his cowl pulled back, his gaze fixed on Indy. As he met Amergin's stare, Indy suddenly remembered his coming into their room. He recalled everything that Deirdre had told him: the newspaper, the gun, and the shooting.

Now he realized something else. He remembered Amergin's saying they were receiving a lesson in what Ceiba was about. This place was ruled by dreams, and that meant the so-called veils were related to dreaming as well. But there was more. They could control memories. That was why Indy hadn't remembered the dream, and Deirdre hadn't recalled seeing Fawcett. That meant they'd been dreaming when Fawcett was in the room, and incredible as it seemed, that they were dreaming now. Then Fawcett's words from his journal came back to him. *They elect the council in their dreams.* It was a dream government.

Someone was talking, a man with a bushy, gray beard, who sat a couple of chairs away from Amergin. He was saying something over and over, and Indy concentrated on his words. Suddenly, he realized he understood. Gray Beard was saying that all significant decisions affecting the people of Ceiba were made in dreams. Indy didn't know how he understood, but he did.

He glanced at Deirdre and saw the shocked look on her face. She leaned toward him, touched his forearm, and whispered, "Indy, I remember seeing Fawcett now."

Rae-la rose from her chair and addressed the council. It didn't matter that she spoke Gaelic. He understood perfectly. He had to be dreaming; he spoke several languages, but Gaelic wasn't one of them. But this was the strangest damn dream he'd ever had, because everything and everyone seemed incredibly real. More than real.

"I want to thank the council for taking up this matter on such short notice. I believe that both of our guests have now realized that the dream state in Ceiba is a special condition with important purposes."

Now he knew what was under the thin ice, as she had said—a world of dreaming.

As Rae-la spoke, Indy wondered if the words he was hearing were exactly what she was saying. Maybe some sort of filtering process was taking place so that he heard them in familiar terms. But he had little time to think about it, because Gray Beard was speaking again.

"Since Amergin has been involved in this matter and is familiar with it in detail, I think it will bode well if he presents his perspective to the council," Gray Beard said.

If this was a dream, Indy thought, couldn't he wake up now? Couldn't he simply snap out of it?

Amergin stood up, but Gray Beard was still speaking in Indy's head. *Your present sleep is particularly deep and you will not wake up for some time.* He focused his gaze on Indy.

Damn. How did he know what I was thinking?

"Thank you for allowing me to explain this sensitive situation," Amergin said, and began retracing his first meeting with Indy and Deirdre.

Do these people take naps every time they have to make a decision? Indy thought. *What kind of society is this? How do they get anything done?*

Indy, in the present circumstances, forceful thoughts and words are essentially the same. This time Rae-la was in his head. *We understand your unfamiliarity with the conditions. However, you must refrain from your questions and comments while others are talking.*

Sorry, Indy thought. *How come I don't hear everyone thinking?*

You two are the focus here, Gray Beard answered. *Your thoughts resonate to us.*

So this is my dream.

This is everyone's dream, Rae-la said. *And to*

*answer your question, the council doesn't make all
of its decisions in the sleep state, only important
ones.*

Indy turned his attention back to Amergin, who
was still recounting the scenario leading to their
trip here. "My action and intent were to bring the
outsiders here to assist our important endeavor. To
prove that they were interested in us, we allowed
them to choose whether or not they would enter
the city, and told them of the dangers that they
would face if they attempted to do so. Yet, as you
know, they came on their own in search of the city.
When I tried to discuss the seriousness of the situation with them in their room, Mr. Jones material-
ized a gun and shot me. What's particularly
disturbing is the fact that he didn't know he was
dreaming."

That comment set off a murmur among the
council members. Rae-la stared coldly at Amergin
and asked to speak as he sat down.

She told her own version, explaining that she
had brought Indy and Deirdre to the Morcego
territory in order for them to accompany Colonel
Fawcett back to his people. Indy noticed that she'd
left out Amergin. She was taking the blame herself. She said she hoped the council would understand her action. She then told them about the
Indian attack, and said that the two outsiders had
fled to Ceiba as a refuge.

"It is my understanding that they would like to
leave Ceiba as soon as possible. Considering that
they are man and wife and do not wish to assist our
needs, I believe they should be allowed to depart.
As you know, the sooner they leave, the easier it
will be to veil their memories of Ceiba. It will
simply seem like a dream to them, one they can't
quite remember."

That's just it, Indy thought. *It's a dream. Are we actually here at all?*

Rae-la paused and gazed at the solemn expressions on the council members' faces. "No one should be forced to do anything against his will. That is a basic rule in Ceiba, and it should apply to outsiders as well as to our own people. I hope you will agree with me."

Amergin was on his feet again. "What Rae-la says is true, but our situation is perilous. We cannot afford such sentiments if we are to survive. We are in dire need of new blood, and must take whatever action is needed or we will not last another generation. I think all of us agree on that, except for Rae-la."

Rae-la's anger rose. "There was no other Indian tribe attacking the Morcegos. You told the Morcegos to attack the outsiders, to force them here, and to kill the ones you didn't want."

"Bernard was not worthy, but the pilot was not supposed to die," Amergin answered in a calm voice.

A goddamn nightmare, Indy thought, and he didn't care who was listening.

20

THE THREE

Indy sputtered, coughed, and jerked awake as water splashed on his face. He rolled over and saw Deirdre sitting up, wiping her wet face with the bed sheet.

"On your feet now. Both of you," a voice boomed. "Time to be on our way."

"What the hell's going on?" Indy looked up and saw a man with a thick mustache standing over him, a nearly empty pitcher of water in his hand. "Who are you?"

"You know who I am. Think."

Indy sucked in his breath as it all came back to him. "Fawcett?"

"Yes, of course."

"I think I dreamed you. I've been having the strangest dreams." Indy was confused. He was trying to put everything together. "I was just at a meeting."

"The Council of Orbs," Deirdre said. "I was there, too. In fact, I feel like I'm still half there."

Indy knew exactly what she meant. He felt the same way.

"Good show," Fawcett said. "You are still there, but you're more here. Now put on these clothes." He handed them two light gray outfits like the clothes he was wearing. Indy started dressing; Deirdre walked into the bathroom.

"I was fortunate to find these particular outfits. The color indicates a member of the higher orb. So now we shouldn't expect trouble unless an alert is sounded."

Indy stepped into the pair of drawstring pants, then pulled the long, loose shirt with an attached hood over his head. He straightened it over his whip, and was pleased that the shirt was large enough to disguise the weapon. "But how can I be dreaming and awake at the same time?"

Fawcett stroked his mustache. "The more advanced Ceibans do it all the time. They can actually be doing two things at once."

"I'm not a Ceiban. I can't do that," Indy said.

"But they can do it to you."

"You mean Rae-la . . . ?"

"Yes, she is holding both of you there. When she realized what Amergin was up to, she knew it would take all of her skills to get us out of here."

Deirdre returned to the room in her fresh clothing. "How do we know we're not dreaming right now?"

"Do something you're not supposed to be able to do. Walk on the ceiling. Float in the air. If you can't do it, you're not dreaming."

"So that's why I understood Gaelic," Indy said.

"Precisely. You wanted to, and you did."

Indy looked at Deirdre. "Say something in Gaelic."

She thought a moment, then said:

"Comnadh tri mo dhuil,
Comnadh tri mo run,
Comnadh tri mo shuil,
Agus mo ghlun gun chlaon,
Mo ghlun gun chlaon."

Indy shook his head. "I must be awake. I didn't understand a word of it. What's it mean?"

"I said:

'May three aid my hope,
May three aid my love-making,
May three aid my eye,
And my knee from stumbling,
My knee from stumbling.' "

Indy looked puzzled. "Three?"

Deirdre shrugged. "It's just an old Scottish prayer. I never knew what it meant."

"Well, the three of us are getting out of here," Fawcett said. "Your arrival and Rae-la's help snapped me out of the spell they've had on me."

"What are we waiting for?" Indy asked. "Let's go."

"Hold it," Fawcett commanded. "Our timing must be exactly right. We've got to wait a couple more minutes until the new guardians come on duty. That's when we'll go."

"I didn't see any guard when we left before with Rae-la," Deirdre said.

"That's because you didn't want to see any," Fawcett said, offhandedly. "You were dreaming."

"I'm not sure I wanted to see that council, and I saw them," Indy said.

"That's different. More dreamers involved. You had to see it."

Indy stomach growled. "What happened to the tea you were going to bring?"

"Oh, that. Rae-la and I drank it. But it wouldn't have satisfied your physical body, anyhow."

Deirdre shook her head. "I don't understand."

"Dreaming is an art here, but like any skill it takes practice," Fawcett said.

"Rae-la told the council that we wouldn't remember anything when we left," Deirdre said.

"That was her pitch to set you free," Fawcett said.

"What about you?" Indy asked. "Can they blank your memory, too?"

"I've been here long enough so that there's a good chance some of my memories may bleed through unless they create false ones." Fawcett looked out the window. The mountain was now outlined in a crimson corona, signaling daybreak.

"How come you didn't write about this dreaming stuff and memory veiling in your journal?" Indy asked.

"I wrote that months ago. I've learned a lot since then."

"Did they make you a breeder?" Deirdre asked.

"Deirdre," Indy said wearily.

"It's all right," Fawcett said. "Yes, they did, but it wasn't like you might think. They imposed dreams on me. I would think I was making love with my wife, only she was thirty years younger."

"You never saw any of the women?" Indy asked, a faint hint of disappointment in his voice.

"Not once," Fawcett said, positioning himself next to the door. "But they tell me I have three children and five more on the way."

"Christ," Indy said.

"I don't like this place," Deirdre said.

At that moment, the handle on the door moved. "Right on time," Fawcett murmured.

The door swung open and two red-haired, burly men with spears peered in at them. One of the men took a step into the room and the moment he did, Fawcett chopped him beneath the nose with the edge of his hand. The impact was followed by the crackle of breaking bone and cartilage. The guardian collapsed with a grunt as blood sprayed from his nose.

The man behind him reacted swiftly, swinging his spear like a bat. Fawcett ducked, grabbed the man's arm, and hurled him headfirst into the wall. He fell to the floor on his face, and his spear rolled away. As the guardian started to stand up, the colonel clubbed him on the back of the neck with an open hand, like a hatchet chopping wood.

"That takes care of those two." Fawcett brushed off his hands. He wasn't even out of breath.

Indy's whip was in his hand, but there'd been no need for it. He was amazed at the sixty-year-old man's agility and expertise. It was obvious that Fawcett hadn't spent his military career behind a desk. "Good show, Colonel. Good show."

"Nothing to it. Let's be on our way." Fawcett turned to the door, but at that moment the guardian he'd clubbed rolled over, pulled a gun from inside his shirt, and aimed it at Fawcett's back.

Indy reacted instantly, snapping his whip and snagging the gun from the guardian's hand. The man lunged for Indy; his hands found Indy's neck. Indy fought to break the hold, but the guardian's arms were powerful, and Indy's neck felt like it was about to break. Then, suddenly, the guardian grunted, his grip relaxed, and the man toppled to the ground.

Deirdre stood over the man, holding the gun by the barrel. "He was going to kill you, Indy."

"Yeah." He rubbed his throat, coughing.

She handed him the gun. "It's yours."

"Hey, my Webley." He tucked it under his belt against his back and pulled down his shirt over it.

"Let's go," Fawcett said.

As they moved across the courtyard, Indy saw two more bodies lying in the thicket. "Who are they?"

"The earlier shift," Fawcett said. "I wanted to wait for the new ones so they wouldn't sound the alarm before we escaped."

Fawcett pulled the hood of his shirt over his head and Indy and Deirdre did the same. When they reached the stairway, Fawcett turned up toward the city. Indy grabbed him by the arm. "We're going the wrong way, Colonel."

"Don't be a fool, Jones. We can't just walk out the main entrance. It's a long shot as it is."

"I thought these outfits would help," Deirdre said.

"Only up to a point."

At the top of the steps, they entered the tunnel again, and Fawcett cautioned them not to say a word. They headed up the now familiar curving incline, but this time, after a short distance, they turned onto a branch that Indy hadn't noticed earlier. But that had been the dream.

Now that he thought about it, he wondered if the dream was really still going on and he was at the council meeting. Instantly, he was aware of himself being elsewhere, even though he knew he was walking through the tunnel.

He was staring at an ogham inscription in large letters on a wall, and was slowly translating it.

"The eye of the great god,
The eye of the god of glory,
The eye of the king of hosts,
The eye of the king of life,
Shining upon us through time and tide,
Shining upon us gently and without stint.
Glory be to thee, O splendid Sun,
Glory to thee O Sun, face of the god of
        life."

Indy realized the inscription was on the wall of
the council chambers next to the Eye of Bel. None
of the council members was speaking. Their cowls
were pulled up, their heads bowed. He leaned
over to Rae-la. "What are they doing?"

"Making their ruling."

Then Gray Beard looked up. "We have considered all the testimony and have reached a judgment. You both will stay with us for a period of five
years. You will be treated well while you are in our
service. After five years, we will release you. At
that time, Colonel Fawcett will also be set free.
Your memories of Ceiba will be erased, and in
their place we will insinuate a false memory of life
with an Indian tribe. That is our judgment."

"There is one other thing you should know,"
Amergin said. He glanced at Gray Beard, who gestured for him to continue. "If you try to escape or
inflict injury on anyone in the city, while dreaming
or awake, your freedom will be restricted, and you
will be required to remain here the rest of your
life."

Gray Beard nodded, then turned his attention to
Rae-la. "It is rare that someone of the Higher Orb
acts against the will of the council. We understand
your feelings about the outsiders. However, we
cannot overlook that you were attempting to assist

Colonel Fawcett's escape. As your penalty, you will be required to remain in Ceiba for the next five years and serve as a breeder with the two male outsiders."

"Okay, here's what we have to do," a voice said in Indy's head.

The instant he realized it was Fawcett talking, Indy's attention snapped back to the tunnel, where the three had reached another door. Fawcett pulled it open and Indy blinked against the sudden brightness.

"Straight ahead is the watchtower, and it may be occupied."

"What do they need a watchtower for if they've got the veil?" Deirdre asked.

"The tower is not used to watch for outsiders," Fawcett explained. "It's a place where they go to commune with those in the Eternal Orb. Let's walk toward the tower as if we were going to join them. But we'll keep going until we reach the cliff."

Indy had heard over and over about the Eternal Orb and the seventh veil, but he still knew nothing about it. "Who belongs to this orb, anyhow?"

"The gods, that's who."

Indy frowned. "They're in the watchtower?"

"Not exactly. From what I understand, you approach the eternal flame, which burns at the top of the tower. Then after performing a ritual, you pay homage and attempt to make direct contact with whichever god you are seeking for help."

Indy's eyes were adjusting to the light, and now he could see a steep incline in front of them leading up to an opening. "Okay, I get it. But what are *we* doing here?"

"This is the quickest escape route. It's dangerous, but there's no other way."

"What way are you talking about?" Deirdre asked.

"Come and see for yourself."

They climbed the incline and stepped outside. The sun was poking between two mountains and flooding the mountaintop with shafts of golden light. Here, there was no garden or plaza. The ground was rocky and, as Fawcett had said, the tower was directly in front of them.

They'd no sooner taken a dozen steps than a man appeared in the doorway of the tower. "Keep your heads down. Look pious."

"How long is the wait?" Fawcett asked as they neared him. Indy hoped he knew what he was doing.

The man wore an outfit similar to their own, except it was green. He nodded to them. "Go right on in."

They stopped at the base of a spiral staircase and Fawcett glanced back at the man in green. "He's looking at us. Guess we'd better go up," Fawcett said.

"Why don't we just take care of him like we did the others?" Indy asked, surprised by Fawcett's wariness of the man, who was older and smaller than the four guardians.

"Because, Jones, that man is not trying to impede our way. The others were trained as guardians and failed in their duties. They deserved what they got." He took a step up the staircase. "Besides, it might bring us bad luck. The poor devil was just up here conferring with his god."

At the top of the steps, they entered a circular room with open windows all the way around. In the center of the room was a huge caldron in which burned the largest candle Indy had ever seen. The wick was as thick as his thigh and the flame was bright and hot.

He gazed toward the city, and was surprised by its size, considering that most of the residents of Ceiba apparently lived on the walls. It would take most of the morning just to walk around the perimeter. The buildings looked as if they had been carved from the mountainside. Some were tiered, a few pyramid-shaped, others rectangular. A grove of trees separated the city from the point on which the tower stood.

He could see the forested valley below them and the mountains beyond the valley. The sight was impressive; he understood why the Ceibans came here to meet with their gods. A sparkling, silver ribbon of water cut through the valley, curved around the base of the mountain, and disappeared in the hazy distance. He wondered if it was the same tributary that they'd followed from the air, the same one they'd crossed on the rope bridge.

"You two are very fortunate to have experienced this place," Fawcett said quietly. "There's no other place like it on earth."

"I'll second that," Indy said.

"The entire mountain range is blanketed in enchantment," Fawcett continued. "You could be literally on top of Ceiba and not see it."

"What about the mountains?" Deirdre asked. "Wouldn't they still be here even if you couldn't see them?"

"Of course they would. You can climb a mountain without seeing it just as you can walk through a forest and only see the individual trees."

There was a more important matter than idle speculation on Indy's mind at the moment. "Just how are we going to get off this mountain, Colonel? Are we going to fly?"

"No, not fly."

"You know some secret way down, right?" Deirdre said.

"It's not exactly a secret route, either."

Deirdre shook her head. "Then what is it?"

Fawcett peered over the side. "You'll see soon enough. Let's go. The fellow's gone." Fawcett started descending the stairs followed by Deirdre.

She stopped at the curve of the spiral. "You coming, Indy?"

"Yeah. Be right with you." Indy stared at the flame in the cauldron. He figured he knew what Fawcett had in mind, and knew they might not live.

"If the gods are here, I hope they help us," he murmured.

He looked past the flame, where an eagle soared high over the mountain. He watched it dive a couple hundred feet, then sweep up, carving a semicircle in the sky. "You make it look easy," he said. Then he headed down the stairs. The eagle was a good sign. He was glad he'd spotted it.

Fawcett and Deirdre waited for him at the bottom of the steps. They moved outside and across the rocky point until they reached the edge. The drop was sheer and at the base of the wall several hundred of feet below them was the foaming water of the river he'd seen from the tower.

"Where's the way down?" Deirdre asked. "I hope it's not on a rope."

"It's not," Fawcett said. "We're going to jump."

"What?" She shook her head. "No! We'll die."

"It's the only way. We can make it if we hold onto each other."

"Or we'll all die."

Fawcett didn't answer.

"Indy. I don't want to do it," Deirdre said.

"I think the colonel's right. We don't have much choice."

"Exactly," said Fawcett. "If we're caught now, we're stuck here the rest of our days, probably in a locked room."

Deirdre stared gloomily over the side. "Just what are we going to do if we survive the jump?"

"All we have to do is float downstream a ways, then cross the river. We'll be outside their territory and safe," Fawcett said.

He made it sound simple, Indy thought.

Deirdre looked worried, but resigned. "All right."

Fawcett patted her on the back. "That's the spirit, young lady."

Indy took her hand, leaned over, and kissed her. "I love you."

She smiled weakly. "Indy, if I don't make it, don't feel sad for me. It's okay."

"Don't say that. Don't even think it. You're going to make it."

"It's just this feeling I have."

She reached out and took Fawcett's hand so that she was between them.

"We'll hang onto you," Fawcett said. "Don't worry, girl."

"Do they have a name for this river?" Indy asked.

"They sure do. I'll tell you when we're down there."

They stood a moment in silence. Suddenly, there were shouts behind them. A swarm of armed guardians rushed toward them.

"Now!" Indy shouted.

The three took a step and disappeared over the side.

21

RIVER OF DEATH

Rae-la came awake in Fawcett's room moments before the guardians arrived. She veiled herself, and skilfully slipped by them into the courtyard. She recalled her dream with perfect clarity. The Council of Orbs had rejected her plea and had admonished her. But now it was going to be worse. She'd committed herself to helping the three outsiders, and standing up to Amergin.

She rushed down the corridor to the main stairway. Even though her abilities allowed her to evade the guardians, she knew that neither she nor anyone else could veil the outsiders from the guardians. But no one would expect them to jump from the cliff, either. By now, if they'd gone through with it, they'd either survived or died in the river. She'd done all she could.

Her own life in Ceiba was over. She must leave immediately. In Bahia, she could seek shelter in a candomblé temple. It was the only place she knew of in the outside world whose ways even vaguely resembled those of Ceiba. But she also knew that

Amergin would come looking for her, and that she would have deal with him. Maybe she'd go to the British Isles and find refuge with a druid group in Ireland or England. Her life would never be the same again; the magic of the outside world was weak, and even a source of ridicule. But it wasn't hopeless.

She reached the steps and dashed down toward the entrance of the city. As she passed another corridor, several more brown-clad guardians rushed by her. Word of the escape had spread. When she finally arrived at the base of the stairs, the open area near the gate was rapidly filling with squads of guardians. She listened to the orders being shouted, and realized that they already knew the three had leaped.

She kept herself veiled, certain there would be orders to find her. She moved toward the gate and waited. As soon as a squad was dispatched, she would sneak through in their wake.

If she had looked carefully, she would have discovered another veiled figure nearby, watching her intently. But in all the activity, Rae-la didn't notice Amergin.

They hit the water feet first, but it didn't matter. The impact knocked the air out of Deirdre's lungs and smacked the side of her head so hard that she nearly passed out. They shot down through the dark water, as if their bodies were made of lead. Fifteen, twenty, twenty-five feet, and suddenly Deirdre's feet were mired in muck to her knees.

She was stunned, battered, and frightened. The thought of dying in the mud at the bottom of a river terrified her. She fought for her life. She forgot all about Indy and Fawcett and clawed the water. She needed air, and fast, or she would die.

* * *

Indy didn't even have time to kick his legs as he rocketed through the water. His feet smacked against a buried log, and his body curled into a ball. His knees buckled and slammed into his jaw, and he lost half his air. He clung to Deirdre's wrist and felt her struggling. The current tugged savagely at him, but Deirdre didn't move along with him. For a moment, he didn't understand. Then he realized she was trapped in the mud.

His grip was slipping as the current dragged him downstream. He reached out and was struck by Deirdre's other hand, which no longer held onto Fawcett. He grabbed her elbow with one hand and squeezed her wrist with the other. His arms felt like they were being pulled from their sockets. Then she yanked free, and they swirled along the bottom, the current spinning them like a top. Indy didn't know which way was up any longer; his lungs were bursting.

Death was swimming in his shadow. He could feel it, but he would die with Deirdre. He wasn't going to let go.

He swallowed a mouthful of water, and suddenly he was frantic, kicking and struggling. He'd be damned if he was going to die without a fight. His hands slashed through the water, no longer grasping Deirdre. He kicked hard, and miraculously, his head popped through the surface.

He sucked in air, sputtered, and gagged. He tried to swim, but it was no use. He was pulled swiftly downstream. He looked for Deirdre, and saw nothing but water and sky. He called her name. He struggled to stay above the water. Where was the shore?

"Indy!"

Deirdre's voice rose above the rush of water

around him. He craned his head, straining to see where she was. Then he stuck something solid, scraping his chest. He was stunned and on the verge of passing out. He'd struck a boulder projecting from the surface, and had washed up onto it.

"Indy! Help!"

He forced away the darkness that was pressing against him. He pushed his body away from the rock face, turned, and saw her, her arms chopping at the water, her head barely above the surface. He felt for the whip at his side and jerked it free. Just as Deirdre was about to sweep past him, he unfurled it in a wide, powerful arc. The end of the whip lashed several times around her outstretched arm. He didn't dare pull her, fearing that the whip would slip off. But then she grabbed it.

"Hang on," he yelled, and he drew her toward him until she was in his arms, pressed against the rock.

Somehow, they were alive. And together.

Deep breaths. One right after another. The sweet, sweet air filled her lungs. She was alive, alive even though she'd sensed death stalking her from the moment they'd climbed the watchtower, had felt its presence when she'd leaped from the bluff, and felt it now, shadowy, hidden.

Indy climbed onto the rock and helped her out of the water. They were in the middle of the river, and the water rushed past them in a foaming fury. She didn't see any way they could make it to shore, but they couldn't stay here.

When Deirdre had recovered enough to talk, she asked where Fawcett was. Indy shook his head. "I don't know. I never saw him after we hit the water."

Something caught her eye, and she stabbed a finger toward the water. It was Fawcett, clutching a log. "Don't count him out yet. Look there."

The log was big enough for the three of them, but Fawcett was at least ten yards away, and he was going to pass them by in a matter of seconds.

"We've got to swim for it," Indy said.

"That's what I was afraid of." Death's chill radiated across Deirdre's chest, making the tropical warmth of the air a bitter joke.

"Jump!" Fawcett shouted.

"Now!" Indy yelled. She plunged. This time she surfaced within seconds, and sliced through the turbulent waters stroke after stroke, kicking with whatever strength she had left. She would make it. She would.

She heard a yell and looked up. She'd misjudged the distance. The log loomed in front of her, and before she could react, it bashed her forehead. There was a moment of bright, stunning pain. Then her body relaxed as she sank into the comforting darkness.

"Stop rolling the goddamn log," Fawcett yelled as Indy climbed onto it.

Indy looked around. *Oh, God. What happened?* "Where is she?"

"Get over here." Fawcett was leaning forward, an arm stretched over the log. Then Indy saw that he was hanging onto Deirdre's forearm.

Quickly, he worked his way around to the other side. Fawcett clutched her left arm, but her head kept bobbing below the surface. "Christ. Pull her up," Indy shouted.

"I'm trying, damn it. I'm trying."

Indy ducked under the water, and grabbed her around the waist, while still clinging to the log with one hand. He pushed her up as Fawcett pulled, but Indy knew the second he let go she'd fall back into the water. He raised himself up on the log while hanging onto Deirdre's right arm, and rolled the log toward Fawcett. As he did, she rose up out of the water.

She hung limply over the log. *Oh, God, she's dead.* "Deirdre! Say something."

He pushed down on her lower back, pressing her stomach against the log. Did it again, and again. Finally, she raised her head, retched, and coughed. She was breathing. She was alive.

"Are you all right?"

Her cheek was pressed to the log, but her hand moved as if to answer him.

"We've got to hold onto her, Jones," Fawcett shouted. "If we hit a strong turbulence, we could lose her."

"I've got a better idea." Indy loosened his whip, and tossed the end of it over the log. He threaded it through his fingers, then reached into the water until his fingers found the knotted end of the whip. He bent down so his lips were near Deirdre's ear. "I'm going to lash you to the log so you don't fall off."

She said something he couldn't hear. He leaned close, listening.

"Am I still alive?" she asked.

"You're not only alive, but we're getting out of here." He fumbled with the whip until he'd slipped it under her arms and around her back. Then he pulled tightly and tied a knot. "That should do it."

"Jones, we've got trouble," Fawcett shouted.

Indy looked up. Three long canoes filled with guardians were paddling away from the shore.

The two men dropped into the water and rolled the log so that Deirdre was no longer on top.

"You think they saw us?" Indy asked. As if in response, a spear pierced the log, missing Indy's hand by inches. "I think so."

"I forgot to tell you, Jones."

"Forgot to tell me what?"

"The name of the river."

"What is it?"

"The River of Death."

"Great."

Indy raised his head up and peered over the log. The canoes were quickly closing the gap. The lead craft was less the twenty yards away. The log was bouncing in the increasing turbulence and it was getting difficult to hold onto it.

Think fast.

He caught one more glimpse of the first canoe, took in a deep breath, and dove down. He swam against the current, his arms shrieking with the strain, then with a final kick he burst to the surface. The canoe bobbed through the water a few feet away, coming toward him. One of the guardians saw him and raised a spear, but Indy grabbed the side of the canoe, pulled hard, and spilled the guardians into the river.

One of them surfaced near him, raised his spear and thrust it at Indy. But another popped to the surface at the same instant and the spear ran through his neck. More guardians surfaced and Indy ducked under the water as one lunged for him. As he came up for air, he heard Fawcett yelling frantically somewhere behind him.

He turned, but Fawcett and Deirdre were nowhere in sight. There was no time to figure it out. He was grabbed around the neck by one man, and pulled under by another who gripped his leg. He twisted, kicked, and pummeled the men, but like sharks with iron jaws set on their prey, they refused to release their holds. He clawed at the face of the guardian who held his neck, but the man only squeezed harder. He elbowed the one gripping his thigh, but the man reacted by ramming his head into Indy's gut.

Air rushed from the archaeologist's lungs. He couldn't last much longer. He arched his back and fought to surface. Then he felt the revolver digging into his back and grabbed at it, tugging at the long shirt that had tangled around it. Finally, he ripped the gun free. He raised the butt over his head and slammed it against the elbow of the man who held his neck. Then he bashed the head of the man on his leg.

Indy kicked free, and gulped a lungful of air. He looked around, and was confused by what he saw. The guardians in the two other canoes were pulling their companions aboard and paddling frantically toward shore.

Indy turned to look for Fawcett and Deirdre again. It seemed as if the river just ended a hundred feet away and met the sky. Was this where the Ceiba territory ended and the outside world began? Then he understood what he was seeing. It was a waterfall, and he was about to be dragged right over it.

Indy swam wildly, but he was still sliding backwards, closer and closer to the brink. There was nothing he could do to prevent the inevitable. He saw the overturned canoe a few yards to one side of him and swam to it. He started to climb on top of it, but a hand grabbed his shoulder and pulled him off.

He shrugged away from the guardian, but it didn't matter. He glanced toward the falls; it was less than ten feet away. The force of the water pulled him below the surface. He reached up just in time to grab one of the crossbars on the overturned canoe. The river suddenly dropped away, and the canoe hurtled over the edge into the roar and spray.

The vessel struck bow first, and Indy was catapulted through the air and into the churning waters. He turned summersaults, twirling like a stick in the vortex of swirling power. He no longer knew where he was or what was happening to him. He thought he heard a voice, telling him something about the seventh veil, but he didn't want to know any more. He didn't care.

The water spat him to the surface. He sputtered and coughed, and realized the river was no longer churning around him. He was drifting with the current, moving slowly downstream. He should be sinking to the bottom, he thought. He wasn't swimming. Then he realized that the water was shallow; his knees were dragging along the sandy bottom.

"Indy! Over here."

Deirdre, not some voice in his head. He stumbled to his feet in the shallow water, and saw her and Fawcett moving toward him from the shore.

"Splendid effort, Jones," Fawcett said, bracing him with an arm. "You did a lot better than that canoe." A piece of the wrecked craft floated past them.

Deirdre slipped an arm around his waist and hugged him. "You did it," she whispered as she and Fawcett quickly ushered Indy into the forest and out of view of the river.

Indy sat down in a clearing. "How did you two make it?"

Deirdre eased down next to him. "I don't know."

"Nothing to it, really," said Fawcett, who remained on his feet. "I hung onto the log and never let go. Deirdre, of course, was tied to it. Before I knew it, we were floating along in the shallows."

"I feel like I swallowed half the river," Indy remarked.

"I did," Deirdre said.

"Well, no sense reminiscing." Fawcett brushed his hands off, and helped Indy and Deirdre to their feet. "We've got to put some miles between us and our Celtic friends. From what I understand, the guardians never cross this river, but let's not count on it. The further we get from here today, the better."

Indy didn't feel like moving, much less hiking through the jungle all day, but he knew Fawcett was right. He also understood why the colonel had finally found his lost city. The adventurer had simply refused to give up his quest, even when others told him it was impossible. The man's unrelenting determination was something worth emulating, he thought as he trudged along behind him.

They walked away from the river, but half an hour later, it appeared again. "This will never do," Fawcett said, shaking his head. "We apparently walked from one bend in the river to the next. We're still dangerously close to the Ceiban territory."

"Look!" Deirdre pointed toward the river.

Indy saw the rope bridge that they'd crossed last night. It seemed like weeks ago.

"My God, I remember this place," Fawcett muttered to himself.

"There's a trail nearby that leads past an Indian

village." Indy told Fawcett about the Morcego guides who had led them here.

"Well, maybe we can pick up a couple more guides who can lead us to Cuiabá," Fawcett said.

"I don't think they're going to be very cooperative. The guardians killed the last ones."

"We'll deal with them when the time comes," Fawcett said, unperturbed.

Indy thought of another option. "Colonel, have you ever flown an airplane?"

"I've got a couple hundred hours of flying time under my belt."

"Good. Let's fly back."

"That's right. Rae-la told me you flew here. That's going to make it a lot easier."

Indy already felt better. They were getting out of here. They'd be back in Bahia in no time and heading back to New York before they knew it. They moved through the jungle in the direction of the bridge, keeping just out of sight of the river.

"Here's the trail," Indy said a couple of minutes later. "Once we get close to the village, I know I can find the lake."

"I'm not so sure we should take this trail," Fawcett said. "We might attract unwanted attention."

"Oh, no!" Deirdre stumbled back into Indy.

Two bodies lay on the side of the trail. At first, Indy thought they were the dead Morcego guides. But then he saw the red hair, and the darts protruding from their backs.

Fawcett took a couple of steps toward the bodies, and suddenly the jungle came alive with painted bodies, armed with blowguns. The Morcegos surrounded them.

Indy raised a hand in greeting, but the Indians put their weapons to their mouths and aimed.

Then the chief stepped forward. White circles radiated from his eyes. Vicious-looking fangs were painted on his jaw. Bat fangs.

"I gave you guides and they were killed. Now you must pay for their deaths."

22

Wings of Doom

They were seated on the ground outside the chief's hut, their hands bound to a pole behind them. The Morcego men were dancing and singing around them, while the women were stacking dried wood in preparation for a feast. Indy had no doubt about the main course on the Morcego menu.

"This is probably the first time in my life that I've hoped dinner is served late."

"Cannibalism is no joke," Deirdre said.

"Especially when we're the guests of honor," Fawcett added.

Two of the dancing warriors were waving decapitated heads by the hair. "I guess they don't shrink heads here," Indy said. The dancers moved closer and he recognized the heads. "My God, it's Fletcher and Bernard."

"We would have been better off drowning than being eaten by these monsters," Deirdre said.

"Indy's got a point, though," Fawcett said. "The longer they parade around, the longer we live, and the better our chances are of getting help from the Ceibans."

"You call that help?" Indy said, scornfully.

"The Ceibans are an advanced people. They not only don't eat humans, they have virtually no crime. In spite of what they did to me, I'm still highly impressed with them. Their civilization is advanced. It just developed in a totally different way from our own."

"If they're so civilized, why do they have so many spear-chuckers?" Indy felt the rope on his wrists vibrating. He glanced back, but he couldn't see anything.

"Those spear-chuckers, as you call them, are all highly skilled in the martial arts and are members of the Outer Orb. The guardians are not considered oppressors, but are the heroes of the average Ceiban."

"Swell. But that doesn't help us," Indy said.

Now Indy felt a hand holding his wrist in place as the vibrating continued.

"Hold still," a voice whispered. Suddenly, the rope around his wrists snapped. A hand touched his shoulder. "Don't move yet."

"Did you say something?" Fawcett asked Deirdre.

"No, but I heard it."

"Quiet," Indy said. "Rae-la's here."

She worked her way around the pole, cutting each of them free.

"Listen to me," she said. "As soon as the guardians attack the village, follow me as fast as you can run."

"We can't see you," Fawcett said.

"You will."

Just then Indy noticed the chief standing in the doorway of his hut watching them. He moved closer and stood in front of Fawcett. "You talk to evil spirits, and they answer."

"Yes. The spirit I talk to said that unless we are released immediately a powerful force will attack the village and many will die."

"I know these evil spirits. I have talked with them many times. I know the tricks they play."

"They want to see us fly away safely," Indy said.

"That's right," Fawcett said. "So let us go, and we'll leave here very fast."

The chief looked warily at Fawcett. "You did not come here from the sky with the others," the chief said.

"No, I was taken to the invisible city many months ago. I am leaving now with them in their flying machine."

The chief pulled out a knife. "I will see if you are a real person or an evil spirit."

He thrust his knife at Fawcett just as Indy jerked his hands from the rope and lunged at the chief. Fawcett's free hands were even quicker. He chopped at the chief's hand, but only diverted the blade to his side, where it sliced through his shirt and slid between two ribs. Indy pulled the chief away, grabbed his wrist, and twisted it until he dropped the bloodstained knife.

Abruptly, the dancing and singing ended. The Morcegos rushed toward their captives, but stopped several paces away. Indy held the knife to the chief's throat, while the Morcegos aimed their poison darts. It was a standoff, and no one moved. Beside him, Fawcett held his side as blood oozed from the wound.

"We've got to get to the plane," Deirdre whispered.

"I know, but I don't think they're going to let us." Indy started edging away from the pole, but the warriors moved closer, blocking their way. "I guess that's their answer."

"Tell them to let us go, or you will die," Fawcett told the chief.

"I am always prepared to die."

Great, Indy thought. Just the kind of hostage they needed.

The chief said something to his warriors, who looked more batlike than ever. They raised their blowguns to their mouths.

Indy pressed the knife to the chief's throat. "What did you say to them?"

"I told them I was about to die, and that it was good. But they must answer my death with yours."

At that moment, a black shaft whistled through the air, slammed into the chief's chest, and passed through it. The tip wedged under Indy's arm. Shouts filled the air. The Morcegos were caught by surprise as the guardians of Ceiba charged across the village, hurtling spears.

Indy dropped the chief and turned to Deirdre, but she was already bolting away. Rae-la was just ahead of her. Indy took Fawcett by the arm, but the wounded Englishman shrugged off his hand. "I'm all right, damn it. Move."

They fled the village amid the cacophony of shouts and cries of pain, and scrambled through the forest. Indy waited once for Fawcett, who was trailing behind, but the colonel waved his hand, urging him on. Fawcett was hurt, but at least in all the confusion no one was following them.

Or so Indy thought.

He glimpsed the silver surface of the lake through the trees. Almost there. What if the Morcegos had burned the plane? Then what? Fawcett would never make it if they had to go by foot.

Rae-la and Deirdre were just ahead of him, blocking his view. Then they emerged on the shore and there it was. Fletcher's plane was tied ten yards offshore where they'd left it. Amergin had been right; the Morcegos had stayed away from it.

"Let me see your wound," Rae-la said as Fawcett hobbled up to the water's edge.

"I've got to get this plane in the air," Fawcett said.

But Rae-la ignored him, and turned to Indy. "Help me take off his shirt. We must stop the bleeding right now."

"She's right," Indy said. "You're in no shape to fly the plane."

Rae-la rolled up the shirt and bound it around Fawcett's midsection. He winced and his muscles tightened, but he didn't utter a sound as she tightened the make-do tourniquet.

Fawcett waded out to the plane with Indy and Deirdre on either side of him. Indy mounted the wing, and opened the door. Then he helped Fawcett climb into the plane, and Deirdre followed. He noticed the surface of the water was glazed with fuel. Was there a fuel leak? *Probably nothing serious,* he told himself.

"Are you coming with us?" Deirdre asked her.

"I have no choice now. I can never return to Ceiba."

Then a voice spoke from the edge of the forest. "You're not going with them, Rae-la. You're going back with me."

"Leave me alone, Amergin."

The Ceiban stepped from the jungle and into full view. His icy blue eyes impaled Rae-la. "You betrayed your people, and you're going to face the consequences."

"You betrayed me," she answered. "I'm going with them."

Amergin made a quick motion with his hand, and two armed guardians appeared at his side. "They can go, but you're staying."

"And what if I don't?" she asked defiantly.

"Then you will all die."

"Go," she told them.

They hesitated. "Now. Quickly."

As Fawcett started the engine, Indy wondered if Rae-la was still going to try to escape. He wanted to help her, but she motioned for them to go. He sat down in the cockpit next to Fawcett as they taxied across the lake and turned around.

"Here, wear this," Deirdre said. She draped the beaded necklace that Joaquin had given Indy over his neck. "It'll bring luck."

"Where did you get that?"

"It was here in my bag."

He pulled her to him, and kissed her. "Thanks. You better sit down."

She squeezed his arm. "We're getting away, Indy."

"Yeah. And with our memories intact," he said.

Indy caught one last glimpse of Rae-la as they picked up speed. She was shouting and waving her arms. It looked more like a frantic wave than a good-bye, he thought.

Then the plane was in the air. Indy watched Fawcett closely as they rose over the trees. "I'll take over now."

"Christ. Let me get a little more elevation, Jones. I'm not dead yet . . . Oh, Christ."

"Are you all right?" Indy grabbed for the steering column.

"Hit your fist against the gas gauge," Fawcett said.

The needle pointed to empty. Indy pounded it, but the needle didn't move. "That's impossible. We had enough fuel to get back to Cuiabá."

Deirdre moved up behind him. "What's wrong?"

The engine sputtered; the plane shook. Fawcett pressed the rudder, and the craft veered sharply to the right. "Sit down," Indy yelled. "Put on your seat belt."

"We've got to get back to the lake. We're going down."

Those were Fawcett's last words. He slumped over the yoke; the plane nose-dived. Indy struggled to pull him away, but it was too late. They plunged toward earth like a wounded bird.

A tailspin.

A blur of forest.

A shout.

Then they slammed into the jungle and earth, and there was nothing.

Indy stared at the smoldering wreckage. How long ago had they crashed? A minute? An hour, two? He looked down at himself. Not a scratch. No blood. No pain. Nothing.

Impossible.

"It happens," a voice said. "But it didn't happen that way to you."

Indy looked around. He didn't see anyone. Was it someone from the city? Someone veiled?

"Where's Deirdre?" The odd calmness he'd felt as he'd stared at the wreck shifted to concern. "I've got to find her." He moved toward the plane.

"Don't go any closer."

He stopped. "Who are you? Where are

you?" The voice was familiar. Where had he heard it?

"Questions, questions."

"I need some answers."

"Patience, Indy."

"You know me?"

"Quite well."

He took another few steps toward the wreck. Then Indy saw it. Something that stopped him dead in his tracks. That something was him. There he was lying on the ground, covered with blood.

"You were thrown free of the wreckage. Unfortunately, you struck your head against a tree trunk."

"What are you telling me, that I'm dead?"

There was no answer.

"I can't be dead. Not now. I've got things to do. I'm too young. I'm just starting my life."

"It's your choice. You can accept your death or go back. There's still time."

Indy looked away from his ruined body. "How?"

Then he glimpsed the figure to his left. A tall, slender robed man with a long, gray beard. An owl was perched on his shoulder. Indy had seen him before, a year ago at Stonehenge. "Merlin?"

"And Churchill." Merlin caressed the bird's downy breast.

"But . . ."

"You can call me Bel, if you like. I have many names, as I've told you before. You've already guessed some of them."

"But who are you . . . really?"

Merlin laughed. "Today you can call me a

*master of the seventh veil, a member of the
Eternal Orb."*

*Indy didn't know what to think, what to do,
what to say. Only one thing came to mind.
"What is the seventh veil?"*

*"Ah. Glad you asked. You're taking a peek
at it right now. It's the veil between life and
death. The masters of the Eternal Orb are the
gods of old, the immortals, who have removed
the veil and move freely between realms."*

Indy looked doubtfully at him.

*"We are also healers extraordinaire, and
that is why you will have another chance, if
you accept it."*

*"What about Deirdre, and Fawcett? Where
are they?"*

*"They cannot join you, if you choose to re-
turn. Their injuries were too extensive. We
cannot heal them."*

*"Why not?" Indy demanded to know. "If
you can bring me back to life, you can do the
same for them."*

*"No," Merlin said firmly. "You've mistaken
me for God. I am immortal, but fallible. I can
do nothing for them."*

"Then I don't want to live, either."

"Suit yourself."

Merlin was gone.

*Indy looked around, and sensed himself ris-
ing from the jungle, away from his body, and
the wreckage. "Wait a minute. I'm not ready
for this. I've got to live. I want to live."*

EPILOGUE

Indy opened his eyes, and rose up on his elbows. He was in a bed surrounded by something filimentous. A blurry figure stood beyond the veil. "Where am I?"

"Son, you are with us," a soft voice said. "How are you feeling?"

"Woozy, and . . ." Indy shook his head to clear the cobwebs, and tried to focus on the white-haired man garbed in black. "Who are you?"

"I'm Friar John Baines. You are at the Mission of Saint Francis near Cuiabá."

Indy realized that he was looking at Baines through mosquito netting.

"How long have I been here?"

"Almost a month. There's someone here who's very anxious to see you. Let me get him." As Baines disappeared, Indy remembered that he'd journeyed to the Amazon. He'd married Deirdre on a cruise ship. Rio. Sugarloaf. Oron. Carino. Bahia.

A moment later, Marcus Brody walked into the

room dressed in a safari outfit. "Indy, my God, I'm so glad to see you awake. I arrived three days ago. I've been worried sick. You can't imagine."

"Marcus, where's Deirdre?"

Brody looked stunned. He glanced at Baines. "You didn't tell him? No, I see you didn't. Indy, Deirdre is dead. There was an airplane crash in the jungle."

"She's dead? No. I don't believe it." Indy tried to sit up.

Baines moved to his side. "Please, lie back. Rest."

"I have to go look for her." Indy struggled, but he was weak. "She can't be dead." He saw a flash of a plane, plummeting toward a fuzzy green carpet.

"Listen to me now," Baines said. "There is a supply plane that is due in a week. It will take you and Mr. Brody back to Bahia, and if you are feeling well enough, maybe you can persuade the pilot to look for the crashed plane."

"Can you remember where you were?" Brody asked. "Where it happened? Can you remember anything?"

Bit of images returned to him. "By a lake and a river."

"There are many rivers and lakes in the forest, Mr. Jones. You'll need more than that."

"What about the mountains, Indy?"

He vaguely recalled something about mountains. "Snoring Mountains."

"That's right. My God. You found them."

"No one has ever found those mountains," Baines said.

Brody patted the air. "Please, Friar, let him talk."

"I only remember you telling me about them. And you gave me a journal."

"That's right. Fawcett's journal. I gave you several pages of it. Did you find Fawcett?"

"The last thing I remember finding is the Hotel Paraíso. It gets sort of foggy after that."

Baines nodded solemnly. "They said you wouldn't remember much."

"Who said that?"

"You were brought here by a man and woman, a most extraordinary pair. A beautiful woman, and a very peculiar older man with a long beard. They took care of you for several days until they were sure you would live. Do you know who I'm talking about?"

Indy shook his head.

Brody grimaced with frustration. "Do you remember anything about Colonel Fawcett?"

"I came to Brazil to look for him."

"Good. What else?" Brody persisted. "You must remember what happened to you in the jungle."

Jungle. Indians. "I was with Indians." Something was wrong with that. The memory had no depth or substance. It was a cardboard image, like a childhood recollection of an incident his parents had described to him, but of which he had no actual remembrance.

But now more was coming back. He recalled the thugs on the cruise ship. "Bernard almost had me killed."

Brody frowned. "Dr. Bernard? It's odd you should say that, because no one knows what happened to him. It's feared he was killed in Guatemala. You know he went back."

That didn't seem right to Indy, but he didn't know why.

"He's still confused," Baines murmured. "Maybe we should let Mr. Jones rest."

"No. I want to talk about this," Indy said. "I want

to know why Deirdre is dead." His voice caught with emotion and he paused. "What else do you know about the ones who brought me here? Where did they go?"

Baines rubbed his jaw. "The woman said she was a nurse working at a wilderness mission. I questioned her about it until she finally gave me the name of the priest in charge. I know him quite well and immediately wrote him. The messenger returned just the other day with a letter."

"You didn't tell me about this," Brody said.

"I didn't want to raise your hopes."

"What did it say?" Indy asked.

"The reverend knew nothing about the old man. But he said that a young woman, like the one I described, stayed several weeks with him last year and helped an Englishman recover from a jungle illness."

"An Englishman?" Brody crowed. "It must be Jack."

"He said the woman left with two Englishmen. One was named Walters, and the reverend was upset that he didn't return."

"What was the other one's name?" Indy asked.

"I don't know. The reverend just said that he was something of a madman with strange ideas."

"It must be Jack Fawcett," Brody said, "and the woman was the one who brought you here."

"Marcus, you know, sometimes you're a little quick jumping to conclusions. If I can't remember her, I doubt if I knew her very well."

"She knew about me, Indy. She told Friar Baines to contact me. She's the one who sent Fawcett's journal. I'm sure of it."

"When they left, the woman said she was going on a long trip," Baines said. "I'm supposed to tell you that you made the right decision, and that everything is going to work out all right."

"I wish she were here to explain it all to me now," Indy said.

"I wonder if she and the man are from the lost city of Z, or rather D," Brody pondered. "You told me the symbol on the note with the journal pages was the ogham letter D."

Indy frowned. "You mean Ceiba?"

"Ceiba?" Brody asked. "What's Ceiba?"

"It's a tree that grows in the tropics," Baines said. "Another name for the kapoc. It's very hardy, with big pods that contain a soft, cottonlike fiber."

"They make clothes from it," Indy said.

Baines shook his head. "No, it's been tried, with no success. They stuff pillows and quilts with the fiber. That's about it."

Brody bent down to the side of the bed, and spoke slowly. "Is Ceiba the name of the lost city?"

"In the story it was."

"What story?" The note of hope in Brody's voice was unmistakable.

Indy thought a moment. "The story the Indians told me. It's one of their legends."

That didn't seem quite right, either. But he didn't know why. Perhaps that was the point. Some things simply weren't meant to be fully understood.

Here is a preview of
the next adventure of Indiana Jones,

and the

GENESIS DELUGE

INDIANA JONES AND THE GENESIS DELUGE
on sale in January 1992.

PROLOGUE

October 1917
Petrograd, Russia

The first snow of the season had started to fall less than an hour earlier as Vadim Popov galloped down the wooded lane. A rope tied to the stirrup of his saddle pulled another horse, and on it rode Vadim's captive, a White Russian lieutenant. Blindfolded and gagged, with his hands bound behind his back, the captive soldier rocked unsteadily atop his steed.

They'd been riding for several hours and Vadim was exhausted. But the young Bolshevik soldier knew he was close to the command post and he was anxious to get there before dark. Until he reached the post he was in danger of encountering White Russian soldiers on the road and becoming a captive himself. So far he'd only passed a few wagons, and the peasants had said nothing. Everyone knew the revolution was underway, and the sight of a captured soldier was not so remarkable as it would have been a year ago.

Vadim was a courier who carried messages back and forth from the revolutionary troops to the command post. He had stopped at an inn last night to meet another courier, who was to pass Vadim messages that he would deliver to the revolutionary leaders. It was late when Vadim had arrived and he'd been unable to find the other courier, whom he knew only by the code name Uri.

The next morning the man joined Vadim at breakfast. As they ate, Uri mentioned that the night before he'd begun talking with a man whom he'd momentarily mistaken for Vadim. They had shared a few shots of vodka together, and soon the stranger was telling Uri that he was an army lieutenant and was on his way to see the czar.

Vadim knew that the only way a lieutenant would

get anywhere near the czar was to be a courier like himself. "Where is he now?"

"Still here, sleeping, I think. He drank too much last night," Uri said with a laugh.

"Let's pay him a visit."

When the White Russian answered his door, he was still groggy with sleep. Vadim jammed his gun into the lieutenant's stomach, and he and Uri bound and gagged him. They found his pouch, and looked at its contents. At first, when they examined the photographs and the useless piece of wood, neither understood what they were seeing. Vadim questioned the lieutenant, but he would only say that he was a member of the 14th Railroad Battalion stationed in Turkey. Meanwhile, Uri read the accompanying documents and excitedly explained the importance of what the man was carrying.

That was when Vadim decided he would take the captive to the command post to be interrogated. He was sure the commander of the revolution would want to thank him personally, and if he did it meant that his future would be bright. The lieutenant suddenly started talking when he realized where he would be taken. He told a fantastic story, but it only made Vadim more eager than ever to get him to the command post.

Finally, Vadim told Uri that he'd made a serious mistake talking to the White Russian. Couriers were not supposed to make idle conversation with strangers, or drink while on duty. However, Vadim said he wouldn't report Uri if he swore to say nothing about what had happened here. Uri considered what he'd said, then grudgingly agreed and went on his way.

That had been hours ago, and Vadim was wet and cold from the snow. He wanted nothing more than to reach his destination. If he'd been alone, he would've been out of the cold and out of danger by now.

Something was wrong.

He felt it like a stab in the back. He glanced over his shoulder.

"Mother of God," he cursed.

The captive was no longer on his horse, and there was no sign of him on the road. Vadim pulled hard on the reins, turned, and raced back. He'd covered fifty yards before he saw the mark in the snow-covered lane where the soldier had tumbled off. He leaped to the ground and dashed into the woods. It was no problem tracking him, but Vadim was surprised by how well the lieutenant was moving through the trees and underbrush. Then he glimpsed him hobbling across a field, and saw that the escapee had managed to lower his blindfold.

Vadim raised his pistol. "Halt!"

The soldier ignored him. Vadim aimed and fired. The bullet shredded bark from a birch tree, missing the lieutenant by inches. He cursed as he raced across the field and plunged into the woods following the man's tracks. If his captive got away, the accolades Vadim expected to receive for seizing the document would no doubt be muted. He might even be chastised for allowing the White Russian to escape.

The man was starting to drag one leg. Vadim was gaining on him; he was going to catch him. Then he heard the report of a rifle, and dived to the ground. How could the bastard have a weapon? His hands were still tied a minute ago.

Voices.

Vadim crawled forward until he saw five or six soldiers, who surrounded a body lying facedown in the snow. For an instant, he thought he'd run into a squad of the Imperial Army. Then he saw their ragged coats and frayed fur-lined hats and knew they were Bolsheviks like himself, and they'd shot the White Russian.

"Comrades," he called out as he stood up. The soldiers turned, and raised their weapons. "That man was my prisoner."

A sergeant approached him. "Who are you?"

Vadim identified himself.

"What's a courier doing with a prisoner?" the sergeant asked suspiciously.

"I was bringing him to the command post. He was carrying important documents to the czar."

"What documents?" the sergeant growled.

Vadim adjusted the leather pouch he carried on his shoulder. "I have them here," he answered in an authoritative tone. "I need to get to the command post immediately."

"*Shloosayu,*" (I am listening) the sergeant said in a stern voice.

Vadim knew that he was supposed to give him the password, but so much had happened today that the word slipped his mind for a moment.

"*Mir,*" he finally said, relieved that he had recalled the simple word, which meant village, peace, the world, or universe, depending on how one was using it.

The sergeant eyed the satchel a moment, then motioned him to follow.

When they reached the road, Vadim remounted his steed and, accompanied by the sergeant on the other horse, continued down the lane. Not more than a mile from where the White Russian had escaped, they turned down a winding drive that ended at a gate where more soldiers waited. The sergeant said something to one of the guards, who looked closely at Vadim, then nodded.

They dismounted and headed along a snow-covered walkway that was scored with boot prints. At the end of the path stood a three-story stone mansion. Smoke curled from a pair of chimneys and soldiers were moving about the grounds. It amazed Vadim that they were barely a dozen miles from Petrograd and the czar's palace, and that the command was firmly ensconced in a baronial estate whose owner had fled from the approaching revolutionary troops.

At the door, there was another exchange with two more guards and they were escorted into an expansive foyer where a fire burned in a huge hearth. Vadim brushed traces of snow from his coat as the sergeant conferred with a captain near the double doors of the mansion's great hall. For an instant, Vadim glimpsed several officers seated around a table. They were probably planning the attack on Petrograd, he thought. The captain, a tall man with a long face, looked over at Vadim, then took the leather pouch and told him and the sergeant to wait.

"What's in the bag? You can tell me now," the sergeant said.

Vadim knew it would be dangerous to reveal anything to the sergeant. "It's not your business."

The White Russian army had made a great discovery in Turkey, almost enough to reaffirm Vadim's faith. But he was a Bolshevik and he knew that religion was an oppressive force. Maybe there was a God, but it didn't matter. The revolution was going to abolish the wealthy bishops and shut down the churches. Religion, after all, had become nothing more than a conspiracy to keep the proletariat in order.

After they had waited about forty-five minutes, the captain returned and asked the sergeant if he'd looked at the documents that Vadim had carried, or if Vadim had told him anything about them. The sergeant shook his head and the captain dismissed him. The sergeant gave Vadim a sour look and walked away.

He was probably hoping he would get the credit for my work, Vadim thought.

"Come with me," the captain said.

Vadim followed him down a hall and into a library with walls rising fifteen feet and covered with books. A fire crackled in an immense fireplace. In front of it was an ornate mahogany desk with gold inlaid trim. The high-backed chair behind it was turned toward the fire. As they approached the desk, the captain cleared his throat. The chair swiveled about. Seated in front of Vadim was a man with a thick handlebar mustache and penetrating dark eyes. The commander of the revolution. Trotsky.

In his hands were the photographs and the accompanying documents. "Sergeant Popov."

"Yes, sir." Vadim stiffly saluted him.

"Tell me how you came upon this material."

Vadim remained standing as he told his story. He embellished it, making the endeavor sound more daring, and he didn't say a word about Uri's help. He said that after he'd discovered he was sharing the inn with an officer from the Imperial Army, he'd snuck into the officer's room and found the document. Then, while he'd been examining it, the White Russian had walked into the room and they'd struggled until he'd overcome the man.

"Excellent work, Sergeant Popov. Has anyone else seen these documents?"

"Just myself." *Uri better keep his mouth shut if he knows what's good for him.*

"Did you tell anyone else about them?"

"No."

"And do you know what these photos are supposed to be?"

"Yes sir. Noah's ark on Mount Ararat."

"Do you believe it?"

Vadim stared straight ahead. He wasn't sure what to say. The question of the authenticity had never occurred to him; he wanted them to be real. He wanted his discovery to be important. "I think they are what they're said to be. Yes, sir."

Trotsky nodded. "You've made an extremely important discovery, and I congratulate you. However, it's unfortunate that you've seen the documents and believe so strongly in them."

Vadim realized he'd said something wrong. The warmth had vanished from Trotsky's face. His eyes turned dark and cold. "Well, sir . . . I believe in the revolution. That's what I believe in."

Trotsky wasn't paying any attention. His eyes shifted toward the captain, and he gave a slight nod.

Out of the corner of his eye, Vadim saw the gun. He turned, held up his hand. The captain fired and the bullet ripped through Vadim's palm, pierced his eye, and buried itself deep inside his brain. He took a staggering step backwards, shuddered, and collapsed, dead.

CELTIC TRAPPINGS

Spring 1927
London

On the blackboard of the classroom were two vertical lines with bars and curls and rectangles drawn at various intervals, some on the left side of the line, some on the right. The young archaeology professor, Jones, pointed at the board with his wooden marker. He was in the midst of a lecture on Celtic ogham to the fifteen students in his class. Some of the students looked bored, while others were enthralled, busily taking notes. A couple of the women in the front row were passing a piece of paper back and forth, and grinning slyly.

The professor's name was Henry Jones, but he preferred to be called Indy. He had just finished discussing the five letters with bars extending from the right side of the vertical line, and now tapped the marker against the letter designated by one bar protruding from the left side of the line. "*Huathe* is the name for the letter H. It was represented by the hawthorn tree. To the Celts, it meant cleansing and protection, and it was associated with a period of waiting in which one kept to himself or herself, away from the hustle and bustle."

Indy could relate to the letter. He felt the same way about himself. He'd felt that way since returning to London last summer after losing the most important person in his life.

He moved down to the letter with three bars extending from the left of the vertical line. "The letter T is called *tinne.* It's symbolized by the evergreen holly. It signifies the will and ability to overcome enemies no matter how powerful. The ancient name for holly is *holm,* and is considered the likely source of the name for Holmsdale in Surrey. It might even be the inspiration for Arthur Conan Doyle's fictional character Sherlock Holmes. As we know, Holmes did quite well in combating his enemies."

He turned to the board. "The letter C is *coll,* which—"

"Professor Jones?" A man with a crew cut and a pencil behind his ear raised his hand. "You forgot the letter D, the one with two bars. You skipped right over it."

Indy tugged at the lapel of his coat and peered through his black, wire-rimmed glasses at the D, *duir,* the oak, which meant solidity and fortification. There was something about it that he wasn't remembering, or didn't want to remember.

He turned away from the blackboard. "You know, the interesting thing about the ogham alphabet is not only that the letters contain complex meanings, but that each one can be represented by a hand gesture. In fact, the language was used as a secret way of communicating in the presence of others, like Romans, who would have no idea what was being said."

Indy glanced toward the two women in the front row. "It saved paper, too."

The class laughed, and it seemed that even the skulls in the cabinets with the pottery shards were grinning at the professor's joke. The two women turned red, and tried to look attentive.

"Didn't that annoy the Romans, when the Celts made these hand gestures?" a man sitting in the second row asked.

"It sure did. No one likes being talked about behind his back, especially when he's standing right there."

He frowned again at the two women, who wriggled uneasily in their seats. When he'd begun his teaching career, Indy had been amused by some of the female students' reaction to him. They apparently expected archaeology professors to be human antiques, not young and virile. But this past year, he'd only been annoyed by his flirtatious students. He definitely didn't want to get involved with any of them. He was still hurting from the loss of Deirdre, the love of his life who had died just weeks after he'd married her.

"The Romans finally had enough of it, and outlawed the use of hand gestures," he continued.

An attractive, dark-haired woman raised her hand. "Does anyone still use the sign language today?"

The question confused him even though the answer was obvious. "What do you mean?"

"Well, I was thinking about the druids who go to Stonehenge for the summer solstice. Do they use the hand signals?"

"Not that I know of."

"I have an uncle who is involved with a druid group," said an attractive, but shy, doe-eyed girl.

"Oh? What's he say about hand signals?" She'd never match up to Deirdre, he thought. None of them would.

"Nothing. But he says that the druids set up colonies in the Americas a long time ago, and that some of them are still alive today. Do you think that's true?"

Why did she have to ask that question? "The subject today is ogham. Let's stick with it, and not waste our time on fanciful ideas that some know-nothing druids pass off as the truth."

The woman drew back in her chair. She had hardly spoken during the entire course, and now when she finally had come out of her shell, he'd attacked her. He turned back to the blackboard and stared at it as if he were preparing to make further remarks about the letters.

He felt bad, but the question had annoyed him. It had made him think of Deirdre again, and their search in the Amazon for Colonel Fawcett, an English adventurer who thought ancient druids had settled in South America.

"Okay. Where was I now? Oh, yes. I got up to the letter C, *coll.* This one relates to creativity, imagination, inspiration, and intuition. You may want to reflect on this one a while before you write your final essay that's due Tuesday."

Everyone laughed, and the bell rang. "Class dismissed."

As the students filed out of the room, Indy caught the eye of the girl he'd snapped at. "Miss Wilkens?" He motioned to her. The two note passers gaped in surprise. "Listen, I'm sorry if I offended you with my comment. I didn't mean it the way it sounded."

The girl crossed her arms over her books, which were pressed to her chest. She looked embarrassed. "It's all right. I know it . . . it must be hard for you sometimes. We all know about Deirdre, of course. I guess I shouldn't have asked that question. I wasn't thinking."

Indy took off his glasses and stuffed them in his coat pocket. "There was nothing wrong with the question. It's just that I'm not feeling so great today." He glanced up at the clock above the door. "That was all."

"Professor Jones, can I ask you a question?" the girl asked.

Indy gathered up his notes. "What is it?"

"Do you think it's worthwhile for a girl—I mean, you know, a woman—to become an archaeologist?"

Indy shrugged. "Why not?"

"My father says it's not a ladylike thing to do. You know, digging the ground and getting dirty. He thinks I should get married and have kids, and forget about going to graduate school."

Indy couldn't help thinking of Deirdre again. He

glanced up at the girl, then looked away. "Maybe he's right."

He strode out of the classroom, and quickly headed to his office. He didn't understand why Deirdre's death was hitting him so hard today. A year had passed since the tragic incident, and he'd been feeling that it was behind him. Maybe the lecture on ogham had opened a door to a buried memory.

Door, *duir*. Something about the ogham word reminded him of the events leading to Deirdre's death. But he wasn't sure what it was. There was a blank in his memory, a result of the airplane crash. He couldn't recall much of anything that had happened in the jungle, and that especially bothered him because he'd lost the memory of his last days with Deirdre. No matter how hard he tried to recall what had happened, the only thoughts that came to mind were vague images of an Indian village.

He entered the office area and greeted the secretary, a frizzy-haired graduate student who worked for three assistant professors. "I don't want to see anybody."

She shrugged. "No one wants to see you. . . . Not now."

He walked into his office and closed the door. Someday he'd have his own secretary and she wouldn't be so damn insolent. He leaned against the door, and rubbed his face with his hands. Then he stared over his fingers at his desk, which took up most of the space in his cramped office. A stack of journals lay on one corner of the desk. His mail was neatly stacked in another. Ungraded term papers were piled in the center of the desk, and a smaller batch of graded ones were to the left. But the papers and journals and mail weren't what caught his attention.

He was peering at two baked clay figurines, one a woman with large breasts and wide hips, the other a man with an erect penis that was half the length of his leg. How'd they get there? They'd been packed away in a box in his closet for months.

The pair had been given to him by Deirdre, who had passed them on from her deceased mother's collection of artifacts. They'd probably been used in Celtic fertility rites, and he remembered how Deirdre had smiled and said: "They represent our love."

But now they were a profanity. They taunted him, and he had an urge to swat them off the desk and smash them against the wall. He moved further into the room and saw that the closet door was open and the box where the figurines had been stored was pulled out of its place on the floor beneath a shelf.

"Francine," he yelled. Then he walked back into the outer office. "Have you been messing around in my office?"

"Don't bark at me, Jones. I haven't been in your office today."

"Then how did my mail get there?"

"Two of your students were here looking for you during your so-called office hours this morning. They were disturbing me with their chatter so I told them to wait for you in there. I gave them your mail and told them to put it on your desk."

"What did they look like?"

The phone rang and Francine picked it up. It didn't matter. He was sure they were the two gigglers who had been passing notes in class. They'd visited him together last week. They'd asked a couple of innocuous questions about the course, then attempted to pry into his personal life.

He returned to his office, snatched up the figurines, put them back in the box, and closed the closet door. He shook his head in disgust, and stopped in front of his bookcase. He stared at the titles, and picked up a book called *Buried Treasures of Chinese Turkestan*. He leafed through it, then put it back on the shelf. He needed a change, a new challenge. Something that wouldn't remind him of Deirdre.

But where would he find it? He couldn't just walk away from his responsibilities. Classes were about to end and he was supposed to teach summer school in another week. Then in the fall back to more of the same. Celtic archaeology.

He had to talk to Pencroft. That was all there was to it. He'd ask for a sabbatical. Maybe he'd go to Egypt or Greece or India. Hell, maybe he'd go dig for the buried treasures of Chinese Turkestan. He didn't know, but he was going to do something, something different, and Pencroft would just have to bend a little.

Indy felt better already. He scooped up the mail and quickly rifled through it, stopping a moment as he noticed a letter from Jack Shannon, his old friend and former college roommate. He put the letter in his pocket, stuffed the rest of the mail in his backpack, and headed for the door.

He recalled that Pencroft had suggested that he save his backpack for the field and that a briefcase would be more appropriate for the classroom. He was about to leave it behind, then changed his mind. His pack was his way of keeping in touch with a part of himself that was important, and if Pencroft didn't like it, too bad.

"Are you leaving?" Francine called after him.

"I hope so."

INDIANA JONES AND THE GENESIS DELUGE. Available soon wherever Bantam Falcon Books are sold.